My Husband's Secret

KAREN CLARKE

ONE PLACE. MANY STORIES

HQ
An imprint of HarperCollins*Publishers* Ltd
1 London Bridge Street
London SE1 9GF

www.harpercollins.co.uk

HarperCollins*Publishers*
1st Floor, Watermarque Building, Ringsend Road
Dublin 4, Ireland

This paperback edition 2022

1
First published in Great Britain by
HQ, an imprint of HarperCollins*Publishers* Ltd 2022

ISBN: 9780008525521

Friends of

GREAT MISSENDEN
LIBRARY

THIS BOOK WAS PURCHASED BY THE 'FRIENDS OF GREAT
MISSENDEN LIBRARY.'

IF YOU WOULD LIKE TO HELP FUND NEW RELEASES FOR OUR
SHELVES, PLEASE ASK ABOUT SUPPORTING US BY BECOMING
A MEMBER.

Search, renew or reserve
www.buckinghamshire.gov.uk/libraries

24 hours renewal line
0303 123 0035

Library enquiries
01296 382415

Also by Karen Clarke

Your Life for Mine
And Then She Ran
My Sister's Child

Books by Karen Clarke and Amanda Brittany

The Secret Sister
The Perfect Nanny

For Tim, with love and thanks

*If you build a relationship on lies
the foundations will crumble*

~ Anon

Chapter 1

Caitlin

I ran into the hospital ward, soles squeaking on the vinyl floor. 'Where is he?'

The nurse at the desk looked up with tired eyes. 'Who are you looking for?'

'Jack Garvey.'

'Mrs Garvey?'

I nodded. 'Caitlin.'

'I'll take you to him.' Her sympathetic gaze presumed my rough appearance was down to hating hospitals – true – and probably the shock of the call I'd received out of the blue about Jack's accident. Also true, but not the full story.

'Thank you.' My voice shook. I knew my face was shiny and pale, eyes red-rimmed from crying while I drove through the night, finally arriving at the hospital as daylight broke through the murky sky.

'He'll be ready to go as soon as the doctor's done his round.'

'Is he going to be OK?' A mix of love and anxiety inflated my chest where my heart was thumping at double its usual rate.

'Like we said on the phone, he has some nasty cuts and broken ribs, and his ankle is badly sprained, but he's lucky it wasn't much worse.' The nurse gave a little shake of her head, short ponytail bouncing. 'He was out cold for twenty-four hours and seemed confused when he came round, but he's been under close observation, and the brain scan showed no signs of damage.'

'And he can't recall what happened?' I held my breath.

'Not at the moment, but that's common after a head injury, even a minor one. He might never remember the accident itself.'

I swallowed a rush of saliva, picturing Jack being tossed like a rag doll through the air, the car that hit him speeding off into the night.

'Good job he remembered your number,' the nurse continued when I failed to respond. 'No ID, no mobile phone. The police were ready to launch an appeal.'

My heart lurched. 'I'm here now.' I managed a weak smile as I hooked a strand of hair behind my ear. Had she noticed I was wearing pyjamas under my coat? It probably wasn't that unusual under the circumstances.

I followed her down the ward, averting my eyes from the patients who weren't curtained off, stuffing my shaking hands into my pockets. 'Did they catch the driver?'

'Not that I know of, but it's early days.' The nurse threw me a resigned look over her shoulder. 'Maybe whoever it was will have an attack of conscience and come forward. It happens, sometimes.'

I tried not to imagine Jack lying, twisted and bleeding, by the roadside. Thank God a passing motorist had stopped and called for help. My chest tightened. Jack had asked for me as soon as he came round. I had been the first person on his mind.

What would he look like?

'The doctor will be along shortly to sign him out.' The nurse stopped by the furthest bed, closest to the window. A man was standing, looking out at a line of trees shaking in the breeze, hands resting on the narrow sill. He was hunched beneath a thin T-shirt, shoulder blades rising, every knobble of his spine visible. *Needs feeding up*, I imagined my mother saying. *He's too skinny.*

'He won't stay in bed, I'm afraid. He's fine but needs to take it easy.' The nurse lowered her voice as she touched my arm. 'Don't worry about the bruising – it'll soon fade.'

My breathing grew shallow. Through Jack's dark hair was a patch of bone-white scalp around a wound that had been cleaned. The sight of it brought fresh tears to my eyes.

'I'll leave you to it, but call if you need me,' the nurse said, her attention diverted by a pitiful cry from a neighbouring bed.

'Thank you.' For a split second I wanted to turn and run. But this was Jack.

As if sensing me hovering, he straightened and turned, his movements slow and stiff as though every part of him hurt.

'Caitlin.' His deep voice was thick with emotion, reminding me of the last time we'd spoken. 'Thank God you're here.'

'Oh, Jack.' A hand flew to my mouth. One side of his face was purple and puffy, strips of tape holding together a couple of cuts on his forehead. I tried to focus on his eyes, deep-set and dark, brimming with love and anguish. 'What happened?'

'I don't know.' He took an awkward step towards me, his angular face contorting with pain. 'I've tried to think but . . . nothing. I woke up in here and thought the nurse was you.' His gaze slid over my pallid face, taking in my same-old blue eyes, childish freckles, the frizz of dark hair pulled into an untidy ponytail, the purple duffel coat I'd thrown on. His brow furrowed as though seeing something he couldn't quite pin down. 'I spoke to a police officer,' he said, haltingly. 'He explained about the hit and run, but it's a total blank. I asked them to call you.'

Instinct taking over, I stepped around the end of the bed, reaching for his hands. They were warm and dry and so recognizable. He had craftsman's hands, sleeves always rolled up, as though ready for action. I squeezed his fingers, heart racing so fast and hard I was worried I might pass out. 'You knew my number.' My weak and wavery voice sounded alien to my own ears.

'Of course I did.' His face was so close it made sense to tilt my head and graze his lips with mine. His breath smelt stale with something medicinal, but underneath he was still Jack, the scent of him dizzyingly familiar. He briefly closed his eyes, lashes brushing the bruised skin beneath. When they opened, they held a question. 'Why wouldn't I remember?' The corner of his mouth twitched upwards. 'You're my *significant other.*'

The words landed like a punch. A laugh erupted from my throat and turned into a sob. It was the term we'd settled on when people used to ask about our relationship. Not *wife* or *husband* – yet – but too old at thirty for *girlfriend* and *boyfriend*. When Jack proposed, four years ago, he'd made a point of asking whether I would officially become his *significant other.*

'That's right.' A smile spread over my face. I reached up and gently touched his cheek, his face swimming in and out of focus through a wave of tears. 'I'm so glad you're OK.'

'I'm a mess.' He sounded wretched with frustration. 'I have to wear this boot thing for a while and will need to use crutches.'

'It's not your fault.' *Was it?* How would I know? 'Come on.'

As I helped him over to the bed, where he dropped down still holding my hand, his other cupping the back of his head, doubt and apprehension flooded in. I studied him for a moment, feeling on the edge of a precipice. *It wasn't too late.* I could leave and not look back, explain there had been a mistake. But was that what I wanted? Jack loved me. I could see it in his eyes, in the way his hand clung to mine like a lifeline. Emotion flowed between us like an electrical current, as strong as it had ever been. It was obvious the accident had affected his memory, but how far back did it go? He clearly had no recollection of the call he'd made, two weeks ago, asking if we could meet.

'I didn't have my wallet or phone on me.' There was a bewildered edge to his voice. 'I don't know what happened to them.'

He looked at his finger, where the gold band that matched mine used to be. 'I've lost my wedding ring too,' he said. 'I don't know how that happened.'

'It's fine – you left it at home.'

I sat beside him, gazing at the clunky black brace-boot encasing one foot, the other bare and vulnerable. *He really had forgotten.* Jack didn't know we weren't together anymore, that we hadn't been a couple for over a year – that he'd placed his wedding ring on the windowsill before walking out and we hadn't spoken to each other until his phone call a fortnight ago.

'Try not to worry.' I pressed my face into his shoulder, felt the warmth of his skin against my cheek and breathed him in as the moment to come clean slipped past. 'Everything's going to be fine.'

Chapter 2

Caitlin

'I really am sorry about this, for panicking you. It must have been horrible getting that call in the middle of the night.' Jack was finally in the car, the passenger seat pushed back to accommodate his stretched-out leg with its protective brace, a brown leather boot on the other foot that I'd never seen before, smarter than the bashed-up kind he used to wear.

'It's fine – don't think about that.' I took the crutches the hospital had issued and laid them in the back, alongside a carrier bag containing the few items of clothing Jack had been wearing at the time of his accident. He fumbled with his seat belt while I tried to calm my breathing and still the shake in my hands.

As we'd left, signed out by a doctor with a harassed expression who gave Jack a letter for his doctor, a prescription for strong painkillers, and instructions for follow-up visits, my heart had drummed with worry that a nurse would beckon us back. *We've just had a call, asking if someone called Jack was brought in over the weekend. She says she's his partner . . .* and then, when we reached the cool brightness of the car park, my ten-year-old Ford Fiesta badly parked in my haste, I half-expected Jack to stop as reality crashed back, crowding out the love on his face as he stared at me in horror. *Hang on. This isn't right. I've just remembered, I left you.*

But here I was, paying the parking fee at the machine, half-wondering about CCTV and number-plate recognition; how quickly I would be found out and what I might be charged with. Kidnapping? Reclaiming my husband? Tricking a former partner into believing we were still together? *Deception.* I'd betrayed Jack once and he'd vowed to never forgive me. He was black and white in that way. *Lying by omission*, he called it. Just as bad, in his eyes.

Back in the car, pulling onto the main road, I almost leapt out of my skin when his fingers brushed my knee. 'You didn't even have time to get dressed.'

'I wanted to get here as soon as possible.'

Shooting him a sideways glance, I saw him looking at my pyjamas – or rather *his* pyjamas. I'd held on to them after he walked out, along with most of his clothes – still wore them sometimes, like I had when we were together, though his scent had long since been washed out.

'They always suited you better.' His fingertips touched my hand, as if he couldn't help himself. 'It's so good to see you, Caitlin, I can't tell you.'

Relief thudded through me. 'I think you just did.' I risked another glance, hardly able to believe he was there, sitting beside me, as though we'd only been in the car together a couple of days ago. 'It's so good to see you too, Jack.' *More than you know.*

'What was I even doing on that street?' I felt the heat of his gaze, like twin lasers on my face. 'Did you report me missing?'

I chanced another quick look, fresh shock rippling through me as I noticed the hollows beneath the bones of his cheeks. He was gaunt – thinner than I'd ever seen him. Sunlight pushed through the windscreen, deepening the colour of his bruises and bloodshot whites of his eyes. *What had happened to him?* 'What do you actually remember?' I tightened my hands around the steering wheel, feeling the sticky heat of my palms. 'Before the accident, I mean.' Waiting for his reply, I fixed my eyes on the road leading out of Brighton where Jack had grown up and where we'd lived together. *He won't know that I've left.*

'I can't remember where I was going, but I think I was walking away from the flat.' His words emerged slowly, edged with frustration. From the corner of my eye I watched his calloused gardener's hands crunch into fists on his knees. He was wearing baggy grey jogging bottoms that the hospital had unearthed, the sort of thing he would never normally choose. *We had to cut him out of his jeans.* I'd lied and said that, in my hurry, I'd forgotten to bring a change of clothes as they'd requested. Jack's things were still in cardboard boxes in the spare room, as I hadn't decided what to do with them. Panic whipped through me, taking the air from my lungs. *Breathe.* I hadn't had an attack for a while.

'Everything's blank after that.' Jack's voice anchored me back in the moment.

'And before?'

'Before?'

'How far back can you remember?' Slowing at the lights, I turned to face him. If he gave it too much consideration, if his memory came back now, the game was up. I would have to confess, say I'd acted in a moment of madness, or instinct, even if it was as good as admitting I still loved him and wasn't over him leaving.

Jack tipped his head back and closed his eyes. I longed to reach over, push a hand through his wavy hair the way I once had, but after all this time it would feel strange – to me, if not to him.

'I think . . . I've a feeling that maybe we'd . . . *argued*?' His voice rose on the word, as though he *felt* it to be true but couldn't quite believe it. We'd rarely argued before that day – the day it all went wrong. 'I've a vague memory of walking around until it got dark. It was raining, I think. I felt . . .' He brought a hand to his forehead, as if the movement might force the memory to return. My breath stalled, pulse spiking. Jack was remembering – or rather *mis*remembering – that day. 'I was annoyed.'

'That's it?' My foot trembled over the accelerator as the lights changed to green. 'What else?'

He lowered his fist, unfurled his fingers. 'To be honest, Cait, I'm struggling. I wasn't completely honest with the doctors.'

Alarm flared along my nerve endings. 'How do you mean?'

'When I woke up, I felt . . . weird.' His hand rose, then fell. 'Disconnected. I knew something awful had happened, but I couldn't think what. They asked me questions: name, date of birth, what year it was, who the prime minister is, about my family – basically checking I hadn't woken up with amnesia, I suppose. Luckily, I knew all the answers, and when I gave them your number they were obviously relieved. They told me having a blank spot from just before the accident was common, the brain protecting itself, but—' He gave a twitch of impatience that was so familiar, so typically Jack, my throat ached with tears.

'But?' I could barely focus, only half-aware of the sea in the distance, sparkling under winter sunshine as though scattered with diamonds. Soon, Jack would ask where we were going.

'It feels like there's something more.' He shifted in his seat, wincing as he adjusted his foot. 'Something crucial I *should* remember but can't.'

I snatched a breath, felt it catch in my throat. 'It sounds as though you've lost quite a bit of time.' Despite my bone-deep regret at not being honest with Jack in the past, I was about to deceive him again. *For the greater good*, I told myself. We should never have broken up in the first place. He would never have left if . . . I slammed a door shut in my mind. 'We did have a disagreement, and you *did* walk out . . .' I trailed off, anxiety fluttering. I hadn't thought this through.

'I remember your birthday.' His tone was lighter now, a note of dreamy recollection in his voice. The opioid tablets he'd taken before leaving the hospital must be kicking in. 'You were commissioned to illustrate that book, about the lonely meerkat.' I could tell without looking that he was smiling. 'You were happier about that than the present I got you.'

My mouth curved automatically in return. 'I loved that necklace.' I still wore it, a tiny, silver hedgehog on a delicate chain. 'I never take it off,' I said, realising he was recalling the last time we'd been properly happy; only a week before my world collapsed.

Jack stiffened as I drove past the end of Atlingworth Street and the converted ground-floor flat we'd called home for nearly four years.

'Where are we going?'

Heart tripping, I said, 'I can't believe you've forgotten we don't live here anymore.'

'What?' I could practically hear the cogs turning as he struggled to work it out. 'Robin Hood's Bay?'

I exhaled and nodded. 'We finally moved up there.' *We.* Jack had only ever visited the little North Yorkshire fishing village a handful of times before my grandfather died and left his cottage to me.

'*That's* why we argued.' As understanding flooded his face, guilt strained across my chest. We *had* disagreed about living there permanently, so far from everyone we knew and his expanding garden-design business. *It's fine for you, Caitlin, you can illustrate books anywhere, but I've worked hard to build the business.*

You can do it again, up there. You'll love it, Jack, and we won't be throwing money away on rent while we save for a mortgage, like we are here. We'll be better off, and we'll still be by the sea. Even closer than we are here. Not that the sea in Brighton had featured much in our daily lives, being more of a background image we took for granted.

'So, we're *living* there now?'

I couldn't bear to see his struggle to remember, waiting for memory to flow in and fill the gaps. 'Well, *I* am,' I said, truthfully. 'You were sorting out things down here, winding up the business.'

Something like relief flashed over his face, as though my

explanation made sense. 'And that's where we're going now? Robin Hood's Bay.'

I nodded, not trusting myself to speak. I was remembering the quality of silence in the flat after Jack had left, how swiftly my life had lost its momentum and sense of direction as guilt and grief dragged me down. Talking to Jack, laughing or being quiet together, sharing jokes, and supporting each other had formed the rhythm of our lives for so long it had seemed impossible that I could continue to function without him.

'I'm sorry I gave you a hard time about it in the first place.' His eyes were on the road ahead now, narrowed as though trying to pinpoint the moment he'd capitulated, to visualise the series of interactions that must have taken place. I was almost on the verge of pulling the car over and blurting out the truth, unsure I could stand the tension – *what had I been thinking?* – when he said, 'I'm really glad you went ahead with it, Cait.' His smile felt like a blessing. 'I've got this feeling I needed to get away, to start over, so it was obviously the right choice. Maybe the business was getting me down. I remember feeling tired all the time, as though I hadn't been happy for a while.'

That wasn't true. He'd loved his job, was committed to it. A quiver passed through me as I replayed the phone call he'd made a fortnight ago, the strain and desperation in his voice – a tone I'd never heard from Jack in all the years I'd known him.

I have to leave London, Caitlin. I made a terrible mistake. All I can do is get out.

What's happened?

It's better if I don't say right now. I'm sorry to call you out of the blue like this but . . . I have to see you. I want to explain.

I had never been more relieved that I hadn't changed my mobile number. *You sound scared, Jack.*

I'll . . . I'll be fine. No one knows where I'm going. I've stopped working and everything's in place. I just . . . I've no right to ask for any favours but—

13

For God's sake, Jack, just tell me.

I'll be in Brighton soon. I'll call you then.

I didn't even have time to tell him I was no longer living there before he hung up, and when I tried to call back, the number was unavailable.

I'd been tormented for the next few days, partly upset that the careful, quiet life I'd begun to build, and even enjoy, had been upended by a single call, but also filled with a joyful, tentative hope that, perhaps if Jack was reaching out, he was ready for us to at least be friends again. I'd missed him so much. He dropped off the radar so completely after he left, and it had taken every ounce of strength I had to not go looking for him, to give him the space he needed, but when one month had stretched into two, became four, then six, I had no choice but to accept he wasn't coming back.

That was when I had my first panic attack.

'So, you drove all the way down from Robin Hood's Bay?'

'What else was I going to do?'

He reached over and stroked a lock of hair behind my ear, the gesture so tender the view in front of me rippled through fresh tears. 'I love you so much, Caitlin,' he said quietly. 'When I was lying in hospital, waiting for you to arrive, all I could think about was your face, about how much I wanted us to be together and for us to have a family.' Shock wrenched every muscle in my body, but he carried on, oblivious. 'I think I might have been a bit of a dick about that in the past, but whatever's happened, I want it more than anything. I want us to move on, to be happy, for this to be a new beginning. I don't even care about the accident, about how it happened, or who it was, or where we live, or who said what. None of that matters.'

I bit the inside of my lip so hard, I tasted blood. It was everything and more I'd longed to hear but assumed I never would. Not from Jack. But even as happiness flowed through my veins, softening my body, something occurred to me.

14

Jack had said that, at the hospital, they asked him what year it was, and he answered correctly – yet he was recalling my birthday from the year before, as if he had forgotten everything since; why we'd split up, the fact we hadn't set eyes on each other in all that time.

Was there another reason Jack wanted to forget the past? Something he was happy to not remember, even if he didn't yet know what it was?

I've made a terrible mistake I can't put right. All I can do is get out.

As I mustered a tearful smile and pressed my cheek to his fingers, resting on my shoulder, a question slid into my head: *What did you do, Jack?*

Maybe it was better that I didn't know.

Chapter 3

Lydia

Before

I hovered outside the police station. Around me, rain bounced off the pavement, soaking my trousers. My umbrella didn't offer much protection but at least it hid my face.

I took a step closer to the building and stopped. If I went inside, if I reported Jack missing, questions would be asked. Questions I didn't want to answer. I'd been in there a month ago, shaking all over, in front of an officer with understanding eyes. He'd spotted the bracelet of bruises around my wrist, the barely healed cut on my hand and gently asked for the name of the person responsible. He told me I should press charges. Apparently, they could arrest him without my permission if I gave a name and address.

I broke down then and cried, wiping my nose on the back of my hand, the memory of Jack's face rearing up in my mind: his mouth a thin, angry line, eyes glazed and unseeing in that moment. But most of the time, Jack *did* see me – he was the only one who truly did. He had done so much for me and Mattie.

16

Mattie. My son's face had replaced Jack's. Sixteen years old, lost, and angry – at least, he had been before Jack came into our lives. Mattie loved him, even if he didn't always show it. And now Jack was gone.

For two days I had waited, knowing he needed time to calm down, certain he would return. He didn't know anyone in London, other than his few gardening clients. I called a couple, but neither had seen or heard from him. Panic had sliced through me. I went looking for him, as though he might be pounding the streets, the words *he's gone, he's gone,* flying around my brain, keeping time with my feet as sweat broke out on my forehead. His friend Mac – the one he'd been staying with when we met – had relocated to Norway for work and Jack didn't know anyone well enough to move in with.

We'd been such a tight unit, Jack, Mattie, and me. Not perfect, not quite – the outbursts, when they came, reminded me how suddenly everything could collapse – but I'd believed we were strong enough to overcome any problems. I wanted us to, so badly. Jack was my soulmate. He'd told me I was his, that we must have been destined for each other. Silly romance-novel stuff that I'd long ago stopped believing in, but I had. Believed him. We were so happy, most of the time.

It had occurred to me in the middle of a sleepless night that he might have gone back to Brighton, to *her* – his wife, Caitlin – and fear sank through me, cold and deep. They hadn't got round to divorcing. It had only been just over a year, though he didn't wear his wedding ring anymore, wasn't wearing it the first time I saw him. I'd have run a mile if I'd known he was married.

The glass doors of Acton police station slid open, spitting out two young women, one supporting the other who had a shredded tissue pressed to her mouth.

'You going in?' The friend, hard-eyed and sallow-faced, stopped so the doors stayed open, one arm tight around the other woman's shoulders.

If I went inside and reported Jack gone and they looked at their records, they might tell me it was for the best, that it was good he was out of my life. They might wonder why I was bothering to report him missing.

'No . . . thank you.' My voice was like a scratch in the rain-soaked air. A gust of wind caught my umbrella, turning it inside out. I shoved it in a nearby bin then hurried away, head down, cutting through Churchfield Road and back to the terraced house on Milton Road where Mattie had been born and raised, the house I'd been able to keep after William – Mattie's dad – died, thanks to an insurance policy that paid off the mortgage with a bit left over. It was a nice house in a villagey part of Acton known as Poet's Corner, a decent size – two bedrooms and a wide garden at the back – but it wasn't a home without Jack, the first man in years I'd allowed into my life.

A sob rose in my throat as I pushed open the hip-high wrought-iron gate that Mattie used to swing on when he was little, watching cars go up and down the road. The gate was rusted and squeaky by the time Jack moved in, but – like so much else – he'd fixed it, oiling the hinges and enlisting Mattie's help to stroke black paint on the metal spokes while I watched from the window, wondering how we'd got so lucky and whether I could hold on to someone like Jack.

I didn't feel lucky now. The sight of myself in the rippled glass pane of the front door was a shock, my dark-blonde hair, which I'd scraped into a knot at the base of my neck, plastered to my scalp, my pale skin almost translucent in the gloomy light. I was thinner than I'd been when I met Jack nearly a year ago at the garden centre I worked at, where we'd got chatting. I was curvier then – too much comfort-eating and wine. Love had killed my appetite for a while, and I hadn't regained the weight, but now my eyes were dark hollows from too many sleepless nights and endless cups of strong black tea.

In the adjoining house a movement snagged my attention. *Harriet Shipley.* Pretending I hadn't seen my neighbour's piercing gaze through her bay window, I stuck my key in the lock with a shaking hand. My nails were bitten and ugly, a habit I couldn't break.

What had Harriet heard lately?

A memory of a scream, torn from my throat a week ago, and Jack's response, more roar than dialogue, brought a grimace to my face. Not easy to explain if Harriet asked. I'd been trying to avoid the old woman, even more than usual.

The house was quiet when I entered, Mattie at school for another hour. At least, I hoped he was. He hadn't skipped classes for ages; not since Jack came into our lives.

A photo by the coat hooks of Mattie, aged seven, smiled shyly at me, his floppy dark hair cut shorter than he wore it now, a cleft in his chin like Jack's. He could easily have passed for Jack's son. Mattie's real dad had been dark-haired too, but ordinary-looking – safe. A solicitor, twelve years older than me, nearly forty when Mattie was born, unaware of the heart condition that would kill him while he was out running one morning, two weeks after Mattie turned eleven. *It's your fault, Mum.* Mattie had screamed at me on the morning of the funeral. *You made him angry. That's why he ran away.* He'd started to lose his way after that, and so had I.

I glanced in the mirror on the wall as I peeled off my sodden coat, blinking rain from my eyelashes, quickly turning away from the sight of myself – the self that Jack had chosen to leave. *He doesn't want you anymore.* A shudder passed through me that had nothing to do with being cold, fear like a fist in my stomach.

What was I going to do? *What if he was dead, like William? Mattie would never forgive me.* I ran into the kitchen and retched over the sink. Nothing came up but bile. I was empty inside. A mug of half-drunk tea sat by the sink. I'd barely been able to force breakfast down, had struggled with food since Jack stormed out. It was hard to imagine ever wanting to eat a meal again.

Do something. The voice rang loud in my head, drowning out everything else. It sounded a lot like my father. He wouldn't have sat around, waiting. Even now, nearly twenty years on, the grief was like a hand squeezing my heart. I missed him so much. *Too much loss,* the therapist had said, after Mattie's dad died, *can lead to unhealthy ways of coping.* But I *had* coped, in my own way. I'd met Jack, let myself fall for him. *Do something.* I couldn't sit around, wondering, waiting for news.

Jack couldn't have disappeared into thin air when he had taken hardly anything with him. His clothes still hung in the wardrobe upstairs, his passport was there with his driver's licence, and so was the book he'd been reading – a tome about horticulture, lying by the armchair in the living room. He'd even left his favourite leather jacket, hanging by Mattie's faded old parka in the hall. He wasn't dead; I felt it in my bones.

I'd searched for a note the first night after he left, the quiet click of the front door worse somehow than if he'd slammed out, feeling under my pillow where he knew I would find it, but not right away, but there wasn't one. Relief had sloshed through me at first, until I realised not knowing where he'd gone, whether it was permanent, was worse.

He wouldn't kill himself, I was sure of that. He loved me, loved Mattie, despite everything. We were supposed to be together, but what could I do if I had no idea where he'd gone? I wanted a chance to try harder to be what he wanted, for Mattie's sake as much as my own. I told myself he'd come back once he'd calmed down. But in my gut, I think I knew even then he'd left for good. He had chosen to go.

But if he was *dead?* He wasn't. I would have heard by now. *Not if he had no ID.* I suspected he must have discarded his phone after trying his number multiple times and hearing it was 'no longer in service'. A number I'd called from Mattie's phone at first, and then a cheap model I'd run out to buy from Carphone Warehouse after searching the house in a panic and realising mine was missing. *Had Jack taken it?* I couldn't think of any other reason it wouldn't be in the house, or my bag.

20

The front door opened, letting in the sound of a road-sweeping lorry chuntering past, and I realised I'd been standing by the kitchen sink, staring blankly through the rain-spattered window, a tea towel gripped in my hand that I couldn't recall picking up.

'Mum?' Mattie's voice was edged with the sullenness I'd hoped was gone for good after Jack had become part of our little family. 'What are you doing?'

Turning slowly, a throb of pain in my palm a reminder of what had gone before, I took in the sight of my son in the kitchen doorway, transformed from the short, gangly boy he'd been into a tall, broad-shouldered sixteen-year-old, his rucksack dangling off his shoulder. Something like fear shrouded the wide puppy-brown eyes that used to look at me with love, back when I was the centre of his world – though even then, he'd been a daddy's boy, face brightening whenever William came home from work. He needed a male role model. He needed Jack. *We both did.*

'He's not coming back, Mum.' Mattie's words switched pitch halfway through. His voice was finally breaking, later than most of his friends' – a reminder he was no longer my little boy. A boy who had seen too much, despite my best efforts.

'He will,' I whispered, but I wasn't sure Mattie heard me, or that the words had even left my lips. He was backing away, a sheen of tears in his eyes.

'I know what was going on,' he burst out when he reached the stairs that would take him up to his room, where he would lock himself away. 'I'm glad he's gone.'

'You don't mean that, Mattie.'

'Yes, I do.' His lip curled, expression hardening. I noticed the beginnings of a moustache along his soft upper lip, and pale wisps of hair around his jaw that made my heart feel as if it was breaking.

'Mattie—'

Instead of going upstairs, he was heading back to the door that was still standing open, a slice of metal-grey sky visible through the gap. 'I'm going to Callum's.'

'What about dinner?'

'I'm not hungry.'

The door slammed and he'd gone, leaving behind his musky scent, mingled with earth and rain.

'Mattie!' But I couldn't seem to move from where I was standing.

A thought crystallised, drying my tears. I would find Jack and bring him home. Make everything right. He couldn't just leave us like this; it wasn't fair. Apart from anything else, I was losing Mattie – again – and couldn't bear it.

And if he had gone to Brighton – back to *her*?

I would fight for him with everything I had.

Chapter 4

Caitlin

'We're here, Jack.' Turning off the engine, I gently nudged his arm. My heart palpitated as I imagined him opening his eyes and instantly recalling everything before the accident. *Was this how it was going to be from now on?*

He'd slept for almost the entire journey, partly the effect of the painkillers, I was sure, but probably the after-effects of his concussion too. My shoulders had dropped a little when he scrunched up the rainproof jacket he'd been wearing when he was brought into the hospital – a jacket I hadn't seen before – to use as a makeshift pillow against the window, murmuring, 'Sorry, Caitlin, can't keep my eyes open,' my relief at not having to ask, or answer, any more questions for a while tempered by anxiety. Was it OK for him to sleep in a moving vehicle? What were his thoughts as he drifted off? What was he dreaming about? He seemed so genuinely relieved and happy to be here, with me, leaving behind whatever had led to him calling me in the first place, that I decided all I could do was take it at face value for now, appreciate the magic of his presence, and concentrate on getting us home.

He stirred once, when I pulled into a service station to fill up with petrol, voice thick as he muttered, 'Thirsty,' and I gestured to the glove compartment where I kept a couple of bottles of water and some snacks – peanuts, a few protein bars – for emergencies. He drank in great gulps, before handing the bottle to me, like we used to on the trip up to visit my grandfather, his muscle memory taking over. I declined, even though my throat was dry and tight with tension, not trusting myself to take my eyes off the road, or even turn the radio on, trying to free my mind of everything but the journey. I was grateful when we were off the motorway, towns giving way to the rolling, North Yorkshire moors, the milky sky darkening to dusk as we finally arrived in Robin Hood's Bay.

Now, Jack stretched, blinking sleep away, peering through the windscreen to see where we were while I held my breath, waiting . . . for what?

'You OK?' I said into the silence, which sounded unnaturally loud after the throb of the engine and vibration of tyres on tarmac.

'Stiff.' He gave a wide yawn and, wincing, eased the leg with the injured ankle into a new position with his hands. 'Everything hurts.'

'You probably need more tablets.' Even in the gloomy light, I could see him gritting his teeth against the pain. 'I'm sorry, I shouldn't have let you sleep so long. You must be starving and—'

'Hey.' Turning, he took my cold hand and stroked my knuckles with his thumb. 'Sleeping's the best thing at the moment, the nurse said, so don't beat yourself up.' The whites of his eyes gleamed as his hand came up to my face and touched my cheek. 'You must be hungry after driving all that way,' he said, once more the old solicitous Jack I knew so well. 'We used to share the driving, coming up here.'

Used to. Not *usually.* As if he sensed there had been a gap, a period of time where we hadn't done what was usual. Or was I overthinking it? 'You won't be driving anywhere for a while.' I wished it didn't sound sinister, the words coloured with guilt at my actions. 'You're in a good spot for healing.'

'You know I'm not great at sitting around.' His mouth curved in a rueful smile. 'Prepare for the world's worst patient.'

An answering smile touched my lips. If only he knew how much it meant to be able to take care of him for a while. 'I suppose you've never had to take it easy before.' I didn't know that for sure though. He could have been ill, or injured, during the past year for all I knew. 'At least you'll be able to get about with your crutches.'

'I probably won't need them once I'm used to the boot.' He dipped his head to look past me, at the shape of the cottage. It was just gone four o'clock, but already getting dark. 'Still seems odd to be here without your granddad.'

'I know.' In truth, although I missed him, I'd had time to get used to my grandfather's absence and put my own mark on the place he'd loved so much. Thinking of the changes I'd made, my muscles tensed. I'd repainted the walls and changed some of the furniture, rearranged the rooms. It was bound to look different to the last time Jack had seen it – not that he took much notice of interior design, always more interested in the garden, which I'd barely touched. 'Shall we go inside?' I couldn't put it off without it seeming strange.

'Can't wait.'

With an uneasy mix of excitement, guilt, and apprehension, I clambered out of the car, stomach growling with hunger all of a sudden. My head pounded, and my limbs ached from sitting in one position for so long. It was hard to see much as darkness gathered, but a rising moon trailed a silvery path across the thrashing sea, and the sound of waves hitting the rocks had its usual soothing effect. It still amazed me how Robin Hood's Bay – despite the harshness of the landscape in winter – had quickly felt like home, even without Jack there.

The former smuggler's haven, which had only a thousand or so permanent residents, a lot of them older than I was, had welcomed me like an old friend, the locals mindful of my grandfather's position as a respected member of the community.

'I'll get your things.' I ducked back into the car to see Jack struggling to put his jacket on. The wind coming off the North Sea was strong and shifted around us, bringing the taste of salt and smell of seaweed. I straightened and breathed deeply, filling my lungs. *We'd made it.*

We must have looked like an odd pair as we headed from the car, parked on a flattened patch of grass. Vehicles weren't allowed on the narrow, cobbled streets of the village, but Sea View Cottage was set apart, closer to the lowest part of the cliff top, with access down a narrow track that wound around to the front of the building.

Jack leant heavily on his crutches, grunting with the effort, while I hovered behind, as if to catch him should he fall.

'I'm fine.' He sounded strained as he looked over his shoulder, hair pushed back by the wind. 'You go and unlock the door.'

Feeling chastened, I hurried ahead, glad I'd left the lights on, so they lit the windows with a welcoming glow.

'Home, sweet home,' Jack said, once he'd negotiated the step into the tiny entrance hall, his foot sticking out in front of him, the boot stiff and unwieldy. In the puddle of brightness from the wall light, his pallor contrasted sharply with his mess of dark hair and stubble. He used to have a neat beard but looked like he'd been clean-shaven until recently, and it was starting to grow back.

'You look exhausted.' The journey had been too much, I could see. We should have stayed somewhere overnight. 'Do you want to go straight up to bed?' I said, dropping the carrier bag I'd brought in from the car, heavy with the weight of his redundant boot.

'Is that a proposition?' A weary smile broke over his face to show he was making a joke, but his words made my breath halt. We hadn't shared a bed in so long. How should I deal with that? In his eyes we were still a couple. In my heart, I wanted nothing more.

'I should stay downstairs,' he said, as though reading something in my face. 'It's going to be difficult with . . . this.' He gestured with his crutch, wobbling slightly. 'You won't get any sleep with me trying to get comfortable.'

Did he sense on some level that we hadn't slept together for a long time? Maybe a part of him was uncomfortable at the thought, but when I said quickly, 'Don't be silly – I don't mind,' relief flooded his features. I rested a hand on his arm and felt the flex of muscle as he tightened his grip on his crutch. Jack might have lost weight, but there was strength in his body, no doubt maintained by his gardening work. *Was he still doing that?*

After he left, I'd resisted all urges to look for him, online or anywhere else. If he wanted to be with me, he would be, I reasoned. He'd made his choice. Seeing that he'd moved on, met someone else, changed jobs even, would have cracked my already broken heart further and if I was to have any life at all, I told myself I had to get over him, stay strong. And now, he was here – but not through choice. He *had* called me though, prior to his accident – had wanted to come and see me. Perhaps to discuss a divorce. *Or maybe he'd wanted to come home.* The thought was comforting, lifting my spirits as I led the way into the living room, a floor-lamp illuminating the white walls where some of my grandfather's watercolours still hung, alongside a series of framed sketches from the first children's book I'd illustrated.

'Wow, you've been busy,' Jack said, as if he'd been away for the weekend to let me get on with redecorating. 'It's really cosy.'

'You like it?' I searched his face, not quite trusting what he was saying was real. 'I know you're not bothered about paint colours, so I thought I'd stick with white. Freshen the place up, you know?'

'Your pictures look great.' He'd been so proud when my art tutor recommended me to an author friend, who was looking for someone to illustrate a children's book about a lonely hedgehog. When the book sold well, she was offered a series and her agent took me on as a client. Since then, the author had switched to adult fiction and I'd illustrated several more books, but those early drawings of Prickles the hedgehog in various guises were my favourites. 'They look better in here than at the flat.'

'I think it's the lighting.' Nerves pinched my vocal cords so that my voice didn't sound like mine. 'The sofa survived the move, as you can see.'

He nodded, frowning slightly at the forest-green three-seater in front of the open fireplace that dominated the small room, as though trying to picture its journey from our Brighton home to here. 'You kept your granddad's armchair.'

My scalp prickled. *You. Not* we. 'Of course.' The chair had grown shabby, the upholstery worn, but I smiled as I stroked my hand across the faded fabric. 'I couldn't get rid of it.'

He hovered in the doorway, face tight. 'I wish I could remember the move,' he said. 'It just won't come.'

'Look, don't worry about it.' I turned and drew the floral curtains, hooks rattling along the pole. I normally left them open, but the reality of Jack being here was overwhelming. The room seemed smaller, or maybe it was the unsaid things between us making the air feel swollen. When Jack and I used to visit, even with the three of us and my granddad's Labrador Toby, and occasionally my mum, the place hadn't seemed crowded at all, but now I was fighting for air.

'It's just . . . one minute we're at the flat and the next we're here with nothing in between.'

I spun to see Jack scrubbing a hand through his hair, his crutch wedged against his side, eyes darting around as if usure where to settle. 'I don't even remember buying new boots.' He nodded to his foot, then bent to ease it off as if he couldn't stand the sight of it, teetering slightly.

'Let's have something to eat.' My hands shook as I unfastened my coat. I didn't take it off. A chill had permeated the cottage, reaching through the stone walls, and leaking around the window frames. 'I'll put the heating on and make us a sandwich while you get comfortable.'

'That sounds good.' Giving himself a shake, Jack hobbled across the sanded floorboards to the wing-backed armchair and lowered himself down. 'You don't mind me sitting here?'

'Of course not, silly.' My voice was high, almost girlish. Seeing myself through his eyes, it was obvious I wasn't behaving naturally, not how he would expect me to be. It would be normal to kiss him, to sit on his lap like I used to and let his arms close around me, but the feelings that had flowed through me at the hospital, pushing me towards him, had solidified into something different – still there, but at a remove, faded by new routines and habits that didn't involve him. 'Put the telly on if you like.' I bent to pluck the remote off the old coffee table made from a piece of driftwood.

'I keep expecting Toby to run in with a sock in his mouth.' Jack propped his crutches at the side of the chair, his gaze still roaming around, pausing on the higgledy row of photos on the mantel above the fireplace, where the one of my grandfather as a young man took pride of place, casting out a fishing net in a glitter of sea spray, eyes crinkled against the sun. Thank goodness our wedding photo was there too, Jack piggy-backing me in the grounds of Brighton Pavilion where our ceremony was held before we headed to the seafront reception close to where we'd met.

'Ham and cheese?' I said to Jack, just as my phone vibrated in my pocket. He was looking at me expectantly and I realised I hadn't responded to his comment about Toby, who had had died a month after my grandfather, and before Jack left me.

Confusion slid over his face. 'I'm vegetarian.'

My heart jumped. 'I meant cheese, sorry.' *Vegetarian?* 'I meant ham for me, it's fresh from the deli. I couldn't resist buying a few slices.' I was talking too much, but his eyes were heavy once more, tiredness closing in.

'And maybe some water for my tablets.' He took the remote control I was holding out. 'My head hurts like hell,' he said, gingerly tracing the cut on the back of his head.

'Of course.' I hurried down the hall to the kitchen, hoping the bread I'd bought a couple of days ago wasn't stale, wondering when he'd given up eating meat. It was something we'd talked about in the past, but never got round to doing.

The TV came on in the living room, an advert jingle for car insurance. I clicked on the kitchen light, blinking at the sight of my dirty dinner plate and tea-ringed mug by the sink from yesterday. It felt like a hundred years ago – a different life.

I opened the fridge, heart thundering in my chest, checking I had cheese and ham, every cell in my body attuned to Jack – *Jack!* – sitting in the next room before knowledge of the text I'd received burned through the image. I couldn't put off looking, however much I wanted to. Fumbling my phone from my pocket, I glanced at the screen and my stomach tipped. *Owen.*

You can't break up with me without a proper explanation, Caitlin. I love you. I'm not going to let you go that easily! Call me, or I'll come over. X

Chapter 5

Caitlin

I couldn't risk ignoring Owen's text.

Give me 5 mins and I'll call you. X

This kiss would appease him, though normally I wouldn't add one. It felt like leading him on, but I didn't want him turning up and have to explain him to Jack. I could hardly explain Owen to myself, other than we had fallen into something I soon realised I wasn't ready for, and he was on a mission to 'win me over'.

I hastily threw some sandwiches together, tearing the bread with the butter, fighting an urge to weep. If I'd allowed myself to imagine a homecoming, a reunion, with Jack, it hadn't been like this.

'Here you go.' When I took the plate through with a glass of water, he was almost asleep, head lolling against the wing of the chair, reminding me momentarily of my grandfather who, in his later years, would nod off after dinner while 'watching' the news.

'You not eating?' Rousing himself with a struggle, Jack took the plate, and I placed the glass of water on the side table.

'I need to make a quick call first.' It wasn't a lie, but when he said drily, 'Your mum?' I nodded. He would naturally assume his mother-in-law would be worried, that I would have told my parents about Jack's accident. They'd been close. Mum had been almost as devastated as I was when he left. 'I won't be long.'

'I'm not going anywhere.' Half-smiling, he took a bite of sandwich. I smiled back, chin trembling with the effort. I wanted so badly to celebrate him being here, wished with all my heart it was just the two of us somewhere remote, away from everyone, from awkward questions and explanations. 'Got your painkillers?'

Jack swallowed his mouthful and nodded, patting the pocket of his jacket draped over the arm of the chair. 'Thank you, Cait.'

His words were laden with emotion, eyes shiny.

'It's only cheese.' The strongest, vintage cheddar. His favourite, not mine, yet still I bought it.

'You know what I mean.'

'Of course I do.' Bending, I gently kissed his cheek, my hair, freed from its band, falling across his face. For a second, I let myself embrace the second-chance feeling dancing between us. For him, it was no doubt about escaping death, rather than the unexpected renewal of our relationship, but either way, it felt precious. And he *could* have died. The thought struck with the force of a slap. Whoever had hit him with their car was still out there. I wanted to feel angrier with them – I'd been furious on the drive down – but now . . . Jack was here because of that person. Did that mean I was *grateful*? Turning the thought away, I straightened.

'Here.' I pulled over a tapestry footstool and carefully lifted his leg, resting it on top, my face throbbing with warmth. After so long, touching him was both familiar and strange.

'That's better.' He let out a grateful sigh. 'Sorry to be a pain.'

'You're not.' The cut and bruised side of his face was towards me, the other white from the light of the television. Suddenly, he was a stranger. 'Back in a minute.'

After leaving the room, I ran up the narrow wooden staircase

32

to the back bedroom, which I'd stripped of its flowery wallpaper and painted pale blue, panic leaping at the sight of the chest of drawers and wardrobe. How would I explain his clothes still being in boxes? Pushing the worry aside for now, I crossed to the window – the farthest point from the living room downstairs – and pressed Owen's number, wishing I could block him.

'Hey, you,' he said, picking up right away. 'I just pulled up outside.'

'What?' Goose bumps bristled my arms. 'I said I would call you back.'

'I'm worried about you, Caitlin.'

'I've got a friend here.' My heart was bounding, my head spinning. I felt half-crazed with tiredness and hunger – and because of Jack being here – and wasn't in the mood for Owen but forced as much friendly brightness into my voice as I could. 'I'll come out.'

I ran downstairs and poked my head round the living room door to see Jack was sleeping, chin on his chest, the plate of half-eaten sandwiches on the floor. The glass on the table was empty, so he must have taken his tablets. Resisting an urge to make him more comfortable, cover him with the furry throw from the back of the sofa, I hurried to the front door and opened it quickly before Owen could march up and knock.

Stepping outside, I was glad I was wearing my coat and hoped Owen would think I'd grabbed it on my way out. The wind tugged at my hair, cold air slapping my face. It was hard to make anything out in the darkness, but I saw the shape of Owen's Land Rover parked behind my car, the interior lighting up as he pushed open the driver's door and stepped out.

'How long have you been there?' I said when I reached him, digging my hands in my pockets. If he'd been watching the cottage, he might have seen me drawing the curtains and wondered why.

'I've only just pulled up.' His earthy Yorkshire accent seemed stronger after talking to Jack, who spoke with a softer, more neutral accent like mine. 'Shall we sit in the car? It's freezing out here.' He gave an exaggerated shiver, teeth flashing in a grin. 'You wouldn't think it was winter,' he joked.

I walked round to the passenger side, flicking a glance at the cottage. Had the curtains twitched? Maybe, due to the breeze that flowed through the old frames. I remembered too late that I hadn't put the heating on.

Owen settled in the driver's seat, as though we were at the cinema. He was big and broad, with a coiled muscularity that seemed to fill the small space. I'd known of Owen Whittaker when I moved to Robin Hood's Bay. He owned an outdoor-clothing and equipment store on the Whitby road and ran training sessions for people who needed to be fit for sports events or expeditions. He lived in a grey-stone cottage next to the store and sometimes drank at the local pub, The Taverner, here in the village. I'd bumped into him there a couple of times with my grandfather before I met Jack. Gramps had known Owen's father, a local, and introduced us, but Owen had been with a couple of friends, and I wasn't looking for a relationship at the time.

Owen remembered me though. He called round the day after I moved in to say he was sorry to hear of my grandfather's death. At that moment, the van containing the furniture from the flat in Brighton rolled up, and he set to work helping me and the removal men to bring in the larger pieces of furniture, and the boxes I couldn't fit in my car.

'I think we've earned a drink,' he said afterwards. I'd accepted, grateful for his help, with no intention of taking it further. Somehow, Owen, while not being pushy exactly, had made his presence felt, turning up randomly to take me out for fish and chips, or a walk on the beach, or to bring me things he thought I might like: a lamp base decorated with seashells, a bottle of his mother's wine – *She makes it herself* – and each time, it would hit me in a dispassionate way how attractive he was, tall and broad with messy, dark-blond hair and gooseberry-green eyes, and I would wonder why he was single, why he was bothering with me.

Over brunch one Sunday – *We do have brunch in Yorkshire, Caitlin, and it's not a date. Just two people enjoying food together* – he confessed he'd never forgotten our first meeting in the pub, had even asked my grandfather afterwards whether I was single. I'd known nothing of this and had met Jack soon after that visit, so presumably Gramps hadn't seen the point in telling me. After Owen's admission, our meetings took on a deeper meaning. Despite being certain I could never feel about him the way I had about Jack, I decided it was time to try. Owen had been patient, seemed happy to let things develop at their own pace, and I had really made an effort. He was kind, interested in my work and in me; my parents hadn't met him, but my oldest friend Dee, who had been to visit just before Christmas, announced she would move up here if I didn't want him, falling for Owen's 'Yorkshire grit'.

But the grit had hardened when I suggested to Owen we would be better as friends. I thought being honest would work in my favour, but it had been a few weeks and he still wasn't taking no for an answer. We had to give it more time; he wasn't the sort to give up; he liked a challenge; I would come round eventually. *You need to relax more, open your heart again.*

And now he was here, his gaze intense, a half-smile twisting his mouth as he studied my face, which I was sure had guilt scribbled on it. 'What's going on, Caitlin? Is it your friend, Dee?' He turned to look at the cottage, and I noticed his normally short hair had grown, curling over the collar of his black sports jacket. 'Is she in some kind of trouble?'

'No, it's . . . it's not Dee.'

'Who, then?' I was pinned by his stare once more. His eyes were harder than Jack's, pupils dilated so they looked almost black. *I mustn't compare him with Jack.* But wasn't that what I'd been doing for the past year?

'Owen, you know I said I wanted us to just be friends. You can't keep turning up whenever you like—'

'Isn't that what friends do?' When his eyes crinkled at the corners, he was friendly Owen again, concerned for my welfare. 'I came up this morning and you weren't here. I was checking in, that's all.'

Checking up on me, more like. 'The thing is, Owen . . .' My heart was a hollow drumbeat in my ears. 'Jack . . . Jack was hit by a car and I . . . he was asking for me, so I drove down there. To Brighton.' For a moment, the silence was so complete I wondered whether the words had made it out of my head.

'Jack?' His large hands came up to grip the steering wheel, knuckles whitening. 'Your ex-husband?'

'I don't know any other Jacks.' My weak attempt at humour was badly judged, and I didn't dare point out that Jack and I were still married.

Owen's jaw tightened. 'He called you, didn't he?'

Owen had been leaving the cottage the night Jack phoned me, after dropping in for a cup of tea, and although he hadn't said anything, I wasn't sure he'd bought my hastily whispered *It's an old friend* excuse as I ushered him out.

'He did, but that wasn't why . . . you and I were already over.'

'Don't say that.'

'It's true.' The window was open a crack, letting in chilled air. The moon-silvered sea had grown wild again, waves surging at the harbour wall. I shivered. 'The thing is, Jack and I are back together.' Better to get it over with, even though the phrase *back together* implied an element of choice on both sides. 'I've never stopped loving him, Owen. I'm so sorry. That's why . . . you and me . . .' I gestured with icy fingers. 'I suppose it's why I never completely let you in.'

My other hand had travelled to the door handle, as if I might need to leap out and run, yet Owen had never given the slightest indication he was capable of hurting me, or would want to hurt anyone.

'You never really tried.' He sounded more sad than angry. I pulled my hand back into my lap and tried to stop my teeth from chattering. 'I won't give up though.' Said quietly, it sounded like a pledge. 'You're worth waiting for.'

'Owen, please.' I swivelled to look at him. 'You deserve to be with someone who loves you properly.'

'The thing is, I don't want anyone else.'

A feeling of dread settled in my stomach. 'That's how I feel about Jack.' Maybe I shouldn't have said it, but I was desperate to get through to him. 'Please, Owen.' I tried to hook his gaze, but he was staring though the windscreen, perhaps not trusting himself to look at me. 'Don't waste any more time on me. I mean it.'

'You say he had an accident.'

'Yes . . .' I hesitated. 'He was hit by a car.'

Owen pulled in a long breath and let it out slowly, tension seeping from him. His fingers drummed the wheel, and he gave a slow shake of his head as he absorbed my words. 'Perhaps he just wants a nursemaid.'

It was a curiously old-fashioned turn of phrase but sent a shard of panic across my chest. 'No, Owen. He still loves me.' No point sugar-coating it. 'The accident brought it home.'

'And now you've brought him home.' *Him.* Slight emphasis, loaded with dislike, though he'd never met Jack.

'I know it might be awkward if we run into each other, but with time I honestly think we can be friends, Owen. I *want* us to be friends.' I wasn't sure I did, not really. Not while I knew that Owen wanted more.

'I have all the friends I need.'

'Then . . .' I struggled for the right words, but could only manage a feeble, 'I guess this is it.'

'I hope not.' Moving his head, he gave me a searching look that I did my best to hold, hoping he could read conviction in my face. Reaching over, he traced a thumb across my eyebrow and down my cheek. I had to prompt myself to breathe.

He leant forward suddenly and gunned the engine, making me jump. 'You know where to find me if you change your mind.'

'Owen, I won't.' I hated the pleading note creeping into my voice. 'Promise me you'll move on.'

'I don't make promises I can't keep.' He flashed me a close-lipped smile that didn't touch his eyes. 'Take care, Caitlin.'

I shoved open the door and almost fell out of the Land Rover in my haste to get away. 'Bye, Owen.'

I didn't wait for him to reply, practically running up the path to the cottage, imagining his gaze burning into me. It wasn't until I was inside, locking the door while peering through the porthole, that he finally drove off; not quickly – no spinning tyres and roaring engine – but with a slow, steady purr, tail-lights flashing red through the blackness like a warning.

Chapter 6

Lydia

Now

'What are you doing?'

I spun round at the sound of Mattie's voice, almost dropping my phone. 'I called the hospital—'

'For God's sake, Mum, he's gone. Why can't you leave it?' The new rawness in my son's voice pushed at my crumbling edges.

'He was taken in,' I burst out, not thinking straight, part of me registering that I shouldn't be telling Mattie. 'He'd been injured but he's fine. He's out now. I told them I was a close friend, that I'd been worried about him, because they weren't going to give me any information.' *Shut up, shut up, Lydia.*

'Injured?' Mattie appeared frozen in the doorway. I only ever seemed to see in him standing in doorways, these days.

'A fall, I think,' I went on quickly, trying to suppress the shake in my voice. 'Badly sprained ankle, cracked rib, concussion but he's . . . he's OK.'

Mattie's face puckered with shock and confusion. 'So, what . . . he's going to come back?'

'No, he . . .' I pressed a trembling hand to my mouth, the nurse's words playing on a loop in my brain. *His wife came to collect him.* Collect him. Like a parcel at the sorting office. 'He's with his wife.'

'His *wife*?'

Mattie knew about her, didn't he? Suddenly, I couldn't remember having that conversation, but he was nodding slowly as though it made sense.

'So, leave it, Mum. He's made his choice.' Something careful and measured in his words made me pay attention. He sounded grown-up, older than his years. 'He doesn't want you.'

'Mattie!' I stared, my phone clutched to my chest, hot in my hand. *His wife came to collect him.* 'I know you don't mean that.'

'He won't come back now you've pissed him off, like you always do.'

Why couldn't he understand? 'He will if I talk to him, Mattie. He loves us both. I know he does.'

'Maybe you should have been nicer to him then.' I felt the coldness of his withdrawal. 'He obviously can't stand you. Just like Dad couldn't, and that's why you killed him.'

'Mattie, *stop!*' Fear gathered in my throat. I held out a hand, nausea rising when he stepped back. 'Please. I just want a second chance to get things right.'

His expression morphed into disbelief. 'Listen to yourself, Mum.' As he turned away, I noticed his eyes were heavy-lidded with exhaustion, the struggle to comprehend. He hadn't been sleeping well. Neither of us had, moving around the house at night like ghosts. Guilt pierced my heart. *I* had done this to him by failing to hold on to the man he'd come to rely on, a replacement father for the one he'd lost. 'And stop calling me Mattie. I've told you, I'm Matt now.'

My heart clenched. I'd tried it out when he decided a few months ago that Mattie was too babyish, but it hadn't stuck. He would always be Mattie to me.

'Shouldn't you be getting ready for school?' I tightened the belt of my dressing gown in an effort to regain control. I hadn't changed out of it for two days and my armpits smelt sour. 'You don't want to be late.'

'Don't worry, I'm going.' He reached for his rucksack, hanging behind him at the bottom of the stairs. 'No point being here now, is there?'

The closeness we'd forged when Jack had entered our lives seemed inaccessible now, and a shiver ran up my spine. Abruptly, I was shaking again, some internal force taking over. It had been that way since the idea that Jack was in Brighton had grown in my mind, the certainty stronger with every breath. I hadn't told Mattie it was the hospital there that I'd called this morning, after ringing the flat where Jack used to live – he'd told me the address once, so fondly it had lodged in my brain – but the woman I spoke to said Caitlin had moved out.

His wife came to collect him, the nurse had said. Where from? Jack must have kept her number all this time and called her. But why would she take him back now?

I wondered whether there had been darkness at the heart of their relationship too. Was that why Jack had been drawn to me? Did I possess similar qualities to his ex? He hadn't discussed her, and I hadn't pressed. I hadn't wanted details. He was with me and that was all that mattered. But now he was with her, and I couldn't stand it any more than I could stand Mattie hating me again. *That's why you killed him.* I'd had moments of hating William, when I had felt my sanity hanging by a thread and worried about what I might do, but I hadn't wanted him dead. *Had I?*

The sound of the door banging shut after Mattie – he hadn't eaten breakfast again – galvanised me into action. I ran upstairs and into the shower room, tearing off my dressing gown. As steam rose around me, a plan began to take shape. First, I would find out where Caitlin lived. Then, I would send her a warning. After that, I would wait to see what happened. Maybe, if she threw him

41

out, Jack would come back and everything would be fine again. I would make sure of it, for Mattie's sake.

I thought of Jack, injured in hospital without me, and tears rained down my face. *I'm coming to get you. Whatever's happened, I can put it right.*

It was less than two hours by train to Brighton. From there I could take a taxi to where his ex-wife had lived. I would easily be back before Mattie got home from school.

I phoned work to tell them I wouldn't be in.

'Again?' My manager was short on sympathy. 'Look, Lydia, I get you're having a hard time after the break-up, but we're short-staffed as it is. Maybe coming to work will help take your mind off things.'

'I'm sorry, Ben. I just can't today.'

The job at the garden centre was only meant to be a stop-gap. I hadn't needed to work when Mattie's dad was alive. William had earned enough for us both, but as much as I'd tried to love being a wife and mum, I needed something to do – I'd just never figured out exactly what it was. At school, I thought I would end up in finance because I was good at maths, but a bullying incident had thrown me off course and I'd never really recovered. I found it hard to settle to anything, convinced I would find my vocation if I tried out different jobs. I had never wanted to be just a housewife – the memory of Mum's martyred submission as she did everything my father asked still made me shudder – but I didn't have any particular talent either. My father hoped I would become an accountant like him, and I considered it, desperate for his approval, but couldn't face the years of training.

The job at the garden centre had been an impulse application. I hadn't expected it to come to anything, but when I got the job, William was pleased for me, Mattie too – most of the other mothers worked – and I ended up staying there. It had been a lifeline after William died, and it was where I met Jack when he came in looking for equipment for a gardening job, our eyes meeting over a selection of neoclassical patio accessories, as we joked afterwards. *Love at first sight.* I'd never believed in it before.

I wanted him back so badly, my body ached as if I was coming down with something. I couldn't shake the mental image of him battered and broken in hospital, even though the nurse had assured me he was OK.

Leaving the house, I pulled up the hood of my coat against a drift of rain and felt Harriet's eyes on me. Spotting her at the window next door, I shot her a smile she didn't return. She used to babysit Mattie when William and I went out, but the sense she didn't like me strengthened after his death.

'Mattie can come round to mine any time he likes,' she told me, after William's funeral, accosting me on the doorstep. 'He's a good boy.' As if I didn't know that. As if she could offer my son something I couldn't.

Her gaze burned into me as I hurried down the rain-slicked pavement, and it wasn't until I was on the train out of London that I felt I could breathe freely.

Atlingworth Street was a long, narrow road of towering, white-fronted houses set behind black iron railings, a glimpse of the sea at the opposite end. The clouds had cleared, and the water glittered in a burst of sunlight. How long was it since I'd been to the seaside? Not since Mattie was little when we holidayed in Cornwall. I wasn't keen on sand, or the sea for that matter – too vast and unknowable – though William had loved it, Mattie too. I'd never visited Brighton, but knew the beaches were pebbly. Jack had grown up here, but his childhood was another prickly subject he rarely touched upon. Why hadn't I asked more questions? I knew his mum was dead, and his dad lived abroad, and they didn't get on. No siblings, like me.

The flat he'd rented with Caitlin was in one of the smaller buildings, crouched beyond wrought-iron gates, on the ground floor of a two-storey building – the only one with a patch of garden behind, which Jack once told me he'd transformed into a tropical haven of plants and shrubs, with a water feature. He'd kept a photo on his phone and showed me one night, as though he couldn't help himself. I'd put the sadness in his eyes down to him leaving all that hard work behind when he left Caitlin, but now I wondered whether it was Caitlin he'd been missing all along.

As I pushed through the gates, it hit me that the likelihood of a neighbour being home at this time of day was small, but if I asked around discreetly, maybe someone would give me Caitlin's address. If she'd lived here for a few years, she must have made friends.

As I approached the black-painted front door, it opened and a woman stepped out, holding the hand of a blond-haired little boy.

'Can I help you?' she said, with a glance of polite enquiry. The boy looked up at me, a finger in his mouth, eyes screwed up against the light. I felt too hot in my coat and pulled the zip down, drawing my mouth into a friendly smile.

'I'm here to see Caitlin Garvey.' I transferred my smile to the little boy, remembering Mattie at that age: full of life, eyes sparkling with mischief. 'I was in the area and thought I'd look her up. We were at school together and I haven't seen her for ages.' When the woman's thin eyebrows drew together, I hurried on, 'I know it's a silly time of day and she's probably working, and I should have called ahead, but I don't have her new number and—'

'It's not that,' the woman cut in, bending to scoop her little boy into her arms, hair slipping from a lopsided bun. 'She doesn't live here anymore.'

'Oh.' My dismay was real. Why would this woman give out an address to a total stranger, even if she knew it? 'Are you her neighbour?'

'No, the tenant.' Turning awkwardly, she pulled the door closed behind her before I'd had a chance to peer inside. 'She's gone to Robin Hood's Bay in North Yorkshire. Apparently her grandfather had a cottage there, by the sea. He left it to her when he died.'

I felt a jump of excitement. 'That's right,' I said, as though I'd just remembered. 'She used to go for holidays there.'

The woman nodded, distracted by the child tugging her hair, his bottom lip sticking out. 'I've got to go.' She flashed a quick smile. 'Sorry I can't be more help.'

'No problem.' Heat crept over my face. 'Thank you.'

She headed at speed to a small car parked outside the garage. While she loaded the boy inside, I slipped through the gates and onto the street, hardly able to believe it had been that easy. Within five minutes of arriving, I knew where Jack was living.

Chapter 7

Caitlin

'I'd forgotten how big the garden is.'

Jack was looking through the window in the kitchen, a crutch tucked under one armpit as he bent over the sink. His hair was rucked up at the back and the sight of it pricked me with tenderness.

'It could definitely do with your magic touch, once you're feeling better.' I tried not to stare as I melted butter into a pan on the stove, the sight of him still a mirage, like something I'd dreamt up through wishful thinking – though the reality of his appearance was a stark contrast to the one I'd held in my mind. I mustn't comment, though, or ask what had happened beyond the obvious injuries from his accident.

'You look good,' he said, turning his head, a smile darting over his lips. 'Rested.'

'Thanks. I am.'

It was true. Despite my unsettling exchange with Owen, and the strangeness of everything else, I'd slept more deeply than I had in months, as if I'd finally won a hard-fought battle. After waking Jack when I came back inside, he'd insisted on spending the night on the sofa after all, too shattered, he said sleepily, to tackle the stairs. He could barely keep his eyes open as I fetched pillows and blankets and made him comfortable, half-relieved when he didn't make any attempt to remove his clothes.

'What if you need the loo in the night?'

'I went to the downstairs toilet while you were outside,' he'd murmured, sinking his head onto the pillow. His words had set off a vibration of panic, as I remembered thinking I'd seen the curtains twitch. Could he have seen me talking to Owen after all? It seemed unlikely, given the darkness outside, and Jack's spaced-out state, his energy seemingly focused on getting out of the armchair, muttering, 'Your mum OK?'

'Sends her love,' I'd said, turning to switch off the lamp so he couldn't read my expression. When I looked back, his eyelids had fallen shut.

On waking, just after seven, I had lain for several minutes, waiting for the rush of guilt, horror, and nerves as I relived the enormity of what I'd done; the concealment of truth. Instead, there was quiet happiness, coupled with a sense of rightness that Jack was downstairs, under this roof with me where he belonged. Swinging my legs out of bed, I decided to stay in the moment, prolonging the anticipation of seeing him again by taking a shower and planning breakfast, imagining us chatting as though things were normal – better than normal. It was a chance to rewrite history. *As long as he never remembers.*

I couldn't completely ignore the voice in my head but told myself I would deal with it when – if – it happened. *Just don't let it be today, or tomorrow*, I silently pleaded, pulling on jeans, a clean top, and a brush through my tangled hair, observing myself in the dressing table mirror. There was a slight wildness in the flush of my cheeks, the brightness of my eyes as nerves circled my stomach. *Let him see how good we are together, how well we fit, and why we got married in the first place.*

'Meant to be,' Mum had said when I took Jack home to introduce him. 'He's just right for you, Caitlin. Kind eyes, like your dad.' She threw my father an affectionate look, which he returned, both taking pleasure in the news that I had found someone I was happy with after a series of short-lived, unremarkable relationships.

Jack had been awake when I ran downstairs, suddenly worried he wouldn't be there, or that something had happened in the night. He was lying quietly, head poking from the puffy duvet, his injured ankle resting on the arm of the sofa. My heart had twisted when his face lit up at the sight of me, his bruises less noticeable in the half-light – more like the Jack I remembered. He slept well too, he told me, a note of surprise in his voice. 'I don't think I moved all night.'

As I served breakfast at the wooden table tucked into an alcove that used to be a pantry, he hobbled over and sat on the chair I pulled out. 'I'd forgotten what a great cook you are,' he said, picking up his knife and fork. I stiffened – *why would he have forgotten that?* – but when he added, 'I can't remember the last time we ate anything but cereal or toast for breakfast,' my shoulders relaxed. Before he wrenched himself from my life, I hadn't made a full English for ages and, often absorbed by work, or a project I was passionate about, I tended to lose all sense of time and forget about dinner. Sometimes Jack cooked, but more often we ordered a takeaway.

'We're a long way from a Chinese or Indian here,' I said, by way of explanation. 'I've enjoyed getting into making meals from scratch again.'

'It's weird,' he said, when he'd swallowed a mouthful of mushroom and eggs, 'that such a long period of time has been wiped out.' He picked up the sheet of kitchen roll serving as a napkin and brushed it over his mouth. 'I mean, forgetting the accident I can understand, and even the hours before that, but a *year*?'

'It *is* weird,' I agreed because it was. And part of me was desperate to know exactly what had happened during that time.

'But remember, yesterday, you said it didn't matter. That you were just glad to be alive.'

He nodded, piling food onto his fork. He seemed ravenous, as though he hadn't eaten properly for a long time. 'The food was terrible in there,' he said, as though reading my mind. It used to be like that between us – each knowing what the other was thinking without having to spell it out. *Until it wasn't.* 'Not that I was in much of a state to eat.'

'I haven't a lot of food in.' I pushed my breakfast around my plate as my appetite waned. 'I'll need to go shopping.' Was I making it sound as though he was a guest I hadn't been expecting? 'I usually go on Tuesday mornings.'

'I'll take your word for it.' He flashed a grin that warmed my heart, then winced. 'I'll be glad when this bruising has gone down. I'm not fit to be seen in public.'

In public. I was going to have to explain his appearance. The locals knew me, and that I was single. Some of them had guessed I'd been seeing Owen as more than just a friend, and his sister Mel had known for sure – had expressed how pleased she was for us both, that I was *just what Owen needed.*

'You need to take it easy for a while,' I reminded Jack, grateful the cottage was off the main track, hidden from prying eyes. I needed time to lay the groundwork for his return, to let people know we were a couple without giving away to Jack that, for more than a year, we hadn't set eyes on each other, let alone lived together.

'Do you think I should call my dad?'

I looked up, surprised. Jack hadn't been in regular contact with his father since Neil relocated to Italy with a younger woman a year before we met. It had been Jack and his dad against the world since his mother's death when Jack was fifteen – his father had taught at a sailing club and took Jack out with him every weekend – but, despite trying to understand his father's new relationship, it caused a rift between them that hadn't healed. I'd met Neil once, when he flew over for his mother's funeral – without his Italian wife – and I'd liked him; an older, broader, more tanned version of Jack, with a ready smile that didn't quite erase the lines of grief etched into his face. Jack's mother had been the love of his life, he told me in quiet tones at the pub after the funeral, but he hated being alone, had wanted to be happy again, to recapture that feeling of being in love, and hoped with all his heart that Jack would accept Rosita one day.

'I think he would want to know what's happened,' I said, carefully. It made sense that when he woke up in hospital, Jack had thought of his dad as well as me. Might he have spoken to him at some point over the last year, told him we'd broken up? It wasn't as if I could ask. 'I'll call him for you if you like.'

'Maybe.' He seemed to reconsider. 'Just . . . not yet.'

'OK.' Relief gave way to a swirl of nausea. All this subterfuge, and we hadn't even finished breakfast. For a while at least, I would be second-guessing everything. The thought shortened my breath.

'Are you all right?' Jack lowered his knife and fork. 'Sorry, that was a silly question. This is all a bit much, I know.' Before I could speak, he added, 'I don't want you waiting on me hand and foot – pardon the pun – especially as you must have work to do.'

How could I tell him I wanted nothing more than to take care of him, to make amends for how much I'd hurt him in the past?

'You would do it for me,' I said with a lightness I didn't feel. He would have done anything for me once. 'And it's not as though you're totally incapable.' I summoned a smile. 'Just a few bruises and a bashed-up ankle. You'll be running around in no time.'

His expression dimmed. 'I doubt whoever hit me is sleeping well.'

'Do you think they knew what they'd done?'

'Hard not to, unless they thought it was an animal, but the police said it was dark, so they must have had their headlights on and seen me.'

'Maybe they were distracted for a moment, a child in the back of the car, or fiddling with the radio.' I'd done it myself once, trying to tune in to a music station, and almost hit a cyclist. It had shaken me up for the rest of the day.

'Maybe.'

'I feel bad that you were even there.' It was true, but not in the way he would assume.

'I chose to stay in Brighton while you got this place ready.' He stretched a hand across the table. I took hold of it, warmth flowing up my arm. 'For all I know, I wasn't looking where I was going and stepped off the pavement. The police think the driver panicked—'

'But you could have been killed.' It hit me all over again that he might have died without me ever speaking to him again. 'I hope they catch whoever did it.'

Jack's fingers tightened around mine. 'Let's not talk about it.' His eyes – one couched in swollen, greenish-purple flesh – were full of compassion. 'As long as I don't have to go back there . . .' A shudder ran though him, as though touched by the ghost of a memory of what had propelled him to be on that road in the first place.

'I never thought I'd hear you say that about Brighton.'

'Yeah, well, I know now that home isn't so much a place as a person,' he said, keeping tight hold of my hand. 'Being wherever you are is all that matters.'

I'd longed to hear those words, had almost accepted the fact that I never would, and hearing them now was almost too much to bear. I'd never got to the stage of thinking about him with nostalgia, reminiscing about good times, because in my mind we hadn't left them until that awful, final day.

Before I could push words past the lump lodged in my throat, he said, 'I can't believe how much you've done here.' His gaze scanned the buttermilk-painted walls of the kitchen, brightened by winter sun streaming through the window, wooden shelves stacked with blue and white crockery that was once my gran's, which my grandfather had stashed in a cupboard for years – the oak worktops, and the windowsill teeming with pots of herbs.

'Well, it needed updating from Gramps's time-warp décor.'

'True.' Jack gave a lopsided smile, releasing my hand to mop up his egg yolk with a slice of thickly buttered bread. 'He never really moved on from your gran dying.'

'He liked being an eligible widower,' I said. 'As long as he had me, Mum, and the dog, he was happy.'

'Especially the dog,' Jack joked. 'What does your mum think about this?' He looked around again.

'She loves it.' I spoke quickly, thankful my parents were currently island-hopping in Greece, making the most of their retirement from teaching. 'She's been . . .' I was about to say, *She's been to visit a couple of times but is still glad to leave and go back to London* but managed to switch at the last second to '. . . really encouraging. You know I felt guilty that Gramps left the cottage to me, not her.'

'She didn't want it,' Jack reminded me. 'She couldn't wait to escape this place for the bright lights of London, remember?'

I smiled. 'She can't understand why I'm . . . we're happy to settle here.'

'I'm surprised she still likes London.'

'Surrey isn't London, though, is it?' I thought of Dorking where I'd grown up – a thriving town circled by countryside an hour's drive from the city – where my parents had settled after they married, first meeting at teacher training college near Wimbledon. 'I think she would like to move abroad now, maybe Spain. You know how she loves the sunshine, but Dad's not keen.'

'Maybe if we hadn't lived in London and Brighton we'd want to live in a city, but I prefer it here.' As Jack's smile broadened, I shrank back a little, knowing instinctively what he was going to say, wanting to push the words away before they were uttered. It would be this, if nothing else, that brought it all back. 'It's the perfect place to raise a family.'

I waited – one beat, two – feeling the frightened beat of my heart.

Puzzlement flitted over his face. 'Caitlin?'

He didn't remember.

'Perfect,' I agreed, heat on my neck, my face. *Look normal.* I let a small smile unfurl, picked up my plate, and rose. 'Would you like to take a shower?'

'I would definitely like to change out of these clothes.'

Turning, I saw him pluck at his T-shirt, wrinkling his nose, the topic of children temporarily forgotten. 'I don't smell great.'

My heartbeat calmed as danger passed, and a lightness now flowed through me as I thought of the cardboard boxes in the back bedroom. 'I'll find some stuff for you,' I said. 'I haven't unpacked everything yet.' I was aware of the gaps; no specific time frames, no mention of where he'd stayed in Brighton while I *got this place ready*, but it felt better than telling outright lies.

His chair scraped back, and he reached for his crutch. Already he seemed capable of managing with one, the other abandoned on the floor by the sofa in the living room. 'Time to tackle the stairs.' He sounded cheerful as if, like me, he was relishing the sheer normality of everything. 'I'll see you up there.'

On my way to help, I stopped as the phone rang, shrill in the quiet of the kitchen. It was the landline phone, fixed to the wall by the fridge-freezer, and had been there as long as I could remember, last updated in the Nineties – almost a museum piece. No one rang the landline.

'Probably a scam call,' Jack said, shouldering his way through the doorway, causing him to inhale sharply and place a hand near his ribs.

'I'd better get it, just in case.' I thought of my parents, fit and healthy in their sixties, keen for new adventures, and imagined one of them toppling into the water, or leaping off the side of a boat and getting caught in a riptide. 'Hello?'

The silence at the other end was disconcerting. It felt alive, somehow. Expecting an automated message to kick in, I went to hang up when a sound, like someone releasing a breath, made me press the receiver to my ear. 'Hello?' I repeated. 'Who is this?'

In the doorway, Jack turned with a wince of pain. From this angle, his face was jaundiced, a purple groove beneath his eye. 'Prank call?'

'I don't know.' Frowning, I listened harder, holding my body still. 'Is somebody there?'

Definitely a breath this time; a sharp intake, as though someone was about to speak. Goose bumps tracked along my arms as the certainty rose that this was to do with Jack.

'Hello?' I spoke sharply to disguise my fear. 'Speak now, or I'm hanging up.' But my words met dead air. Whoever it was had gone.

Chapter 8

Lydia

He was with her.

I hadn't been completely sure at first, shocked when she answered the phone as the reality of what I was doing slammed into me. Robbed of speech, I didn't even ask for her by name. *Caitlin.* I hadn't planned what to say, still couldn't believe it had been so easy to find the number. To find *her*.

C Garvey, Sea View Cottage, Robin Hood's Bay.

There in plain sight for anyone to see, courtesy of an online phone directory. She hadn't even reverted to her maiden name, and I wondered whether she'd hoped that Jack would find her, one day.

I'd assumed he no longer had her mobile number. I went through the contacts on his phone once, not snooping, exactly. He'd left it behind and rang me from a payphone to ask me to call a client and let her know he was running late. I'd recognised all the numbers in there: mine, Mattie's, the garden centre, his handful of customers and a couple of gardening contacts.

'Not worried I'll discover you still have your ex's number, under a different name?' I'd joked, heart thudding at the idea.

'How would you know if it was under a different name?' He'd tried to match my tone, then told me he'd deleted her number as soon as he left Brighton.

Was it stored in his memory all along, or had he given the hospital her name and they tracked her down for him?

I'd expected the search to be harder, that if there was a phone number assigned to a cottage in Robin Hood's Bay, and there were many, it would be under her grandfather's name, which I didn't know. But in the end, I struck lucky. No need for plan B, which I hadn't thought through but had vaguely involved calling local pubs and asking for her in the hope someone would say, 'Oh yes, Caitlin's here, I'll put her on.' *As if.*

When she picked up after several rings, during which I nibbled the ragged skin around my thumbnail, feeling sick and dizzy, I froze.

'Hello?' Not suspicious the first time, just curious.

I pictured her as I'd seen her online, a profile picture on her Facebook page: wild, dark hair around a heart-shaped face, deep blue eyes, and lightly freckled skin, her slightly self-conscious, white-toothed smile suggesting she wasn't keen on having her picture taken. She was beautiful. Jack clearly didn't have a type, but maybe he was attracted to me because I was her opposite.

The Facebook page, like her website, contained nothing personal, relating only to her job as an illustrator of children's books, and links to other work she'd done. One was a mascot logo that I recognised for a children's charity, in the form of a little boy dressed as a superhero.

Immediately, I wanted to wipe my mind clean of Caitlin Garvey. I didn't want to build up a picture of her, or even think her name. I didn't want her to be a flesh-and-blood person with thoughts and feelings, when up until now she'd been nothing but an abstract, a smudge, a hazy blur in a corner of my mind that I kept closed.

Resisting the impulse to look for more, I'd come offline and called the number of the cottage, trying to read into that first *Hello* what kind of person she was.

'Hello?' The second time, something trickled into that single word; a wrinkle of discomfort. 'Who is this?'

Had he told her about me? If so, what had he said? Maybe he hadn't mentioned me at all, but she knew . . . *something*. That my silence represented a fact she didn't want to face: Jack had been with someone else since they broke up. Had loved somebody more than her.

So why had he gone back? Then, a different voice broke through the film of ice that seemed to have coated my veins.

'Prank call?'

Jack. Bitterness had flooded my mouth and I bit my knuckles to stop a cry escaping. He was there.

Caitlin spoke again, but her words seemed to come from underwater and all I heard was a third *Hello* before cutting the call.

I threw my phone across the room where it bounced off the wall and skittered along the floorboards. Pushing my hands into my hair I tugged it hard and let out a yelp of anguish, but the storm in my brain wouldn't settle.

'Mum, what's wrong?'

My heart gave a startled beat as Mattie came in. He rounded the sofa and picked up my phone, studying the screen. 'It's not broken.' He looked at me. 'What were you doing?'

'Sorry, I . . . I got impatient trying to download an app. I couldn't get it to work.'

His gaze was wary. 'What app?'

I huddled into the oversized cardigan I'd pulled on earlier and pushed my feet into my slippers. Despite turning up the heating, I was cold to my bones. 'I didn't hear you come in.'

Mattie reluctantly placed my phone in my outstretched palm, a sulky set to his mouth. 'I told you, I had a free study period this afternoon. I came home to get changed, then I'm going to the cinema with Callum.'

'Doesn't study period mean you're supposed to study?'

'I'm on top of it, Mum.'

Jack had been keen to instil in Mattie the importance of an education, just as William had, especially impressed by Mattie's talent for art, which I'd joked he must have inherited from an unknown, distant relative. Mattie needed direction and encouragement, both of which coming from me, a college dropout, meant nothing.

I need you, Jack.

'Have you been off work again?' Mattie took in my lank ribbons of uncombed hair, ancient jogging bottoms and vest top under my cardigan, and the mugs of half-drunk tea littering the surfaces. When he looked at me again, his eyes sparked with fear.

'Mum—'

'Look, Mattie . . . Matt.' I reached for him. 'It's going to be fine, I promise.' To my surprise, he let me take his hand. 'It's not going to be like after Dad died,' I said, recalling the bleak months after the funeral when it took every ounce of energy to get out of bed in the mornings and see Mattie off to school before crawling back under my duvet, ignoring Harriet from next door when she called through the letterbox. 'I just need a bit of time to get my head around everything that's happened – that's all.'

He tugged his hand from mine, his guard up. 'How much time?'

I forced a smile but let it drop when he recoiled slightly. 'I might go away for a few days,' I said impulsively.

'Away?' His brow lowered. 'What do you mean?'

'Go to Aunt Shona's.' My tone brightened. 'I haven't seen her in ages. It'll do me good to get away, clear my head a bit.'

Shona – not a real aunt but a friend I'd known since school – constantly issued invitations to visit during our semi-regular text catch-ups. She wanted to meet Jack, but we hadn't got to that stage, just as I hadn't met anyone in Jack's circle. I preferred it that way, the three of us in our little bubble, no need for anyone else, and when things got a bit difficult, it was better that we didn't have to explain things to people who might not understand the nature of our relationship.

'I could come too.' Mattie's voice rose with a boyish excitement that summoned a flashback to him as a toddler, a butterfly landing on his pudgy arm in the garden, and the way he'd stared at it with a look of pure delight. 'I like Aunt Shona.'

It was true they got on well. Even William had liked her company – a bit too much, I sometimes thought. If I was honest, it had been a relief when she met Connor, fell pregnant and moved to York, where his family was from.

'You have school,' I told Mattie, swallowing a barb of guilt. 'It's important with your A levels coming up if you want to get into university.'

'We can go at the weekend, or during next half-term.'

'Half-term's too far away, and I don't want to wait until the weekend.'

His face grew rigid with resistance. 'Is this about Jack?'

'It's not about Jack.' I injected the words with as much conviction as I could muster. 'Look, I'll prove it.'

Unlocking my phone, I found Shona's number and typed **I know it's short notice, Sho, but can I come up tomorrow and stay a few days? Desperately need a break and would love to see you xx**

'See?' I showed Mattie. 'No ulterior motive.'

'So you're just leaving me here?' He glanced around the living room which, not long ago, had felt alive, the television tuned to *Love Island* – my guilty pleasure – Jack's wallet and keys on the mantelpiece, Mattie hunched over his homework at the dining table, smiling ruefully at one of Jack's 'dad' jokes – *I used to hate facial hair, but then it grew on me*, stroking the fledgling beard I kept asking him to shave off – the smell of a casserole floating from the kitchen, or pizza boxes scattered across the coffee table. 'I don't want to be here on my own.'

'It'll only be for a few days. I'll ask Harriet to come in, or you can eat at hers. You like Harriet,' I reminded him.

'I'm sixteen, Mum. I don't need a babysitter.' Even so, he didn't protest any further. When he was younger, I'd overheard him ask Harriet if she had any grandchildren. When she said no, he told her that all his grandparents were dead, which had made me feel both sad and angry at the unfairness of life. 'I've never been to York,' he said, knuckles white around the strap of his rucksack, still dangling from one hand.

'You can come with me another time, Mattie, I promise.' I battled a surge of irritation. 'I'll be there and back before you know it.'

He didn't know that Jack was only an hour or so further up the motorway from York. That I could easily get there and back in a day. 'You can phone me – or Shona – any time if you don't believe I'm there.' Mattie wasn't stupid. It was obvious he wasn't entirely convinced by my story, but if I could convince Shona to say I was with her if Mattie called, it would put his mind at rest. The last thing I wanted was for him to worry about me. And once Jack was home, Mattie would be so happy he wouldn't care how it had happened. I would have my son back again, smiling and carefree, full of hope for the future.

'What if she says no?' Mattie said, just as my phone pinged with an incoming text.

Of course you can come!! I can't wait!! Let me know approx time of arrival. I'll get the wine in 😊 **XX**

'She said yes.' I knew Shona wouldn't be able to resist.

'I bet she doesn't know it's just you.'

'I'll explain everything when I get there,' I said. 'It'll be good to talk to a female friend, someone who knows me well.'

'How come you haven't got any friends around here?' It came out accusing, but before I could respond, Mattie dropped his gaze to look at his scuffed black school shoes. 'I'm going to get changed.' He sidled past me, into the hall. I wanted to wrap him in a hug but knew he wouldn't let me.

'What are you going to see at the cinema?' I called, but he was already upstairs, and the only response was the slam of his bedroom door.

He refused the twenty-pound note I pulled from my purse when he emerged half an hour later – *I'll use my savings, thanks* – and watching him go in his loose jeans and too-white trainers, the tug of sadness in my chest became a storm of tears as he turned the corner at the bottom of the street without looking back. His hatred was so hard to bear – and so unfair. Relationships were complicated; he couldn't be expected to get it, hadn't had a girlfriend yet – as far as I knew – but it wasn't right that I should take all the blame for Jack's leaving. Bringing him home was the only way to make life bearable again.

Once the tears had stopped, I grabbed a bar of chocolate from the fruit bowl in the kitchen – *to balance out all that fruit,* Jack used to say – and ate half of it quickly, the sweetness melting on my tongue and burning my throat.

Energised, I perched on a stool at the breakfast bar and looked around for something to write on. I tried to think whether there were any envelopes or stamps in the house. I couldn't remember the last time I'd posted anything but a Christmas or birthday card. I wanted to send Caitlin a message – give her time to rethink her decision to take Jack back. Hopefully, when I next saw him, he would be only too happy to come home with me.

Chapter 9

Caitlin

Sorting through Jack's clothes while he showered – I could hear him humming an old Bruce Springsteen song under the stream of water – I thought about the phone call. If someone knew where Jack was, had followed us from the hospital, what would be the point in calling the landline then hanging up? If – my blood ran cold at the thought – it was the hit-and-run driver, what did they want? Had they been hoping Jack would answer the phone? Maybe they wanted to know what he'd told the police and to threaten him into keeping quiet, not realising he had no memory of what had happened. Perhaps whoever it was wanted to apologise. *Unlikely.*

A scarier thought took hold: what if they'd meant to hurt Jack and were here to finish the job? Feeling shaky, I hurried through to the bedroom with a bundle of jeans and T-shirts and dumped them on the bed. *What had Jack been running from?* What if he was in danger and by keeping the truth from him, I was putting myself in harm's way too.

I sat on the end of the rumpled bed, clutching a jumper I'd bought Jack a few Christmases ago, after he joked we were at the age where festive-themed knitwear was appropriate on Christmas Day. I was being overdramatic, my guilty conscience summoning unlikely scenarios. Jack had been with me for less than twenty-four hours and I was panicking over a single, silent phone call that had probably meant nothing.

'You OK?' I called, realising the water in the bathroom was no longer running. It had felt natural hearing him in there, as though no time at all had passed since he'd last showered within earshot.

'All good.' He appeared in the doorway with a white towel wrapped around his waist, ruffling his damp hair with another. I couldn't help smiling at the supermarket bag I'd helped tie over the boot brace to protect it from the water, unwilling to risk removing it just yet. 'Not my finest look.' He rested against the doorframe with a rueful grin.

'It's not that bad.' I tried not to flinch as my gaze skimmed his torso. He'd lost his wiry muscularity and his ribs were visible, the skin around them badly bruised.

'I'd ask for a hug, but I think it would hurt too much,' he said, but something in his voice, his eyes, pulled me towards him. When his arms folded around me, I leant into him gently, closing my eyes against a rush of tears.

'You smell a lot better.' I pressed my lips against the skin of his collarbone. He felt different, and I wondered whether I did too, though my weight rarely changed. Jack was all bones.

'I used your shower gel,' he said. 'I like it.'

I remembered how he used to smell of bonfires and leaves, and as if picking up my train of thought, he added, 'I feel as if I've missed you,' his breath warm against my scalp. 'Does that sound silly?'

Could he feel my rapid heartbeat? 'You're here now.' I pulled back and lightly kissed his lips, feeling a tug of desire in the pit of my stomach. It was a feeling I thought had died for good after he left; a feeling Owen had tried to resurrect. The thought of Owen brought a lurch of apprehension. 'You should get dressed.'

I moved away from Jack's scrutiny, sweeping my arm towards the array of clothes. 'You could do with some new ones,' I said when he limped to the bed and plucked out a plain, white T-shirt, sniffing it before pulling it on with careful movements. His head reappeared, hair already starting to curl as it dried.

'The bed looks so inviting.'

It wasn't a hint to join him there, I realised, watching him stifle a yawn. I wondered whether he'd slept as well as he claimed. His colour had drained, his bruises livid.

'Why don't you get some more sleep while I go shopping?' I lifted the clothes to the chair by the window, then pulled back the duvet and plumped the pillows. 'You're still recovering,' I reminded him. 'The doctor said it was normal to sleep more than usual for a while.'

He sank down with a grateful smile, gravitating to the side of the bed he'd always slept on – the side I'd got used to sleeping on after he left – shedding the towels as he pulled the duvet to cover himself. His moment of modesty made me pause. It was as if on some basic level he sensed we hadn't been intimate lately. Unless I was reading too much into it – into everything.

I opened the drawer by the bed and took out his wedding ring. 'Here,' I said, taking his hand and slipping it onto his finger self-consciously. 'It's a bit big.' It was true. He'd lost weight everywhere.

'Must be why it fell off.' He frowned as though trying to recall why that might have happened. 'Good job you found it.' He gazed at it for a moment, a soft smile on his lips, but didn't ask me where I found it. 'Must have been the stress of moving out and closing the business.' It was an obvious reference to his worrying new skinniness. I nodded quicky, trying not to make too much of it.

'A few good meals and it'll fit properly again.'

He clenched his hand, eyes still on the ring. 'Are my books here?' He sounded sleepy as I slipped the plastic bag off his foot and gently eased his leg onto the mattress.

'Of course.' I would remove the books from the cardboard box they were stored in and put them on the shelves downstairs. 'Did you want something to read?'

'Not right now.' He masked another yawn with the back of his hand. 'Nice lamp.' He squinted at the seashell-covered base that had been a gift from Owen and I made a mental note to move it into the spare room.

'Shall I fetch your painkillers?'

He moved his fingers to his temple. 'Actually, my head feels better today. I just have to remember to keep it turned while I'm lying down.'

'That's great, Jack.' I hoped it didn't herald the return of his memory and hated myself for the thought. 'It's a good sign.'

'Caitlin, you don't have to worry.' He reached for my hand, and, for a crazy second, I thought he knew what I was thinking and was going to tell me it didn't matter – that whatever had happened, he understood and forgave me. But Jack wasn't big on forgiveness, as I knew only too well. My insides shrivelled as I imagined his reaction if – when – he put the pieces together and discovered the truth. 'I won't be like this forever,' he said, the corner of his mouth turning up. 'I know you don't like playing nurse.'

Washed with relief, I gripped his hand in both of mine. 'That was when you had man flu,' I said, running my thumb over his knuckles. 'This is different.' Leaning over, I stroked a damp lock of hair off his forehead. 'Let's take things a day at a time.'

'Sounds good to me.' When our eyes met, he seemed to be searching for something in my gaze. Was I was being different, acting all wrong? Heat travelled up my neck, but then he sighed with a dozy smile and weaved his fingers through mine as though happy – *relieved?* – to be there, before turning his head to the window. 'I can't believe how noisy those seagulls are.'

'I suppose I'm used to it.' Smiling, I untangled my fingers from his and went to close the window, which I normally kept open to let in the salty air, so much fresher than the traffic-fumed wafts that had drifted through our flat in Brighton. Despite its proximity to the beach, the road outside had been busy and our position at the furthest end of the street meant we were barely aware of the sea. Even so, the seagulls there had made their presence known. 'You should be too,' I added. He must have got used to not hearing them in London. 'Perhaps you're sensitive to the noise, because of your injury.'

'Probably.' He threw an arm across his eyes as though to block out the light.

I looked at the sea, a wrinkled expanse beneath a pearlescent sky, and caught a movement below the window: a flash of dark clothing. Pressing my forehead to the glass, I strained for a closer look but there was nobody there. Visitors wouldn't come into the garden, which was accessed by a locked gate at the side of the cottage; they would come to the front door. The only other way into the garden would be via the steep cliff path from the beach and to scale the wooden fence, which seemed an unlikely situation.

Unsettled, I drew the curtains across and turned. 'I'll leave you an old mobile phone,' I said, unwilling to leave Jack on his own. 'I'll put my number in. If you need anything, call me straight away.'

He made a noise of assent but didn't move and I couldn't be sure he'd heard me. A strip of light fell through a gap in the curtains onto the bed and I longed to slide in beside him and hold him close. Instead, I forced myself downstairs where I unearthed the phone in a kitchen drawer – the one I'd had when I was with Jack. Would he recognise it and think it odd I had a different one, or assume its appearance was another memory his brain had sealed away?

I left the phone on the bedside cabinet with a glass of water and a blister pack of tablets in case Jack's headache returned, watching the rhythmic rise and fall of his chest for a couple of minutes as he slept, before heading out, double-checking the door was locked behind me.

Everything seemed different: brighter, the air sharper, colours more vivid. I paused, drinking in the scenery I normally took for granted: the sweep of bay, the rock-pools – where I'd spent happy hours as a child with my grandfather, hunting for fossils – the brooding cliffs that towered over the village, and precipitous coastal path leading to Boggle Hole. The village was still sunk in winter hibernation, but in summer the bay's population would be swollen by thousands of visitors, every guesthouse, hotel, and campsite filled to capacity, the air overlaid with the tang of fish and chips, the cobbled streets and alleys hard to navigate.

The road at the bottom of the hill led into the sea at high tide, but this morning the water was far out, the light picking out the ridges and ripples in the sand where seabirds strutted about. There was woman at the water's edge with a dog that kept charging at the waves and a man in a canary-yellow waterproof walking with his head down, hands in his pockets. For a second, I thought it was Owen, but he wasn't tall enough. All the same, I scanned the area again, as if Owen might be lurking somewhere, though by this time he would no doubt be at the store, counting stock while it was quiet, or working out in his gym.

With a final glance at the grey-stone cottage behind me – the curtains gaping slightly at the bedroom window – I fastened my coat and walked up the hill, propelled by an urge to get back as soon as possible. As I passed the old stone house that used to be a police station, the gift shops, bakery, and pub, my thighs began to burn. Despite walking up the hill regularly, I never seemed to get any fitter, and I unfastened my coat as I overheated.

I barely registered the woman coming towards me until I heard my name.

'You're in a hurry this morning,' she said, stopping in front of me.

It was Owen's sister, Mel. She ran the Hill Top guesthouse which had a prime view of the cluster of houses below, right down to the sea. She must have seen me coming.

'Hi, Mel.' At the sight of her stormy expression, my stomach flipped. 'Are you OK?'

'Owen tells me you're back with your ex.'

I tried to catch my breath, pushing aside my windswept hair. 'Look, Mel—'

'Is that why you broke up with him?'

Mel was tall and broad, like her brother, with the same greenish eyes and dark-blonde hair, which she wore in a thick plait. Six years his senior, she was protective of Owen, and her normally friendly features were hostile.

'He knew I still cared about Jack.' I decided it was better to get the conversation out of the way. 'I never made a secret of it, Mel.'

'I thought you'd got him out of your system and that's why you were with Owen.'

'I thought I had.' I realised only now how deeply I'd fooled myself. 'Jack was in an accident recently and it made me – *us* – realise we wanted to be together again.' *Forgive me, Jack.*

'Just like that?' Mel must have rushed out without realising how cold it was. The sleeves of her flannel shirt were rolled up, her forearms prickled with goose bumps. She didn't seem to notice.

'I suppose we never got over each other.'

'For God's sake.' Mel curled her lip, a look I'd never seen before. She'd been wary when Owen took me to the guesthouse for dinner one Sunday at the end of the summer season, when business had slowed down. He announced to her that we were taking our friendship to the next level, getting family involved, though he'd told me we had been invited because his sister was an amazing cook and loved an excuse to show off. Mel had seemed almost startled to see me walk in behind Owen, her eyes darting to our hands as he laced his fingers through mine. His smile had been a little shy and shot through with pride as he said, 'This is Caitlin, be kind.'

'I know who she is, you idiot.' Mel was a whirlwind of activity, constantly busy with her two young children and the business she ran with their mother – her husband was a solicitor in Whitby – but she seemed to thrive on the adrenaline. We hadn't become close friends exactly, but after that first, rather awkward visit, she'd warmed up to occasionally dropping round to the cottage for coffee, and to admire my illustrations, and had even commissioned a mural for the children's bedroom wall.

'I knew you'd hurt him,' she said now, the edges of her shirt flapping in the wind. 'I told him . . .' She looked away, eyes narrowed. 'I said you weren't ready.'

'Mel, I'm sorry. I really am.' I couldn't bring myself to tell her Owen had been to see me the night before, or what he'd said. 'Owen's great, but he's not right for me.'

'He hasn't taken it well.' Her vowels were broader than usual, flattened by anger. 'You led him on.'

'Come on, Mel.' Annoyance flared. 'That's ridiculous. People break up all the time and it's not like we were engaged, or even living together.'

A man passing by, piggy-backing a small girl crying, 'Faster, Daddy!' gave us a curious look, as if sensing something combative in our body language. My hands were clenched into fists, and I straightened my fingers. All I wanted was to run back to the cottage.

'He won't give up easily, you know.' Mel's voice was quieter, her gaze shrewd. 'You know he's in love with you?'

Unease slid through me. 'He'll get over it.' I spoke lightly, feeling the burn of hypocrisy. I hadn't got over Jack, had I? But that was different. We'd been together a long time, were married; had planned a future together. 'Please, Mel. I don't want to fall out with you over this.'

'Bit late for that.' I was shocked by the bitterness in her voice, but supposed she was entitled to be upset.

'He had his heart broken once before and it didn't end well.'

'What?'

Mel bit her lip, as though regretting her words. She tugged down the sleeves of her shirt. 'I'd better get back.' She smoothed both hands over her hair, a single strand caught in the corner of her mouth. 'Mum will be wondering where I am.'

'What did you mean just now?' I was unwilling to let her comment go, recalling Owen's words in the car the night before, how determined he seemed to hang on to our relationship. 'What didn't end well?'

Mel looked at the ground for a moment, dark with overnight rainfall, small puddles rippling by the kerb. 'Just be careful, that's all.' Not looking at me, she backed away.

A shiver rippled through me as I watched her stride to the top of the hill, her words ringing in my ears as I hurried to the grocery store.

Was it a threat, or a warning?

Chapter 10

Lydia

'I should have known you had an ulterior motive for finally coming to visit.' Shona's smile couldn't quite disguise her disappointment, or the glimmer of disapproval I glimpsed when I told her I was planning to visit Jack. 'I suppose if I'd moved to Cornwall, you wouldn't be here.'

'Don't be like that, Shona. I wanted to see you too.' It was hard to keep my tone upbeat, the differences between us more marked than I'd expected.

On arrival, my friend had gathered me into a perfumed hug, telling me her children were with her mother-in-law for a few hours so we could catch up in peace, but her grin had faltered as she stood back to take me in, eyeing my hastily scraped-back hair that showed oily roots, not fooled by an attempt at a healthy glow with make-up, or my smartest jeans and silky top, both of which hung off me. I couldn't seem to eat more than a few bites of anything, my stomach perpetually churning.

'What's on earth's happened, Lydia?'

Over freshly ground coffee in her newly installed kitchen,

71

where the glossy, snow-white tiles made my eyes hurt, I filled her in, playing down the seriousness of the break-up. 'If I can just see him, I know we can sort things out.' I didn't tell her that Jack was back with his wife, only that he was taking a break to get over an injury.

'Why Robin Hood's Bay?'

'He likes it there.'

'It's a long way from Brighton,' Shona said, knowingly. 'Shouldn't you leave it to him to decide whether he wants to come back, instead of running after him?'

'He's not thinking straight.' My shoulders were high and tense. 'When he sees me, I'll be able to talk him round. I can be very persuasive, as you know.' It was an attempt to draw her in with a reminder of the past, when she'd envied my ability to attract male attention with not much more than a smile and a bit of flattery.

Shona assessed me for a moment in silence, the only sound in the kitchen the hum of the fridge, and the incessant rain that had followed me from London hitting the bifold doors that led to the garden. With her amber eyes, high-cut cheekbones, and deluge of long red curls, she looked years younger than me. At school she'd been sporty and easy-going with a wicked laugh, and I briefly longed for the uncomplicated friendship we'd had before my father died, and the world became dark and unpredictable. 'What does Mattie think?'

Mattie.

He'd been asleep when I left the house that morning, or at least pretending to be. He hadn't stirred when I pressed a kiss on his rumpled hair and glanced round his room – not the teenage den I assumed most boys his age occupied, but almost spartan, the floor clear of clutter, clothes hung neatly in his wardrobe, books stacked by the laptop on his desk where the angle-poise lamp cast a dim pool of light. The only remnants of his younger self was the blue carpet William had put down one weekend, while Mattie was at a friend's house, and a photo of him on his father's shoulders in the garden, surrounded by the rainbow of bubbles I'd blown before snapping the picture.

I switched off the lamp on my way out and left Mattie a note on the kitchen table before going next door to ask Harriet to keep an eye on him.

'Everything OK?' she'd said, seeming unsurprised to see me on her doorstep before seven-thirty on a weekday morning.

'I have to go away for a couple of days. Mattie says he doesn't need babysitting, and I know he's sensible, but I would really appreciate you looking out for him.'

'Of course.' She gripped the edges of her pink furry dressing gown against the chill whisking through the open door. 'He's welcome here anytime for his dinner – he knows that.'

Her bright blue gaze was hard to read, a mix of curiosity and pity and something close to judgement that stirred a flame of anger. 'Will you check he goes to school?'

'I'm sure he doesn't need me to tell him, Lydia. He's a good boy, in spite of . . .' She trailed off, no doubt remembering the days and nights I'd hammered on her door before I met Jack, not knowing where he was. 'Has he gone then?' she said, unexpectedly. 'Your . . . young man?'

I wanted to say that Jack was thirty-five, but supposed he looked young compared to William, who used to chat to Harriet on his way in from work, or before he went for a run. 'I'm sure he'll be back soon,' I said. No point denying that Jack had left. Mattie would probably fill her in – though not on everything, I hoped. 'It's just a break.'

'Maybe it would be better if he stayed away.' Harriet spoke with an air of defiance, as if deciding to speak her mind and be damned. 'These walls aren't soundproof, you know.'

A creep of shame made me mumble, 'I don't know what you think you've heard, but it's not—'

'I know what's going on,' she cut in, voice hard. 'It's the same as before.'

73

William. Maybe she'd seen the bruises, no doubt had me down as the sort of woman drawn to a certain type of man. Maybe she was right. 'I love him,' I said, suddenly unsure whether I was talking about William or Jack, desperate to get to the station and away from her knowing eyes. 'Relationships are complicated.'

'Mine wasn't.' Her gaze fogged over with sadness, as if seeing her long-dead husband, Graham. 'We liked and respected each other, pure and simple. None of this power struggle, one trying to control the other. That's not love, it's . . . I don't know what it is, but it's not healthy.'

'I have to go.' Hitching my holdall onto my shoulder, I hurried away from the torrent of words she'd plainly been holding on to. 'Thank you for watching Mattie for me.'

Hearing her door slam, I turned when I reached the pavement, and saw with a jolt that Mattie was watching from his bedroom window, his face a stark, white oval.

He didn't return my wave.

'Mattie wants Jack to come home as much as I do,' I told Shona now. 'Jack's been so good with him.'

'Is Jack a lot different then? From William, I mean.' Why did everyone keep talking about William, making me think about him when I didn't want to?

'Very different.' I swirled my cooling coffee around the porcelain mug. I rarely drank the stuff; preferred black tea with two sugars. It had made Jack wince the first time he made me a cup at my house, saying he couldn't bear it without milk. No doubt Caitlin was making him tea with milk right now. 'I don't want to talk about him.'

Shona's face dropped before she rallied. 'Fancy a tour of the house? The kids will be back soon, making a mess everywhere.' I could tell she didn't mind. Shona had happily given up her career in marketing to be a stay-at-home mum, supported by her husband's hedge-fund manager's salary, which also paid for their live-in nanny who was currently on holiday. 'Connor's taking them bowling this evening so we can have some wine and watch a film if you like?'

'I'd love that,' I said, though truthfully, I couldn't think of anything worse. I wished now that I'd booked a cheap hotel to stay in, or even gone straight to Robin Hood's Bay regardless of Mattie's feelings on the matter. I was wasting time in York, pretending to admire the parquet floors and special-edition William Morris wallpaper in Shona's listed house, listening to her detailed plans for a fountain in their garden-cum-orchard, and how the twins were showing a flair for interior design – both, or one of them, I instantly forgot – when all I wanted to do was get to Jack.

'Is that a new car?' Shona said, after showing me the family bathroom – a cavernous space with a giant, claw-footed bath at its centre, a big chrome showerhead lying in its cradle. She was on the thickly carpeted landing, looking out of the front window. 'Nice,' she said, though the nippy VW Golf was no match for the gleaming 4X4 parked on the gravelled driveway. 'You got over your fear of driving, then?'

She knew I was terrified of driving in London, but I rarely needed to. 'Just about.' I decided not to mention that I'd taken the train up to York then hired a car for the journey to Robin Hood's Bay. 'Mattie will be taking lessons soon,' I said, to divert her.

'I can't believe it.' She pressed a French-manicured hand to her chest. 'I can remember him as a teeny-tiny baby. Do you remember when he was little and used to imitate William saying, "Right-ee-ho!"'

I smiled, softening as my mind scrolled back to those briefly happy years, when bright bursts of optimism had filled my chest every day and life was good. Right up until the time that William started taking too much interest in Shona and she'd eventually stopped coming round. 'He went off the rails a bit a few years ago.' I hadn't meant to say it, keen to keep up the illusion that my life was, if not half as perfect as Shona's, at least not the chaotic mess it had become before I met Jack. 'Mattie says I killed his dad and that Jack's left because of me,' I blurted out, then pressed my fingers to my mouth and shook my head. 'Sorry.'

Shona bit down on her lower lip before saying quietly, 'William had a heart attack out running, didn't he?' One hand went to her collarbone, as though feeling more words leaping to her throat. I wished I hadn't said anything. 'Mattie probably saw and heard a lot of things he shouldn't have—'

'He's fine now, really,' I cut across her. 'We both are.' Shona's face worked with sympathy, and something I couldn't interpret. 'Mostly down to Jack,' I hurried on, affecting a small laugh that sounded fake. 'It's different with him, I promise. I can't give him up.'

Shona blinked several times, looking as if there were a thousand things she wanted to say before settling for, 'Well, let's hope he's worth it then.'

The rest of the day passed in a blur of lunch with wine, the kids arriving home – both chatty, red-haired mini-replicas of Shona – a stilted catch-up with Connor, who, though unnervingly good-looking and smiley seemed wary of me, as though I'd come to whisk Shona back to the alcohol-fuelled, flat-sharing, singleton's life we'd led in London before I fell pregnant and settled down with William. Shona kept up a steady stream of chatter, seeming to sense that dissuading me from going to see Jack was pointless, mostly reminiscing before falling silent during *Love Actually* – once our favourite film – casting me sideways looks before I pleaded exhaustion and was shown to an immaculate spare room straight from an interiors magazine.

'Shona, if Mattie calls tomorrow, would you tell him I'm here?' I said, tongue loosened by the couple of glasses of rosé we'd drunk. 'He doesn't know I'm going to see Jack. I don't want to get his hopes up,' I added when a frown settled on her brow. 'I need him to concentrate on school.'

Shona regarded me steadily, her easy smile fading as she nodded. 'I'll do it for Mattie,' she said. *Wasn't that what I'd said?* 'I hope you know what you're doing Lyddie.'

Her use of my childhood nickname brought tears to my eyes. After she'd gone, I stared at the door for a long moment, wishing I could go back in time and do everything differently.

After digging out my phone, I dropped onto the enormous, comfy bed and messaged Mattie again. **Sleep well, sweetheart. Love you XX** He hadn't replied to my earlier text, letting him know I'd arrived safely, but the two blue ticks told me he'd read it.

I imagined him in Harriet's cosy living room in front of the television eating one of her meaty casseroles – the sort of meal Jack had enjoyed before I persuaded him a vegetarian diet was healthier and more ethical – while she did her ironing. It was a shame in a way that my mum was no longer around but Harriet – as nosy and annoying as I found her sometimes – was the next best thing to a grandmother he had.

I looked up Robin Hood's Bay again, though I'd already done my research on the train journey up. It was a small place, but out of season it had been easy to book a room at one of the guest-houses. I shouldn't be there long, two nights at the most – one if I spoke to Jack right away and persuaded him to come back with me. We could even stop in at Shona's on the way back and I could introduce him. Maybe we could take a walk around the city, which I'd barely noticed driving through, hands clamped hard around the steering wheel of the unfamiliar car.

Settling back on the bed, a pleasant dreaminess now cushioning my thoughts, I impulsively brought up the number of the cottage and pressed dial, then hung up before it rang. If Jack answered, what would he say when he heard my voice? Far better to be face to face. And I didn't want to risk *her* answering again and getting suspicious. I might end up revealing who I was and then anything could happen.

How was Jack? I wondered, leaning forward to ease off my socks – Shona had a no-shoe policy in the house – before shuffling under the duvet. I thought back to what the nurse had said at the hospital, words I'd barely taken in at the time. *Cracked ribs, badly sprained ankle.* Something else. *Concussion.* A worm of suspicion wriggled through my brain. Throwing off the duvet I swung my legs to the floor and padded to the window, the moonlit view interrupted by the black skeleton of a tree in the garden. *Concussion.*

I found the number of the hospital, half-aware it was getting late to be calling – though the twins weren't back yet with their dad – and asked to speak to someone about Jack Garvey.

'I'm his wife,' I said, heart thumping. I glanced at the door, but could hear Shona moving around downstairs, the clink of glasses. Outside, headlights brightened the darkness. Car doors slammed, followed by the babble of voices and crunch of feet on gravel.

'Can I help, Mrs Garvey?' came a voice down the phone.

'Oh, yes please. My husband was discharged a couple of days ago and I wanted to double-check we have all the right medication and there's nothing more I should be doing.'

'One moment.' There was the sound of a keyboard being pressed. 'Have you registered with a doctor up there?' the woman said, clearly seeing the address was a long way from the hospital where Jack had been treated.

'I'm onto it.' I forced a smile into my voice. 'There's a lot to think about.'

'Well, it was mostly prescription painkillers for his ankle, and for the headaches he might be suffering after his concussion, which, as I'm sure was explained, can be taken every four hours, if necessary. Be careful not to exceed the dose, and if he shows any more signs of memory loss, do get in touch, and speak to the consultant here.'

I was barely breathing, my heart a rapid drumbeat in my chest. 'Memory loss?'

'As we explained Mrs Garvey, it's common after a head injury. Your husband might never remember the accident, or the events leading up to it, but if there are other areas of amnesia, he will need further examination.'

'Of course.' Her words seemed to have sucked the life from my limbs. 'Thank you, that's very helpful.' I rang off and stood motionless, trying to work out the implications. *Amnesia.* Was that why Jack was back with his wife?

Had he forgotten I existed?

Chapter 11

Caitlin

I swam towards wakefulness the following morning, chased by a dream of the police calling, pushing their way into the cottage, looking for Jack. I lay still for several moments, listening to his steady breathing until my heartbeat slowed. It was worth it, I told myself, turning to face him. It was worth a bad dream to have Jack lying next to me. I wondered whether they would become a regular feature, guilt surfacing while I slept. I strained my eyes but couldn't quite make out Jack's features in the grey light pushing against the curtains.

I'd left them shut the day before, after checking on Jack when I got back from the grocery store, happy to let him rest while I put away the few items I'd bought, still shaken by my encounter with Mel. In the store, I'd received another text from Owen.

Does he know about us?

My heart had leapt into my throat as I quickly replied: **Yes.**

I decided in that moment I would have to tell Jack some version of the truth in case Owen turned up at the cottage, intending to stake his claim, or to engineer a chat with Jack. I couldn't keep them apart forever, short of packing up and leaving in the middle of the night. Even then, I wouldn't put it past Owen to find us.

It didn't end well. I couldn't get Mel's words out of my head.

Jack had eventually made his way downstairs at lunchtime, just as I was stirring a pan of vegetable soup on the stove.

'Smells good.'

His gentle smile, and the touch of his hand in the small of my back as he kissed my cheek, weakened my resolve. I didn't want Owen souring things between us. I would talk to Jack about him later.

The rest of the day had passed in such a companionable way it was hard to fathom there had ever been any distance between us – though of course, as far as Jack was concerned, there hadn't been, other than his brief spell in hospital.

He seemed happy to be close to me, first at the kitchen table while we ate bowls of soup together for lunch, chatting about this and that, then on the sofa in the living room with his ankle propped on a footstool while I attempted to focus on some illustrations I had a deadline for, stealing glances at him as he flipped through one of the gardening books I'd pushed onto the bookshelf, a mug of milky tea in his hand.

The absence of his smile had been like missing sunshine, but finally, everything felt restored. A return to how it had been before I ruined everything, his presence bringing a new sheen to the cottage, a new liveliness to my movements. When he asked to see what I was working on, I'd snuggled close to him on the sofa and showed him my sketches, talking him through the story I was working on. The strangeness of contact after so long had quickly passed. I felt renewed, as if a missing piece had been slotted into place, and when Jack's hand closed around mine, the rightness of it had drowned out the niggling whispers of conscience.

After we had eaten dinner in front of the television, answering questions to *The Chase*, like old times, and night fell, the air became charged with chemistry. Helping Jack up to bed, laughing as we stumbled on the stairs, had felt like the most natural thing in the world. When he traced lines across my skin with his fingertips, desire had risen like a ball of electricity, and the gentleness and familiarity of his lips on mine reinforced my certainty: I had done the right thing. We'd moved together carefully, tenderly, as if we were designed to fit together, laughing softly whenever he flinched or groaned with pain, rather than pleasure.

Tell me if it hurts too much and we'll stop.

I don't want to.

Now, watching him sleep as seagulls skittered on the roof above, I tried to hold on to that feeling as the nightmare faded, reluctant to face the day and the possibility of a confrontation with Owen. At least Jack would be confined to the cottage for a few days, so there was no chance of him bumping into Owen by chance.

Pushing doubt aside, I considered getting out of bed. Normally, if it wasn't raining, I would go for a run on the beach to set me up for the day. I wasn't a natural when it came to exercise and preferred to get it out of the way, but I didn't want to leave the warm confines of the duvet, or Jack. I reached out, intending to lay a hand on his naked chest but froze when he stirred and mumbled something that sounded like 'lids'. His head twisted on the pillow, and I wondered with a chill whether his head was hurting. He hadn't taken any painkillers last night. Settling my palm on his warm skin, I jumped when he roared, *'No!'* and his fingers clamped around my wrist. He flung my arm back onto the pillow, twisting it painfully.

'Jack!' I tried to wriggle away. 'You're hurting me.' He was up on his elbow now, leaning over me, eyes wide and black in the half-light, the bruising on his face giving him a devilish appearance. 'Jack, what the hell are you doing?' There was power in his grip, so much more than I had ever realised. *Was he still asleep?* He didn't look like Jack.

'Lids.' That word again, almost a growl.

With a superhuman effort, I wrenched free, flailing for the

82

switch on the bedside light. As the room illuminated, Jack blinked, his weight on my arm easing. I shot away from him, collapsing to the floor with the duvet over me, and lay panting on the rug.

'Caitlin?' Squinting down at me, tangled in the bed sheet, Jack was familiar again, his face creased with bewilderment, hair sticking out at odd angles. 'What are you doing down there?'

I stared, ice in my limbs, trying to impose logic on the situation. 'I . . . you were having a nightmare, I think.' My voice was more of a bleat. 'You attacked me.'

'*What?*' Jack shuffled to the edge of the bed, grunting with the effort. 'Caitlin, I would never—'

'You grabbed my wrist and twisted my arm back.' I closed the duvet around my shoulders, feeling vulnerable, before scrambling to my feet. 'You looked like you wanted to hurt me.'

'Hurt you?' He sounded aghast as he dropped back onto the pillow. 'Caitlin I . . . I'm so sorry. I was dreaming. I was being chased, but I don't remember who by, or . . . My God, I'm so sorry, Caitlin.' His eyes – Jack's eyes again – implored me as he held out a hand. 'You know I would never hurt you. I love you.'

'Maybe it was something to do with your head injury.' Ignoring his hand, I gripped the edges of the duvet. I'd opened the window a sliver the night before, and a cold draught snaked across my neck. 'Should we talk to the doctor?'

'My head isn't hurting, but yes, maybe I should.' Jack covered his face with both hands. When he spoke his voice was muffled. 'The last thing I want is to hurt you, Caitlin. I can sleep in the spare room until we know I'm not going to lash out.'

'Don't be silly.' Softening in the face of his distress, I sat gingerly on the bed. 'Apart from anything, it's still full of packing boxes in there.'

He shifted a hand, bringing it to rest on my arm. I tried not to flinch at the memory of him twisting it back. It throbbed where he'd grabbed me, and I was certain there would be a bruise there later. 'Caitlin, I promise it's not—'

'What if it is though?' I instantly knew what he meant. 'The accident might have . . . I don't know. Dislodged old memories. Brought it all up again.'

'I don't think it's that. I really don't.'

We fell silent, remembering a night not long after we'd moved into our flat together, when Jack broke down and confessed how, after his mother died, he'd struggled with anger issues. Her death had been the result of medical negligence, a cancer diagnosis that came too late. He'd struggled to deal with the injustice, seeing her suffer unnecessarily, and with accepting her loss too early as well as the effect it had on his bond with his father.

I'd held him while he cried, my heart breaking for him, so thankful my own parents were alive and healthy, that my memories were packed with sunny days and laughter.

He used to lash out, he said, punching walls and – once – a so-called friend who told him to 'get over it'. He had counselling after that, worked hard to escape the net of grief and anger, but during the course of our relationship there had been moments when a darkness would cloak him – frustration over a gardening job that hadn't worked out, something he'd read in the news, or his dad relaying cheerful snippets from his new life in Italy – *as though Mum never existed* – and I would sense something coiled within him, waiting to spring free. He'd never once directed any physical anger towards me, though, not even on the day he walked out.

'It was probably a one-off,' I said at last, desperate to push the past back where it belonged. 'I touched you and it triggered something, that's all. You're not yourself, yet.'

He levered onto his side and propped himself back on his elbow. 'If it happens again, slap me, kick me, whatever you have to do. And I'll get help, I promise.' He was deadly serious, his face stricken. 'I can't bear to think of you being scared of me.'

'I'm not.' I wasn't . . . at least, not now. 'You kept mumbling a word,' I added, wanting to move on, yet not quite able to let go. 'It sounded like "lids".'

'Lids?'

I watched his expression for some spark of awareness but saw only puzzlement in his creased-up face. 'That doesn't even make sense.'

'I know, right?'

'Lids?' He turned the word over as if trying to taste it.

'Can you remember any more of what you were dreaming about?'

He closed his eyes for a moment, forehead furrowed. Then he exhaled and shook his head. 'It's gone.'

The thought came without warning: *He's lying.*

'Let's forget it.' I dropped the duvet over him and reached for my dressing gown. I pulled it on quickly, wanting to cover my nakedness, though Jack was now staring at the ceiling. 'I'll make us some tea.'

The morning had brightened, pale sunlight flooding the kitchen when I entered. In the brightness, my worries shrank. Jack had suffered a nightmare he didn't care to recall and touching him had triggered a visceral response. It didn't have to be anything more sinister than that. No need for a doctor – unless it happened again.

I checked the kettle was filled and switched it on. The letterbox rattled and I glanced at the clock on the oven: 8.30 exactly. The postman was rarely late, but it was unusual to get anything other than junk mail these days. Probably a postcard from my parents. It was the sort of thing they did, despite sending streams of photos of their trip from their phones.

Tightening the belt of my dressing gown, I slipped into the hall, checking the heating had come on and wondering whether I should light a fire, or wait for Jack to do it – something he'd always enjoyed when we visited my grandfather. *It must appeal to the caveman in me.*

There was a single white envelope on the mat in front of the door, my name and address written in neat, block capitals.

The postmark was hard to make out. I stared at it for a moment, as if it might magically reveal itself.

'Do you want a hand?'

I jumped at the sound of Jack's voice from upstairs.

'It's OK,' I called back. 'I'll be up in a minute.'

I tore open the envelope and pulled out a little card with a cartoon dog on the front, blowing a kiss – the sort that someone might write *Thinking of you* or *Thank you for the gift* inside. I opened it, mouth drying as the words inside travelled slowly to my brain. Only a few, but the message was loud and clear: **Let him go, Caitlin. He doesn't love you, and he's not the man you think he is.**

Chapter 12

Lydia

'This is your room. I hope you find it comfortable.'

'Thank you.' My smile felt stiff.

'Breakfast is served between seven and nine. If you'd like a meal in the evenings, let me know before you go out.' The guesthouse owner looked at my bag as I placed it on the end of the double bed. 'Are you on holiday, or visiting relatives?'

It was probably unusual to host holidaymakers at this time of year – especially a woman on her own – but I resented her curiosity.

'I needed a break,' I said, glancing around the room. It had a restful air, with soft green walls and a view of the sea through a tall window. 'Someone I know used to live around here and I remembered her saying how nice it was.' The woman seemed to be waiting for more. 'I like being by the sea.'

'Well, there's plenty of it here, and lots of good walks if that's your thing.'

'I just want to relax.' I spoke gently, hoping my smile reached my eyes. I didn't want her gossiping about the 'strange' woman staying in room six. 'I'm a bit burnt out,' I added. 'Work, you know?'

'Oh, tell me about it.' Her eyes swept over me, greenish-grey like the restless water in the bay outside. 'I could do with a break myself.' Sympathy softened the lines of her face. 'I have two children under five, so even out of season there's no rest for the wicked.'

'I can imagine.' I slid my coat off and draped it over my bag. 'My son is a teenager now, but it doesn't get any easier.' *Shut up, Lydia.*

She nodded but didn't probe. 'I'm Mel, by the way.' A warm smile lifted her eyes.

'Nice to meet you, Mel.' *Go away.*

'You too, Lydia.'

I wished now I'd made up a name but booking online had made it impossible. I felt a leap of fear. I should have picked somewhere further away from the village. This wasn't like London, where I didn't know most of my neighbours and everyone kept to themselves.

'And don't worry, you'll have all the privacy you need.' As if sensing I wanted to be left alone, Mel left the room at last, a trace of vanilla lingering. Her perfume, or the waft of baking I'd detected on arrival, I couldn't tell.

I sank onto the bed and let out a long breath, shaky with adrenaline. *What now?*

Since my conversation with the hospital, I bitterly regretted sending Caitlin the stupid card I'd found in the dresser from a pack I had no memory of buying. It would have been better to orchestrate a meeting alone with Jack first. If he really had amnesia, seeing me might be enough to bring his memory back and, once we'd talked, we could have returned to London without the need for warnings.

My stomach turned over. *What if he didn't remember me?* I could walk away, of course I could, but why should I? Jack was mine now, for better or worse, even if it wasn't in the eyes of the law. I couldn't pass up the chance to make things right, to show him we had a future worth fighting for – that we had Mattie to think of.

I would talk to Caitlin first and explain my relationship with Jack. All of it. She wouldn't want him by the time I'd finished, I was certain. She might wonder why I did, but that was none of her business. Wasn't there a saying about all relationships being strange in their own way? Or was it families? And maybe it wasn't strange – *unhappy*, that was it. Only, I hadn't been unhappy with Jack, contrary to what Harriet would probably say if anyone asked.

Thinking of Harriet, I dug out my phone and texted Mattie. **Have a good day at school. Miss you XX** To my surprise, he replied straight away.

Where are you?

Out shopping with Shona XX My heart thudded. I hated lying to him. I waited a moment, looking for the dots that would tell me he was typing a reply, but they didn't come. Would Shona go along with it? I quickly sent her a message.

Mattie might call. I told him we were shopping. Thanks, Sho. X

Are you OK?

Good, thank you. Don't worry X

She would let me know if Mattie called. As far as I could tell, her loyalty to me still outweighed her disapproval.

I checked the time. Only ten-thirty. I'd left Shona's house after a hasty breakfast of coffee and toast while she was dropping the twins at school, unable to settle or attempt conversation with Connor, who had the morning off.

He'd eyed me warily as he came downstairs in a paisley dressing gown, giving a nod of what looked like relief when I said I was leaving.

'Be careful,' he'd said, making it sound like a warning, a cool-ness in his gaze.

I felt a stab of annoyance that Shona must have told him where I was going and why. 'You too,' I replied, flashing a pointed glance at his groin to let him know Shona had confided she didn't want another baby, despite his constant cajoling. 'Be happy with what you've got.'

After a few moments of adjusting to the sounds of seabirds close by, and faint thrum of voices below, I made an effort to unpack, placing my toothbrush and toiletries in the en-suite bathroom. I paused at the window to take in the turbulent sky and rolling sea, but all the time my hands shook, the throbbing behind my eyes threatening a headache.

I had to get this over with.

I smoothed my car-crumpled clothes and drew my black, quilted coat back on, glad I'd thought to bring it as the wind blustered against the window. I pulled a grey beanie over my hair, tucking the tendrils inside, and stared at myself in the wardrobe mirror until my breathing had calmed and my eyes were focused. *You're not doing anything wrong. You're fighting for the man you love, the man your son sees as a father.*

Why isn't he fighting for you? Shona would argue. *It doesn't sound like an equal relationship to me.*

But it seemed as if Jack might have lost his memory, plus our relationship wasn't like hers and Connor's. Only Jack and I understood what we meant to each other.

Checking I had my room key – an actual key on a metal fob – I slipped out of my room and stood for a moment on the landing. I was one of three rooms on the second floor, the others currently vacant.

I ran down the flight of pale-carpeted stairs to the first-floor landing, stopping when I heard voices in one of the rooms. The door was ajar, and I caught a glimpse of movement, a hand waving, a flash of a pale face.

'I know it's hard, Owen, but you have to let her go.'

'I just think something's off,' a man replied. 'You didn't see her, Mel. What if he's wormed his way back and is threatening Caitlin?'

I shrank against the wall, breath stuck in my throat.

'Why are you looking for complicated reasons?' Mel sounded exasperated. 'She never stopped loving him, Owen. She told me that. I know it's horrible for you to hear, but I believe her.'

'She cares about me; I know she does.'

'I'm sure she does, in her own way.' Mel's voice grew gentle. 'But I get the sense that Jack was – *is* – the love of her life, and now he's back it's definitely over between you two.'

I pressed my fingers over my mouth to stop any sounds escaping.

'I don't buy it.' The man's voice was a low growl. 'There's more to it – I know there is – and I'm going to find out what it is.'

'For God's sake, Owen. You should be at work, not skulking about here, plotting and planning.' Another slice of movement in the gap between the door and its frame. I pulled my head back, straining to hear. 'Focus on what you love doing. You'll meet someone else soon enough.'

'I don't want anyone else.'

'You feel like that now—'

'I'm not giving up without a fight, Mel.'

'Look, Mum and Dad don't need you going all brooding and moody like you did last time. They're getting on now. They want a quiet life.' Mel's voice rose. 'We all want a quiet life, Owen.'

'Fine,' he snapped. 'I'll leave you out of it.'

'Owen, wait . . .'

I pressed back into the shadows as the door flew open and the man stormed out. He swiped a hand through his hair and thundered downstairs, slamming the front door as he left.

Hardly breathing, I watched Mel come out, her profile pensive. There was a defeated slope to her shoulders as she walked slowly downstairs where she was greeted by a tousle-haired boy in denim dungarees, dragging a box of Lego behind him.

'Where's Uncle Owen, Mummy?'

'He had to go back to work,' Mel said brightly, ruffling the boy's hair. 'Let's go and find Granny.'

They drifted out of view. I heard a door open and close somewhere along the hallway, releasing a smell of baking bread and the sound of music playing.

Breathing hard now, I peeled away from the wall, replaying what I'd heard.

The man – Owen – had obviously been in a relationship with Caitlin quite recently. Had she ended it as soon as she heard from Jack? Did Jack know about him?

Dizzy with new knowledge, heart beating erratically, I dashed downstairs and through the front door, shivering as a blast of cold air hit my face. I dragged my hood up over my hat, turning away from the double-fronted guesthouse, its windows staring like accusing eyes.

I felt exposed at the top of the steep hill that I knew would lead me down to the cottage where Jack was staying. I'd already looked it up on Google Maps.

The air felt so much colder than in London, the sky bigger and currently crowded with steel-grey clouds and wheeling seagulls. How could Jack stand it? He'd told me that, in Brighton, he'd barely been aware of the sea. Growing up there, he took it for granted and preferred city holidays, or visiting the countryside; somewhere with lots of greenery.

I huddled into my coat and made my way down the hill, which sloped so steeply there were railings to hang on to.

I jumped as a delivery van beeped, stepping aside to let it pass. The roads were narrow, little alleyways leading off the cobbled main street and hardly designed for vehicles.

There weren't many people around, but my heart was racing, my face burning by the time I reached the bottom of the hill, hoping no one had taken any notice of the figure in the black coat.

The sea felt too close down here, almost reaching the top of the harbour wall as the wind pushed high waves onto the deserted beach, which was pitted with water. When I touched my lips with my tongue, I tasted salt.

I looked around for the cottage, which was set above the harbour wall; one of a scattered row of grey-stone buildings. From my online search, I knew Sea View was the cottage set apart from the others, at the far end, accessed via a muddy track.

I set off down it, wishing I'd brought waterproof footwear as I stepped in muddy puddles, dampness seeping through my black suede ankle boots.

The few cottages I passed seemed unoccupied, the owners perhaps at work, unless they were second-homes, left empty during the winter. I didn't look too closely, keeping my head low until I reached a patch of churned-up mud that was patterned with tyre marks. Beyond that was a wooden fence and I looked over, into a wild-looking garden – Caitlin clearly didn't have Jack's green-fingered touch – with a raised patio area to one side, where a couple of wicker chairs were stacked next to a bistro-style table. I imagined the pair of them there on a summer's day, a bottle of something chilled on the table between them. My ribcage tightened, my cheeks pulsing with heat.

All around me was the sound of the sea, the rush of it seeming to echo inside my head. I glanced at the cottage, its windows small and old-fashioned – no double glazing to keep out the draughts – and walked past, trying to look purposeful instead of suspicious. The front of the cottage faced the sea from a different angle, with a wide patch of grass in front that led to the winding coastal path.

Feeling exposed, I kept walking, taking mental snapshots: a bottle-green front door, tubs of dead plants either side of the step; a wooden sign on the pale stone wall with *Sea View Cottage* engraved in white letters. Was Caitlin inside? Her job meant she probably worked from home, and with Jack newly out of hospital, she wouldn't want to leave him.

But I realised I didn't want to talk to Caitlin just yet, after all. I wanted to see Jack's reaction when he set eyes on me. It would tell me everything I needed to know for now.

The door to the cottage opened suddenly, and a woman emerged.

My heart skipped a beat. *It was her.* She was wearing knee-length boots and a purple duffel coat, winding a long scarf around her neck with one hand, stuffing something in one of her coat pockets with the other. A sheet of dark hair blew across her face, and she pushed it away, glancing around as if looking for someone.

Panic ripped through me. I quickly retraced my steps and peered around the garden fence, willing her to leave. She was still for a moment, then turned and called something through the half-open door. I thought I heard her say Jack's name, and anger bubbled in my chest. How dare she speak to him as though he was hers? I bit my knuckles, reminding myself that she didn't know any different – *yet.* I briefly wondered whether it was possible to intercept the post, but even if I wasn't too late, I doubted it would be possible to steal back the card I'd stupidly sent.

Caitlin finally closed the door and scurried away, past the black Fiesta parked nearby. She couldn't be going far if she was on foot. I thought of the conversation I'd overheard at the guesthouse and wondered whether she was on her way to see Owen. He didn't sound like someone willing to slip peacefully out of her life, and as I watched her retreating back, it occurred to me that I could use that information if necessary.

Once she had disappeared in the direction of the hill, I hurried out from my hiding place. I might not have much time before she returned, but this shouldn't take long.

As I approached the front door, a burst of optimism warmed my insides. Whatever had happened in the past, it could be explained and forgiven. Images fell through my mind like glass beads: Jack beside me in bed, his arm curled around my waist; the tilt of his head when he laughed at one of Mattie's jokes; his look of deep concentration when cooking, as if in that moment, nothing else mattered but getting it right and feeding me and my son.

I couldn't do without him. *I wouldn't.* And I wouldn't risk Mattie hating me and blaming me again. I'd had enough of that after William died.

My knuckles rapped the door, surprisingly firm. I held my shoulders back, a sense of anticipation straightening my spine. For the first time in days, I had a sense of rightness, of being where I ought to be.

There was no sound from inside. I imagined Jack, debating whether or not to answer. Unless he was in bed. Maybe he was in too much pain to come downstairs. I tried to look through the little porthole set into the wood, but it gave a distorted view and there was no sign of life.

I sidestepped one of the dead plants and peered through the window, cupping my eyes as I peered inside. An ordinary living room, sofa and chairs grouped round a coffee table, a television in one corner, a log fire blazing. Then a movement caught my eye – someone passing the living room.

I darted back to the front door and rapped again, my heart a frantic beat against my breastbone. A pause. Dry-mouthed, I raised my fist again as the door swung open and there he was. *Jack.* My eyes fixed on him like magnets, and I couldn't stop them widening in horror. He looked dreadful. Badly bruised, pale, and puffy-faced, with tangled hair. He was leaning heavily on a crutch, wearing an olive-green T-shirt that hung from his thin frame, and below his joggers a clunky black boot-like contraption hugged his ankle. A glint of gold on his finger caught my eye. *He was wearing a wedding ring.* Caitlin must have kept it and given it back to him. It looked too big, sliding around his knuckle.

While I struggled to contain my emotions, Jack glanced down at himself. 'I know, I look terrible.'

Words blocked my throat. I wanted to throw myself at him, weeping, to bundle him back to London, but he was looking at me again – not with startled, loving recognition but with an expression of polite curiosity.

'I'm afraid Caitlin's not here at the moment,' he said. 'Can I help?'

Chapter 13

Caitlin

'You look different, Caitlin.' Beverley gave me a beady look as I swiped my card across the reader. 'Everything OK?'

I nodded, stuffing more groceries into my shopping bag. I'd dropped the card I'd pushed in my pocket when I pulled the bag out and felt my face flush when I bent to pick it up.

'I'm fine.' I threw the older woman a smile. 'Something unexpected has happened, that's all.' This was why I'd come out again, after all. To tell someone guaranteed to spread it around that I'd reconciled with my husband. I guessed Owen wouldn't have mentioned it to anyone but Mel because he didn't want it to be true.

'I'm all ears.' Beverley rested her fleshy forearms on the counter and bent closer, her expression avid. I smelt tea on her breath from the flask she kept under the counter. 'It's something nice, I hope.'

'My husband and I are back together.' I stretched my smile, hoping it looked more natural than it felt. 'He was in a car accident . . . he's fine,' I added when Beverley's pale blue eyes widened. 'But he called me from the hospital, and we realised we wanted to be together again.'

'Well, isn't that just lovely.' Beverley had never married, but at sixty still hoped to meet a man who would match up to the heroes in the romance novels she devoured. I knew she would be sympathetic, even if others were less accepting – friends of Mel in particular – and was bound to play up the romantic angle. 'They say true love always finds a way.' A broad beam plumped her rosy cheeks. 'Sometimes you have to let somebody go for them to find their way back to you.'

'Exactly.' I knew she wouldn't dig for specifics that might spoil the magic of our reunion. 'Jack sustained a bit of a head injury in the accident and can't remember the details,' I ploughed on, putting my purse away to hide my face in case she read guilt in my eyes. 'We don't want any fuss, or questions, just to be treated as though we've never been apart.'

'Poor love.' Her round face collapsed into concern. 'So handsome, though it's a long time since I've seen him. Your grandfather thought very highly of him – I remember that,' she went on. 'He'll be OK with you to look after him.'

'I hope so.' It was hard, keeping my smile in place. 'He can't get out and about too much at the moment. He's hurt his ankle, and has a bump on his head, but I'll bring him in to say hello when he's feeling better.'

'That would be lovely.' The smile was back, crinkling Beverley's eyes. She smoothed plump fingers over her loose grey curls, as though picturing Jack in the shop. 'And don't worry, I won't mention . . .' she lowered her voice and tapped the side of her nose '. . . the accident, or anything else.'

'Thank you, Beverley.' I hesitated, fiddling with my scarf. 'If anyone asks, could you play it down a bit?'

'Of course.' She straightened, ready for her next customer. 'Don't worry about a thing. I'm happy for you, love.'

As I headed for the door, the words from the card rushed back at me.

He doesn't love you, and he's not the man you think he is.

For a stupefied moment, I'd thought it might be from Owen. Another attempt to 'win' me back, but I knew his handwriting – unless he'd disguised it. It was a ridiculous thought. The truth was that Jack had been seeing, and probably living with, someone else while we'd been apart. And whoever it was, she knew about me, and knew Jack was at the cottage. *Let him go.* How had she found out? Did she want him back? Why not just confront me?

Was she the one who had phoned the day before? I'd stood in the kitchen motionless until Jack had jokingly called to ask where his cup of tea was. I couldn't show him the card, or ask what it meant, without admitting I'd brought him home under false pretences. And I wasn't prepared to risk losing him again.

So what had it meant? Could it be a warning from whoever hit Jack with their car, or was that genuinely an accident? Tired of trying to untangle the implications, I decided that if the caller rang the cottage again, I would talk to whoever it was. Explain that Jack was staying with me now, and there was no going back. Surely if it was someone who Jack had been seeing, she wouldn't want to be with him if he couldn't remember her. Mine was the face that Jack had wanted to see when he woke up in hospital. Mine was the number he'd remembered. He loved *me* – I was certain of it.

As I'd made Jack a mug of tea I had an overwhelming urge to put things on a firmer footing and after taking it up to him, I'd showered and dressed while he slipped back into a doze, and then called Mum from the downstairs toilet to tell her the news.

'Caitlin, that's wonderful!' Against a background of clinking cutlery and muted chatter, guessing they were breakfasting in a hotel, I heard her call to Dad, 'Caitlin and Jack are back together, Michael. Isn't that great?' Her voice came back to me. 'He's helping himself to croissants. We stock up, so we don't need to buy lunch.'

Seconds later, Dad was congratulating me in his typically down-to-earth way. 'About time,' he said. 'I'm glad you've put whatever it was behind you.' He left a pause for me to finally tell them what it was and when I didn't respond, gave an affectionate laugh. 'Are you sure it's what you want, Caitlin?'

'Positive,' I told him, knowing I would have their support no matter what, grateful they were an ocean away and not due back for a couple of months. 'We don't want any references to our break-up, Dad. We've moved on.'

'I knew it would happen one day,' Mum interrupted in the pragmatic way she approached most things in life. 'You're obviously perfect for each other. My God, those wedding vows he wrote for you.'

I love you for always believing in me, for making me feel strong, and for helping me to believe in myself. I vow to love you openly, honestly, and forever. Jack's face had blurred through a haze of tears as I made my promises in return.

Except, I hadn't been honest.

'I just wish you hadn't had to go through all that heartbreak,' Mum said.

'I suppose there was a reason.' I knew the sentiment would appeal to her. 'I'm a stronger person now.'

'You must be, living up there.' I heard the shudder in her voice. 'Why don't the pair of you fly out here for a visit?'

'I'm a bit busy right now,' I told her, relieved they hadn't asked what Jack had been doing while we'd been apart. 'And Jack is looking for work.' It wasn't a conscious decision to not mention his accident. By the time they returned, I could fashion it into a funny story if I needed to mention it at all.

After promising to pass on their love – *we don't want it to be awkward* – I sent my oldest friend Dee a message – she was a secondary school teacher in Richmond-on-Thames and would be in class now – and relayed a shortened version of the same message, knowing she would call the minute she was free. Dee had been there from the start, knew why Jack had left. It would be harder to convince her I was doing the right thing.

Certain I'd heard a noise outside the door, I poked my head

around. No one was there, but it took several minutes for my pulse to decelerate.

I wondered again now, as I left the grocery store and made my way down the hill, whether I was going to be constantly looking over my shoulder?

On impulse, I darted into the little newsagent's and picked up some of Jack's favourite chocolate bars, almost cannoning into a hunched figure as I came out. Whoever it was seemed in a hurry, walking fast, swaddled in a padded coat, head down.

It was spitting with rain, which blew into my eyes as I continued back to the cottage with a growing sense of urgency. What if whoever had sent me the card was here already, in Robin Hood's Bay? They could have been watching the house, waiting for me to leave. Would Jack have answered the door? I'd told him I was popping out, and he'd assured me sleepily he would be fine, but I was panting with something close to terror as I reached home.

Buffeted by the wind, I jabbed my key at the lock, swearing when it missed and dropped to the step. My hands shook as I retrieved it and tried again before bursting indoors.

'Jack!' I called, dropping my bag of shopping as I took the stairs two at a time in my rain-soaked boots. 'Are you OK?'

'In here.'

I followed his voice to the spare room, hands gripping the doorframe as I looked inside to see him rummaging through one of the cardboard boxes, his crutch propped against the wall. A hot wash of relief gave way to anxiety when I saw him flipping through a plastic folder of documents. 'What are you doing?'

'It's the weirdest thing.' He half-turned so I could see the undamaged side of his face. 'I can't find my passport.'

My stomach flipped. His passport was one of the few things, along with his driving licence, that he'd taken when he left. I'd wondered at the time whether he was planning to fly out and visit his father, perhaps make up with him. I half-hoped he would – that Neil would talk him down, persuade him to come home, but when I spoke to Neil a fortnight later, he hadn't heard from his son, and I didn't mention that Jack had left me.

'Why do you need your passport?' I tried out a laugh as I moved into the dusty room and took the folder from him, rifling through old insurance papers and a few bank statements, kept as a link to our past because everything was digital now. I pulled out my own passport to buy myself time to think.

'It's not that I need it,' he said, leaning against the stack of boxes and gingerly stroking the back of his head. 'I had this . . . I don't know. I woke up with a panicky feeling that my passport was missing and thought I'd look for it.'

'Planning to do a runner?' My voice rose on a surge of adrenaline and Jack gave me a strange look. 'Actually, you're right. It is lost.' I opened my own passport and studied the photo of my serious face – eyes big, mouth a straight line – so I didn't have to look at him. 'Mum would love us to fly out for a visit,' I said on impulse. 'I spoke to her earlier.'

'I can't do that without a passport.' When I risked a glance, my heart clenched. His gaze was darting about, a groove between his eyebrows. He seemed to be trying to grasp hold of something just beyond his understanding.

I have to leave London, Caitlin. I made a terrible mistake that I can't put right. All I can do is get out.

Was there a reason he'd needed his passport? Had he left it wherever he'd been staying by mistake? *With her?* I swallowed a bubble of fear. 'A few things got lost in the move,' I said, with a brightness that felt alien. 'I can pick up an application form for a replacement from the post office.'

Relief flashed over his face. 'I don't remember it being lost.'

'There are a few things you don't remember,' I said, skin crawling with shame as I tucked my passport away. 'At least it's not important.'

'It felt like it was.' He ran the heel of his hand across his

101

forehead. 'I just don't know why.' His shoulders sagged. 'No driver's licence either.'

'You didn't have your wallet or phone at the hospital,' I reminded him, wondering for the first time whether it had been deliberate, part of the 'leaving' plan he'd spoken about on the phone. *Everything's in place for me to leave.* 'You can get new ones.'

He nodded, distracted. 'Also, there's no internet.'

Another jump of alarm. 'There is, but it's not reliable.'

'I was going to check my emails.' He gave a slight shake of his head. 'I couldn't get a signal on that phone you gave me.'

So he hadn't been sleeping while I was gone. Instead, he'd been overwhelmed with an urge to search for his passport and check his emails. My skin felt cold. If he remembered his email address, different to the one he'd had when we were together – I'd tried it once and the message bounced back – there was bound to be something there from the past year. Even if he didn't recall the details, it would be game over. He would know he'd been living a different life before he was hit by that car. *A life without me.*

'You can use my laptop if you like.' My casual tone belied the frantic thump of my heart. I shed my coat and ran downstairs to the living room where the fire was dying. Jack must have risen as soon as I left to get it going, and I couldn't work out how I felt about that. 'Do you know your email address?'

As I heard the clump of him making his way downstairs, I wondered whether it was possible to fake a power cut. The fuse box was an old one in the cupboard under the stairs. I could get in there and flick the switch on the pretext of putting my boots away. But that would only buy me a certain amount of—

'It's the usual one, isn't it?'

I twitched with fright at the sound of Jack's voice behind me. 'No.' *Of course he would expect me to know it.* 'You hadn't used that one for a while, remember?' Blood rushed to my face as I headed to my Mac on the dining table. 'You'd been having problems with it and were going to set up a new one when we moved here.'

'That's . . . right,' he said in a doubtful way that made me hate myself. When I dared to look, his teeth were digging into his bottom lip. 'I don't suppose you can remember what it is?'

I looked through the window where the clouds had parted, revealing patches of blue sky. A figure was silhouetted against the glimmer of sea in the distance, seeming to stare at the cottage before striding out of view.

'I don't know whether you got around to changing it,' I said. 'We can check your old address if you like.'

'It doesn't matter.' As though losing interest, Jack hopped across to the fireplace and poked the embers in the grate. 'A fresh start,' he said. 'Out with the old, in with the new.' He turned, throwing me a half-smile. 'Who emails anymore, anyway?' he said. 'Much easier to text, if and when I get some clients.'

'You will.' Relief rinsed away some of the tension in my bones. 'I'll start putting it about what a brilliant gardener you are. Gramps used to tell people that, and you know his word meant a lot around here.'

Jack curled his arm around my shoulder as I joined him in front of the fire, watching the orange flicker leap into a blaze, the warmth quickly spreading through the room. 'I miss the old man.'

I leant into him. 'Me too.'

We were silent for a moment, gazing at the photographs on the mantelpiece, a gallery of memories. My limbs felt bloodless. The danger wasn't over. There would be more questions, and what about when his memory returned? Or when the person who had sent the card turned up on the doorstep?

'By the way, someone came over while you were out.'

Ice washed down my spine. It was as if he'd read my thoughts. 'What?'

Jack shifted, his arm dropping away. He crossed to the window, levering himself on the furniture, one crutch still on the floor, the other propped by the door. 'A woman,' he said. 'She seemed shocked by the state of me.'

Chapter 14

Lydia

I hurried along the beach, head down. My encounter with Jack had left my heart pounding and tears burning my eyes. *He didn't recognise me.* How was that even possible? All the memories we'd built, erased as easily as pencil marks from paper.

The injustice of it wrenched a sob from my throat, the sound lost among crashing waves and wailing seagulls as I stumbled across the sand.

It's me, I'd wanted to cry. *Come home, Jack. You don't belong here.*

But something had stopped me as I drank in the sight of him, thinner than I remembered. Despite his crutch and the bruises he'd seemed unnervingly relaxed . . . like someone already at home. There had been a looseness to his shoulders and jaw that made me realise how clenched he'd been the last time I saw him, when his eyes had blazed with fury, and I'd run into the garden, aware too late that Mattie was watching from his bedroom window. If there were some things that Jack had forgotten, I was glad. But *everything* about our time together? *Even Mattie?*

I'd waited a beat before speaking, trying to compose myself, checking his face for signs it was a trick, that any second recognition would flash over his face and the smile I loved so much would break out. *Lyds! Oh my God, I've missed you so much.*

Instead, a wrinkle of confusion had appeared on his brow. 'Are you OK?'

'I'm fine.' My voice had emerged thin and high, and I had to clear my throat. 'I'm visiting the area and was out walking. I saw a man in your garden.' I'd pointed to the side of the building. 'He looked like he was casing the joint, so I thought I would come up and scare him off.'

'A man?' Jack's gaze had moved beyond me, as if the fictitious figure might materialise, while I tried not to stare at the growth of beard covering half his face. He'd mostly been clean-shaven with me because I loved to see the little cleft in his chin, and the angle of his cheekbones. 'Did you see where he went?'

'He'd gone by the time I got up here.' I gestured vaguely behind me, wondering whether Jack could tell that I was shaking. 'I was on the beach.'

'Right.' The frown was still there, as if he was trying to put two and two together. Had my voice, my accent, evoked something deep in his mind or was he thinking about the man that Caitlin had been seeing – the one who wasn't prepared to give up on her. *Did he know about Owen Whittaker?* 'Thank you for letting me know,' he said, scanning the immediate area with worried eyes. Eyes that used to fill with emotion when they looked into mine, and dance with laughter when Mattie teased him.

'Round the back,' I said quickly.

'There should be footprints.'

'Sorry?'

'It's been raining and it's muddy, so he's probably left footprints.'

Heat travelled across my face. 'Are you going to call the police?'

'I don't think so.' He spoke quickly, pulling back a little from the doorway. For a wild moment, I wondered whether he was going to invite me in, but instead he adjusted his crutch and said, 'It could have just been a nosy passer-by.'

106

'Maybe.' I saw an open door behind him, a glimpse of kitchen. A bonfire-night smell of burning wood drifted out from the log fire I'd seen in the living room.

An open fire is too dangerous, he'd said when I asked about opening the Victorian fireplace that William had bricked up after Mattie was born. *And bad for the environment.* Maybe the environment up here didn't matter.

'What happened to you?' I couldn't stop the words erupting, my voice stronger this time.

'I was hit by a car.' He related it blandly, as if it was nothing – as if he really couldn't remember it happening. 'I was lucky, I guess.'

A rash of goose bumps had raised the hairs on his arms. It was cold and his T-shirt was old and faded, nothing like the ones I'd bought him, with their discreet logos and heavy material, as well as a pair of expensive leather boots, even though he preferred things that were 'worn in'. *Where were his boots, and the North Face waterproof jacket I'd bought for his birthday?* I hated that Caitlin must have kept all his things, as if she'd expected him to come back.

I wanted to fold myself against him, bury my face in his neck and breathe him in. Would I detect a trace of the Paco Rabanne aftershave I'd bought him for Christmas? *Probably not, with the beard.* 'Unlucky, more like.' My voice quivered. 'Those bruises look painful.'

'I'm a bit bashed up, but it's not as bad as it looks.'

Except you've lost your memory.

'Have you lived here long?' *Stop it, Lydia.* 'It's nice,' I added, holding on to my hood as a gust of wind threatened to drag it down. 'Apart from the weather.'

'It can get wild.' A smile uncurled, the sight of it squeezing my heart. 'We've not been here long, but the cottage has been in my wife's family for a couple of generations. Her great-gran was evacuated here during the war and ended up staying.'

My wife. Two simple words that made me want to howl, to throw myself down and beat my fists on the ground. 'Nice,' I managed. 'Robin Hood was obviously a fan of the area.' *Stupid, stupid thing to say.*

'According to a local ballad, he arrived at the bay to help local fishermen fight French pirates before taking their booty.' He gave a self-conscious shrug when I didn't – couldn't – respond. 'My wife's grandfather was a mine of local information, used to give tours after he retired. The place was a smuggler's hotspot back in the day. There's a network of passages and tunnels under some of the houses, and one of them opens directly on to the slipway if you fancy exploring. But you probably know all that stuff anyway.'

Barely anything had registered apart from the words *my wife*. 'I'm up from London.'

Nothing, except a slight movement of his eyebrows. 'That's a long drive.'

'I stayed with my friend Shona in York on the way.' I'd mentioned her to him, told him we'd been best friends, but there wasn't a tremor of recognition. 'I'm having a few days away from being a mum,' I blundered on. 'Staying at the Hill Top guesthouse.'

'Nice.'

'I'm hoping my son isn't missing me too much.'

A ripple of confusion crossed his face, as if wondering why I was telling him so much. 'I hope you enjoy your break.'

Frustration battled with a feeling of helplessness. 'I'd better leave you to it,' I said, turning away as my mind crumbled.

'Thanks again for knocking,' he called after me. 'I'll keep a lookout in case he comes back.'

I looked over my shoulder once, certain he was watching me, but the door was shut and the windows empty. Sorrow clutched my insides, but as I hurried away, it struck me that my story about the man in the garden had been a stroke of luck. *Or had I already known on some level that I would use it?* I was certain when Jack told Caitlin, she would think of Owen; the man she'd dumped when Jack called because he'd forgotten they were no longer together.

My ankle boots were filling with cold, damp sand, and my legs beginning to ache. The wind was like an assault, biting my cheeks, yet in my thick coat and hat I felt feverishly hot. A strange sensation prickled across the back of my neck. I swung around, certain there was someone behind me – *Jack?* – but the arc of beach was deserted. I scanned the rim of the sloping clifftop and got the impression that someone had dropped out of sight. *Caitlin?* Maybe she'd seen me leaving and was watching . . . wondering.

I lingered a moment, cold air pushing like hands at my back, but nothing stirred, and I couldn't be sure I hadn't imagined the whole thing.

I walked for a while, losing track of time as my mind circled back over the conversation with Jack, and the shock of his appearance, before retreating to the guesthouse, relieved no one was around as I emptied my boots of sand outside the door before heading up to my room.

On the first landing, I paused, hearing a sound from one of the vacant rooms. The door wasn't closed properly. Maybe a new guest had arrived, or perhaps Mel was in there cleaning, but, for some reason, the hairs on the back of my neck had lifted.

'Hello?' I wasn't sure why I'd spoken. Perhaps to prove to myself that I wasn't being paranoid, my conscience summoning sinister scenes out of nothing.

There was no response, but I sensed a presence behind the glossy white door. As though hypnotised, I moved forwards and gave it a shove. It opened slowly across a carpet identical to the one in my room, above. It was the room I'd heard Mel and her brother arguing in. She must have forgotten to lock it after Owen left.

'Hello?' I felt a tick of panic in my chest. The room was empty yet seemed to be holding its breath. My gaze flicked over the double bed, the rustic wardrobe and matching dressing table, snagging on the neatly folded throw across the bottom of the duvet. There was a barely discernible indent in the middle, as though it had been recently sat on.

Reluctant to step over the threshold, I sniffed the air just inside the door, my heart speeding up as a vaguely familiar scent filled my nostrils. *Jack?* My legs went cold as I breathed in the earthy, masculine traces left behind. I'd mentioned to Jack that I was staying here. Could he have headed up to the guesthouse after I'd gone, perhaps wanting to talk some more? But why, when he hadn't remembered me, and why would he have been in this room? For a wild second, I imagined him hiding under the bed, a hand snaking out to grab me, and backed away, pulling the door shut. I was being ridiculous. It was probably Owen's scent, lingering from the day before – that was all.

Hearing movement downstairs, I bolted up to my room, out of breath, realising as I opened the door that I wasn't the only one forgetting to lock up. My mind had been too full of Jack when I left earlier to think about security.

Glancing around, a tremor ran through me. Someone had been inside. My bag, which had been on the chair, was now on the floor under the window, and there was a scent in here too, faint but unmistakable. *Or was I imagining it?* I inhaled, a pulse throbbing in my neck, but could only detect the stale tang of my own perspiration, mingled with the laundered perfume of the bedding.

Mel. My shoulders sagged. She must have been in to clean and moved my bag. But the bed hadn't been straightened, and the towel I'd used was still slung over the back of the chair. Could she have started and got called away, perhaps by one of her children? I had to stop letting my imagination run riot, or I would be no use to anyone.

For a while, I paced tight circles in front of the window, still in my coat, arms clutched around my middle. *What should I do?* Returning to London without Jack wasn't an option. But if I went back to the cottage now and explained who I was, wouldn't he wonder why I hadn't told him in the first place? He hated subterfuge of any sort. The first argument we'd had was after Mattie told him – on Valentine's Day of all days, when I was trying to hide feeling upset because Jack's card had been jokey rather than romantic and he hadn't bought me a gift, just booked a table for dinner at a restaurant I wasn't keen on – that it was my fault his dad was dead, that I'd sent him out the day he died because I didn't like him being in the house, and that I was glad he was dead.

Jack demanded to know why I hadn't told him my relationship with William had been rocky, instead of making out that we'd been happy, and although I'd tried to explain, I sounded defensive. In that moment, I saw a look cross his face that William had worn many times, had felt the slight shifting of power. I knew, looking back, that was the moment things changed between us, even though I'd done everything I could after that to show Jack I loved him.

Now, if I arrived on his doorstep again, how could I explain why I hadn't been honest with him in the first place? The thought of him disbelieving, or rejecting me again, pushed tears to my eyes. His return had to be a choice, but with Caitlin in the picture, and me not even a distant memory, how was I supposed to make that happen? I let out a groan of frustration. *Why hadn't I introduced myself?* It would have seemed weird, but my name might have triggered something. I had a sudden, vivid memory of my mother snatching a black cat out of my arms when I was eight years old. I'd found him at the bottom of our garden and wanted to keep him, already planning to rename him Salem like the cat in *Sabrina the Teenage Witch*.

He belongs to someone, Lydia. You need to think before you act, or you're going to get into trouble.

Hands trembling, I made some tea, using the kettle provided, dropping a bag of English Breakfast into a china cup. I got out my phone, and threw myself down in the tub chair by the window. No point looking for Jack online. He hadn't used social media while we were together, even for business, and the photo on his website was years old, his hair shorter, face fuller than it was now. A stranger.

Instead, I typed in *Owen Whittaker, Robin Hood's Bay.*

He owned an outdoor clothing shop and fitness centre a few miles away. There was an image of him on the website, sitting on a fallen tree trunk, a couple of weights spilling out of a rucksack as though he worked out in a forest every day. He was smiling and windswept, ruggedly attractive with a bulky physique. Not my type, and presumably not Caitlin's either. *Maybe I should pay him a visit.* I had no idea what I would say to him, if anything, but he was a link to her.

Relieved to have a plan of sorts, I drained my tea and grabbed the pack of complimentary biscuits – homemade, according to the card attached – then entered the address of the shop into Google Maps. As I scooped my keys off the dressing table, something out of place caught my eye through the half-open door to the en suite. I whirled around, pulling the light on as I entered the nautical-themed bathroom, nerves pulsing with fright as I stared at the mirrored cabinet over the sink. Someone had written on the glass using toothpaste. Two words: **GO HOME.**

Chapter 15

Lydia

'Is anyone else staying here?' I asked Mel when I reached the foot of the stairs, heart still racing with the shock of what I'd seen. I was relieved to catch her coming out of the kitchen, so I didn't have to seek her out. 'I was sure I heard someone moving about in the room under mine a while ago.'

'Oh?' Frowning, she glanced past me, shaking her head. Her cheeks were flushed, and she seemed distracted. 'You're our only guest at the moment.'

'Perhaps someone was cleaning in there.' I adjusted my hat, hoping she hadn't noticed the wobble in my voice. I could hardly ask whether she knew who'd graffitied my mirror with toothpaste, which I'd already wiped clean – not without raising questions I didn't want to hear and had no idea how to answer – but maybe I could prompt some sort of explanation.

'We only clean while guests are staying, and only if they request it,' she said. 'We ask on the booking form.' Concern flared in her eyes. 'You ticked the box for privacy.'

Did I? 'Of course, it's fine,' I said. She hadn't seen the message

113

then – and surely wouldn't have put it there herself. The thought that it might have been Jack was unbearable, but who else? *Caitlin?* But how would she know I was here, or the purpose of my visit?

'It's funny you should say that though.' Mel's brow furrowed. 'I thought I heard the front door earlier, but there was no one here but me.' She shook her head, mouth turned down. 'I looked outside and saw someone heading towards the hill.' From her rush of words it had clearly been bothering her. She sounded unguarded, anxious almost.

'You think there was an intruder?' I gripped the banister, my knuckles white against the wood.

'No, no, not in that sense,' she said quickly, unconsciously smoothing a hand down her plait and twisting the end. 'I had a look around and there was no sign anyone had been upstairs. It's just . . .' She pulled a wry face. 'I don't always drop the latch on the front door. My family tells me off about it, but I've always felt safe here.'

I didn't feel safe. Not at all.

As if sensing my growing unease, Mel added, 'Of course I'll make sure the door's locked from now on. I came in with some shopping and must not have dropped the latch before I went into the kitchen. I normally come in through the back door, but it sticks sometimes and—'

'You saw someone leaving?'

'Not necessarily.' Her flush deepened. I got the impression she was struggling to regain control. 'It's fairly unusual to see someone I don't know around here, that's all, though . . .' Another quick shake of her head. 'I have a feeling I know who it might have been. He's a newcomer.' Her lips tightened. 'He's been in an accident recently, and the man I saw had a limp.'

My heart tripped. *Jack.* It had to be. 'You think he came in here?'

'No, no.' Mel held up a hand, wide-eyed, misunderstanding my tone. 'I thought he might have been looking for my brother, but . . .' She straightened her shoulders, seeming to make a

114

decision. 'Look, whatever it was, it's a family issue.' Finally, a smile warmed her eyes, no doubt meant to reassure. 'I promise you don't need to worry.'

I drove out of the car park with Mel's words playing on a loop in my mind. *I promise you don't need to worry.* If only she knew. But if Jack had been in my room and left the message on the mirror, what did it mean? That he had remembered who I was and wanted me gone? Why not just talk to me? Then I remembered our last argument – how it ended with me going to the police station in desperation. Perhaps he thought leaving was for the best, that being apart was better, but he was wrong. *So* wrong. I thought back to our conversation earlier, reassessing everything he'd said, but couldn't recall so much as a flicker of recognition. Jack wasn't an actor. I was certain he hadn't recognised me. That only left Caitlin, who might have been told about a woman staying at Hill Top, and put it together with the card she'd received, telling her to let Jack go.

A hard ball of anxiety bounced around my stomach as I drew closer to Fit For Out – surely a play on words. My northern grandmother used to say *'owt* meaning *anything* – and Owen Whittaker. The clothing store was set back from the road a few miles from the village, backed by rolling countryside. It had been built to look like a giant log cabin with a smoky-glass-fronted extension to one side, where I could make out someone pounding a treadmill. On the opposite side was a small, stone building I guessed must be where he lived. How sad, that he lived and worked in the same place, and probably would for the rest of his life.

I had no idea why I'd come, other than Owen was part of Caitlin's life and, by extension, Jack's too.

I was clammy with nerves by the time I'd found a space and wedged the car between two bigger vehicles. The sky was restless with flapping birds and scudding clouds, and I kept my woolly hat on as I stepped out, some instinct to keep my hair covered kicking in.

Inside, the store was warm, and I risked unzipping my coat, crumbs from the shortbread biscuits I'd eaten on the way over falling to the weathered oak floor.

'Can I help?'

'I'm just looking,' I said to the pink-cheeked assistant tidying a rail of fleece-lined jackets nearby. 'Thank you.'

'We've a good selection of walking boots if you're interested,' she persisted, nodding to the far wall, where footwear was arranged on shelving designed to look like a rock face.

'Maybe.' I glanced at my worn boots, still rimmed with sand. I wouldn't be buying any walking boots, but I had noticed a man talking to a customer in front of the display, who looked like he might be Owen Whittaker. Throwing the assistant what I hoped was a friendly smile, I made my way over, pausing by a stand of thermal socks so I could check it was him.

His broad, tanned face was smiling as he spoke to a pumped-up man with a shiny bald head, and for a second, I could understand why Caitlin had been drawn to him. He was nicer-looking than his sister, without the lines of tiredness around his eyes, which even from a distance I could see were a mossy shade of green. He wore his cargo trousers and fleecy top well, and the expressive way he talked, hands moving as he explained some detail, was appealing, but once the man had smiled his thanks and moved away, Owen's expression changed.

About to step closer – unsure what my approach was going to be – I found myself shrinking back and picking up a pair of socks as his gaze moved away from mine. It was as if a shutter had come down, turning his face to granite as he stood for a moment, eyes seeming to stare at nothing. Then he pulled a phone from a side pocket in his trousers and studied the screen. A wince contorted his features before he shoved it back with an angry movement. *Was he checking for a message from Caitlin?*

'Are you looking for anything in particular?'

116

I felt a hook of fear in my throat. He was addressing me, coming closer. His smile had returned, wide enough to see a chipped tooth further back. He was tall, as well as powerfully built, and I couldn't help thinking how hard it would be to escape if he were to grab hold of me. 'Just the socks,' I said in a falsely bright voice, waving the pair I'd picked up.

Turning, I hurried to the till before he tried to talk me into buying something else. I had no doubt he would be good at it, but despite the vague plan that had started to form, to find out more about Caitlin, and maybe even get him onside, tell him the truth and enlist his help, I'd glimpsed something in him that made my skin crawl: repressed anger, coupled with a sense of entitlement that I recognised only too well. I knew how dangerous it could be if unleashed, and it was the thought of that anger being turned on me that had me paying for a pair of men's socks I didn't want before rushing back to my car, hoping he wouldn't remember our encounter.

Chapter 16

Caitlin

'I don't think we're going to find anything.' My heart hammered as I stared at Jack peering around the garden. 'And you shouldn't be out here.'

Hovering his booted foot above the ground, he wobbled as he pushed his hair off his face and resumed his scrutiny. 'There should be some footprints.'

'I can't see anything.' It was hard to keep the strain from my voice, his words from earlier rattling around in my head. *She saw someone in our garden. A man, looking through our windows.* My vision had danced, the walls receding as images flooded in: Owen coming round and forcing a confrontation, driving Jack to flee or – much worse – hurting Jack and bundling him into his Land Rover.

Now, seeing Jack stooping over the straggly flowerbed in his old, hooded jacket, supporting his weight with a hand on the damp stone wall, I was struck by the wildness of my imagination. Owen wouldn't hurt Jack, knowing how I felt about him. Even so, the idea that he could have turned up, or spoken to Jack on the phone while I was out, made my knees sag.

'Come inside.' I tugged Jack's sleeve. 'It's freezing out here.'

Straightening, he looped his arm around my shoulders, letting me help him into the cottage. He smelt of toothpaste and coffee. 'Maybe she got it wrong,' he said, as I tried to unzip his jacket with shaking fingers.

'Here, let me do that.' He shed his coat and I did the same, hanging them together on the hook by the door.

'By the way, what happened to the jacket you were wearing when you came home?' I said, more to push the conversation in a different direction.

Something flashed over his face, as if he was trying to catch hold of a memory. 'I put it in the cupboard under the stairs,' he said tightly. 'I don't even know where I got it.'

As I didn't know either, I didn't respond.

He followed me to the kitchen, grabbing his crutch, which tapped the tiles behind me. 'If there was someone outside,' he said, pulling out a chair, the scraping sound setting my nerves on edge. 'They're long gone.'

Turning, so he couldn't read my face, I filled the kettle. 'Who was this woman who came to the door?' I'd managed to put off asking as my head had filled with thoughts of Owen.

'Just a tourist out walking.' He spoke neutrally. 'I suppose it was good of her to let us know.'

My lungs deflated. His use of *us* was like a balm, and the woman . . . she couldn't have been the one who had sent the card. Surely the sight of her on our doorstep would have triggered a memory, perhaps even brought it all back, and though Jack looked troubled, he didn't seem agitated – and surely he would have said something if he'd recognised her.

Fear sliced through me again as I remembered thinking I'd seen a figure in the garden earlier. I swivelled to see Jack ruffling his hair, an exhausted set to his face. 'Did she say what the man looked like?'

'Why?' Jack's gaze sharpened. 'Do you know who it was?'

119

I dragged a hand across my forehead. 'No . . . only, I . . . maybe.' *For God's sake.*

'What is it, Cait?'

For a moment, I imagined telling him everything, but my mind tangled with the possible outcomes. 'You probably don't remember, but there's a man – Owen Whittaker.' My face flushed and my scalp prickled. 'He had . . . has a bit of a thing for me. It's embarrassing, really—' I stopped. Jack was nodding slowly.

'I do remember, vaguely,' he said to my surprise. 'Your granddad mentioned him once. Said I should look after you because the man whose family owns the guesthouse at the top of the hill was waiting in the wings. He pointed him out in the pub the first time we came up here.'

I'd completely forgotten about that. Gramps had gone into overprotective mode, practically warning Jack to look after me, or else. Owen had been chatting to the landlord and hadn't seemed to notice me, so the exchange had barely registered. Now, I was filled with a twisted gratitude towards my grandfather for making it easier to lie.

'OK, well . . . I haven't said anything, but since I came up here, he's kind of been on the scene.' Every word burnt my throat like acid. 'He heard I . . . we were moving into the cottage and while you were in Brighton, he helped move some furniture in and asked me out for a drink.' At least that was true. 'I thought it wouldn't do any harm to go, as a friend, but it was a bad move.'

'And you didn't think to mention it?' Jack eyed me warily.

'Do you remember the day I drove up here, Jack?' *Of course he didn't.*

He squinted, then let out a sigh and shook his head. 'It's gone.' He lifted a hand and let it drop to the table. 'It's like . . . there are so many gaps.' He prodded his temple. 'Like a jigsaw with pieces missing.'

I swallowed the tears creeping up my throat. 'It's not your fault.'

'So you think it was him?' Jack's face darkened. 'He's been pestering you?'

'It's fine – I can talk to him.'

'He does know we're married?'

A coldness spread down my back and my airways shrank. I spun around and switched on the kettle, then gripped the edge of the worktop. 'Yes, he knows.' My arms and fingers were tingling, my legs watery. There wasn't enough air in my lungs, and I panted for breath. I couldn't have a panic attack now. They started a few weeks after Jack left. The first time, I thought I was having a heart attack and called my friend Dee in a sobbing frenzy. She understood instantly what was happening and talked me down but, for a while, the fear of it happening again had prevented me going out. I was scared of having an attack in the supermarket, or while I was driving, but they came randomly – in the middle of the night, or while I was washing up and, once, at my parents' house after Sunday lunch. I'd managed to make it to the bathroom and hid there until it passed, practising the breathing exercises I'd looked up online.

I hadn't had one since moving to Robin Hood's Bay, which I'd taken as a sign that I'd done the right thing, leaving behind my old life with its tainted memories.

As I squeezed air out of my lungs while the kettle came to the boil, I wondered whether bringing Jack back into my life had been a bad idea, but when I felt his presence behind me, I turned to let him hold me and knew I would do it all again.

'It'll be OK,' he said softly, as my panic receded. 'Even if there was someone outside, it could have been the postman.'

'He came earlier.' I spoke without thinking, my voice muffled against his chest, stiffening as I remembered the card in my coat pocket. 'Not here, I . . . I saw him on my way out.'

'Do you want me to have a word with this Owen? Warn him off?'

I shook my head, pulling away. 'Really, it's fine.'

Jack stroked a strand of hair behind my ear, eyes searching my face. 'I shouldn't have left you up here on your own.'

'It's what we agreed.' I reached past him for the carton of milk in the shopping bag. If only there was a way to fast-forward a few weeks, so this was behind us, and our lives here were established. 'Let's not think about it now,' I said firmly. 'You're not going to get better quickly if you're worrying all the time.'

He puffed out a breath and nodded, absently picking up one of the bars of chocolate I'd bought. After a moment's silence, he sank against the worktop and ate it quickly as he watched me make the tea. 'I was thinking, while you were out,' he said, when he'd finished. 'I could have some flyers printed and deliver them around the village, get some work lined up.'

'That's a good idea.' My mood lifted. 'In a month or so, people will be thinking about their gardens.'

'It's weird, but I checked my website and saw that I'd posted a testimony on there from a couple I don't remember doing a job for.'

'How did you check your website?' I thought of everything he'd been doing in the short time I'd left him alone – including talking to a stranger on the doorstep – and my lungs tightened again.

'On your laptop.' When my head snapped round, he gave a rueful smile. 'You did say I could use it, and it's not as if we have private passwords.'

I should have changed mine but was hopeless at remembering new ones. I'd kept our combination of wedding date and surname with two z's on the end for added security, which Jack had found hilarious.

I don't think a hacker would have much trouble getting into your accounts.

They wouldn't find them very interesting.

Except . . . my phone was linked to my laptop, giving access to my messages. How many exchanges were there with Dee, the only one privy to my private life, who knew all the ins and outs, how devastated I had been about my break-up with Jack and the reason it had happened? *And my last few exchanges with Owen would be visible.*

'I can't remember the last time you looked at your website.' Somehow, I kept my voice steady as I spooned sugar into his tea. 'Were you thinking about updating it?'

'Maybe.' He picked up his mug and took a sip, wincing slightly. He always drank his tea too hot. 'I felt like I wanted to do something productive.'

Heart racing, I opened a drawer and looked inside. 'The testimony,' I prompted. 'You said you can't remember the job.'

'It was from a couple called Eric and Jean, thanking me for bringing their garden back to life and saying they would happily recommend me to anyone.'

I rattled some cutlery and shut the drawer. 'That's good, isn't it?'

'Why can't I remember them?'

I gave him a look and he briefly closed his eyes. 'Forgetting the accident is one thing, Cait. Why would I forget a gardening job?'

'Like you said, there are missing pieces.' The job must have been in London. *Eric and Jean.* A dart of anguish pierced my heart. They'd seen more of my husband than I had in the past year.

'You don't recall me mentioning them?'

A siren of anxiety went off in my head. Jack used to talk to me about the houses he went to, what the owners were like, show me before and after photos, which he occasionally put on his website. 'Honestly, no,' I said, unable to summon another lie. 'I'm sure it'll come back.' Thank goodness Jack wasn't on any social media sites. There was no way he could stumble across updates on Facebook or Twitter and wonder what they meant, unless . . . *What about the woman he'd been seeing?* She could have posted pictures of them together – but unless she'd included Jack's full name there was no way of checking.

Even so, when he manoeuvred himself towards the living room to check on the fire, I took out my phone and keyed his name into a search engine, adding *Facebook* then *Twitter*. Several Jack Garveys came up, but none was my husband. I checked Instagram too, where I sometimes posted pictures of my illustrations, but no images appeared of a woman entwined with Jack somewhere with the hashtag *living our best life*. I felt a pull of tension across my neck and shoulders. *How was I going to live like this?*

I jumped when my phone vibrated with a message from Dee, who had tried to call a couple of times while I'd had my phone on silent.

Cait, I'm worried. Why aren't you picking up? Has he forgiven you? CALL ME! X

I looked at the image she'd sent of her 'worried face' – no doubt to make me smile. Her naturally wavy blonde hair, pale skin and full lips made her look like a Forties film star, which she played up by wearing full-skirted dresses with nipped-in waists, little cardigans, and ballet pumps, but her demure appearance belied the steely core that made her a such a good and loyal friend – and also a formidable opponent on the netball pitch, a game she played at county level. *A good way to blow off steam after trying to teach kids who would rather be somewhere else, how to paint.* We'd met on a fine art course at London Art School and became friends based on a mutual appreciation of the lumpy cakes made by another student, Louise, which everyone else found inedible.

I was through Dee that I'd met Jack, when she dragged me to her sister's hen do at a pub in Brighton, where he'd been equally miserable at a friend's raucous birthday party, nursing a pint at the bar where we got chatting, bonding over our mutual dislike of big gatherings, the fact that neither of us had siblings, and exchanging silly snippets about ourselves.

Do you have any special talents?
I know all the Latin names for plants. You?
I can sketch you in thirty seconds.
Go on then.
Pass me that napkin.

Dee had been heavily invested in our relationship, was deeply upset when Jack walked out. *He should have forgiven you. Everyone deserves a second chance.* It hadn't occurred to me to fight for him or plead for forgiveness back then. As far as I was concerned, I'd got what I deserved. Yet here I was, acting out of character to grab that second chance. Or maybe this *was* my character. With my easy upbringing, taking all the love and support in my life for granted, my character – my *mettle* as Gramps would have put it – had never been put to the test, until the moment I'd chosen to deceive Jack.

It's all good, don't worry! Adjusting to each other again. I added a winking face. **Will talk soon, I promise XX.**

I took a selfie, grinning and giving a thumbs-up, hoping my face didn't betray my seesawing emotions, holding my breath until she replied: **I'm guessing by the bed hair it's going well, you minx! XX** then I exhaled a shaky sigh, hating myself a little more as I unlinked my phone from my laptop so there was no chance Jack would see the conversation. On impulse, I deleted Owen from my contacts folder, erasing the few texts and WhatsApp messages, including one he'd sent late at night, after being at the pub, asking what I was wearing, accompanied by a love heart emoji, to which I'd replied, *A frown at being woken up!* It seemed like a lifetime ago.

For the following few hours, I focused on behaving like a wife who had just brought her beloved husband home from hospital and was nursing him back to health, trying to calm the scurried beating of my heart.

'Let's watch a film,' I said, in a perky way that didn't feel like me. Jack didn't seem to notice. After moving away from my laptop – to my relief – he'd taken a couple of painkillers and retreated to the sofa in front of the fire, under the furry throw. I drew the curtains, surreptitiously checking no one was hovering outside, and brought popcorn and orange juice through before curling up beside him.

He rested his head on a cushion on my lap as I found *The Grand Budapest Hotel*, which we'd enjoyed seeing at the cinema when it came out, and I buried my fingers in his hair to gently massage his scalp the way I used to, careful to avoid the healing wound. We munched our way through the popcorn until Jack fell asleep and my legs went numb, and the fire dwindled to embers, and I almost managed to forget about everything else as my eyelids drooped.

Jack woke as the credits finished rolling, pushing himself upright as he blinked and yawned. He looked rested, a brightness to his eyes. There was a moment of gut-churning worry – *had his memory returned?* – before he looked at me, his gaze soft with love. 'Shouldn't you be working, Mrs Garvey?'

'That's the best thing about being my own boss.' I leant over and touched my fingertips to the bruise across his cheek. 'I set my own hours.'

He took my hand, a look of intent in his eyes as he drew closer. 'What did Dee mean in that text message?'

My stomach dropped. 'Sorry?'

'She asked why you weren't picking up and whether I'd forgiven you.' His grip on my hand strengthened. 'I know I shouldn't have looked, but your phone's obviously connected to the laptop and the messages popped up while I was on there.'

Forcing myself to keep my hand in his and not leap up, I managed a feeble laugh. 'You've been going through my messages?'

'Of course not.' He looked genuinely hurt. 'I wouldn't have known they were there if Dee hadn't texted you.'

Why hadn't I unlinked my phone sooner? 'I haven't got round to calling her back since I brought you home, that's all.' My heart rate rose along with a sense of panic. 'You know what she's like.'

'And you're supposed to forgive me because . . . ?' He dipped his head. 'What did I do?' His tone was seductive – *a trap?*

'Oh, it's nothing,' I said. 'Just a silly argument you and I had before . . . before the accident.' My face was stiff with tension, my lungs constricted. 'I can't even remember what it was about to be honest, something to do with—'

A knock at the front door made us jump.

126

'What time is it?' Jack peered at the old carriage clock on the mantelpiece, releasing my hand at last. 'It feels like the middle of the night.'

'Only four-thirty.' Light-headed with relief at being let off the hook, I rose as the knock came again, more insistent. 'I'll get it,' I said, stumbling as my legs prickled with pins and needles 'Stay there.'

But Jack was rising too, not bothering to grab his crutch before limping after me into the hall. I snapped the light on, glancing through the porthole as I opened the door a crack. *Owen.* My heart crashed against my ribs. He was looking up at my bedroom window, hands on his hips.

Why won't you let me stay over, Caitlin? I promise I don't snore.

I'm not ready to take that step.

When do you think you will be?

I don't know. Soon.

Was he imagining me up there with Jack? It had frustrated him that I held back, that I'd only visited his home a few times, where the spartan neatness, prison-grey walls and tiny windows had made me feel strangely dislocated – as though I didn't know him at all.

'What do you want, Owen?'

He brought his face close to the door, trying to see past me. 'To check you're OK.' I willed Jack to move away but knew he wouldn't. 'What's going on in there?'

I felt my pulse in my throat. 'Nothing's going on,' I said. 'I'm fine.'

Owen clenched a loose fist and rested it on the doorframe, eyes glowing with suspicion. It was raining again, a fine drizzle misting his hair. Behind him, the sky was darkening to slate. 'Why are the curtains shut?'

'I don't think that's any of your business, mate.' Jack reached past me, pulling the door further open so I was forced to take a step back.

Cold air flowed in as Owen looked from me to Jack, shock briefly blanking his face.

'You should see the other guy,' Jack said in acknowledgement, a thread of humour in his tone; an attempt to defuse the situation I'd created.

'Does he know about us?' There was a hint of menace in Owen's voice I'd never heard before.

'Owen, I've told you. There is no "us".' I hated that I sounded desperate, that I was trying to tell him to back off with my eyes while keeping my face averted from Jack's gaze.

'You do know that Caitlin is my wife?' Puzzlement leaked into Jack's question. 'She's married to *me*.'

'Nice of you to remember, *mate*.' Owen squared his shoulders, and the movement brought a ripple of fear as I thought about all the ways he kept fit. He could easily have vaulted over the fence into our garden earlier. 'You didn't think of that when you—'

'I shouldn't have left her up here on her own – I get that.'

For a second, I thought Jack had remembered everything, and my insides turned to water, but I realised he was talking about the day I moved in. 'I appreciate what you did, but I'm here now. You can't be hanging around the place.'

'Hanging around?' Owen's brow gathered into a frown. 'What's that supposed to mean?'

I desperately wanted the encounter to be over, but had to ask, 'Were you here, this morning?'

'I've been at the store until now.' His lip curled as he glanced at Jack, the words *some of us have to work* hovering in the air. 'You can check if you don't believe me.'

I didn't. 'I do,' I said quickly, putting out a placating hand. 'Sorry, Owen.' I felt the burn of Jack's stare at my appeasing tone and banished a memory of Owen's lips pressed against mine. 'Please, can you just go. I've nothing more to say.'

Owen looked at me for a long moment, as though trying to draw out something more – an admission that something was

128

wrong? *Did he think Jack was holding me against my will?* The thought was almost laughable, until Mel's words floated into my head. *He had his heart broken once before and it didn't end well.*

'Thank you for checking up on me.' I forced myself to hold his narrowed gaze and keep a smile in place until I'd closed the door, resting my hand on it and praying he would leave quietly. I started when Jack spoke.

'He's definitely got a thing for you.' I turned to reassure him, but his eyes were fixed on the door with an expression that made my stomach sink. 'I've a feeling he's going to be trouble.'

Chapter 17

Lydia

When my eyes shot open the following morning, I knew what I had to do.

Firstly, I called Mattie. I'd fallen asleep on the bed when I returned to my room the day before – after double-checking that nothing had been disturbed and my toothpaste was in my toiletry bag where I'd left it – waking in darkness to find it was close to midnight and too late to ring home. I'd lain awake instead, my mind awash with questions as I listened to the wind for what felt like hours before drifting into a doze.

'Hey, Mum.'

His voice in my ear was a shock, bright and clear as if he was in the room with me. 'Mattie, how are you? How was school?' I felt a prickle of tears as I pictured him getting dressed and eating breakfast without me. 'Did you eat dinner with Harriet?'

'When are you coming back?'

When he was little, he would ask me that if I went out without him, not in a plaintive way because he loved spending time with his dad, but with mild curiosity, as though working out how long they had together. Now, his question was loaded with suspicion.

'Mum?'

There was a heavy feeling in my stomach. 'I thought I might stay another day or so.' I pinched the bridge of my nose, wishing I could tell him I was here for him as well as myself but knowing he wouldn't understand – not yet. 'I'm really starting to unwind.'

I resisted the urge to fill the silence with words that would sound like lies. That *were* lies. *Other mothers don't behave like this.* 'I'll be back by the end of the week, I promise.' As I pictured his joyful reaction to me returning with Jack, daring myself to imagine us hugging, Mattie's eyes brimming with love, there was a commotion in the background, the blast of a car horn. 'Where are you?'

'On my way to school.'

I glanced at the time on my phone: 8 a.m. 'The bus doesn't come until eight-thirty.'

'I've got study leave this morning. I'm meeting Callum to revise.'

'Mattie, that's great.' I felt a rush of love and relief. 'I'm so happy you're taking your exams seriously.'

More silence, then: 'What are you doing today?'

I swung my legs out of bed and crossed to the window. I'd stripped to my underwear the night before, but the heating was on, the room a nest of warmth. Outside, the wind had dropped, and lemony sunlight glittered off the sea.

'I might go for a long walk,' I said, cringing as a pair of seagulls flew past with loud, mournful cries. Did they have seagulls in York? I remembered Shona telling me they'd started encroaching on the city, re-establishing themselves, and prepared to relay this information to Mattie, but he didn't ask.

'I'm going to stay at Callum's tonight, if that's OK,' he said.

'Of course, I should have—' He cut the call before I could finish.

I pressed the phone to my chest. He hadn't asked after Shona or answered my questions about school and eating dinner with Harriet.

Talking to Harriet was next on my to-do list, but first I forced myself into the shower – averting my gaze from the mirror over the sink – then pulled on jeans and a navy, cable-knit sweater of Jack's before heading downstairs. I'd eaten nothing since the biscuits the day before and hunger was making me feel untethered.

'Cooked breakfast?' Mel appeared with a friendly smile as I settled at a cloth-covered table in the dining area, where the boy I'd glimpsed yesterday was zooming a toy car along the oak floorboards, reminding me of Mattie at that age, and his fixation with an old yellow Tonka truck that used to belong to William. 'The bacon, eggs and mushrooms are locally sourced.'

I returned her smile. 'Just eggs and mushrooms, please.' Now I had another plan, things seemed brighter, despite a flutter of nerves in my chest and the words *GO HOME* etched behind my eyes. Once I'd eaten I was going to talk to Jack. Explain who I was, with proof if necessary – proof I hadn't thought existed as Jack had taken my phone with all my photos, also deleted from the Cloud, and our text exchanges. I'd woken earlier to find the answer sitting at the front of my mind. *His passport.* It was still at home with mine and Mattie's. I would ask Harriet to let herself into the house to find it and send a picture. Only as a last resort would I call Mattie and persuade him to speak to Jack. If he really didn't remember me, he would surely remember Mattie? The only problem was Caitlin, but I planned to watch the cottage first. If it looked like she wasn't going out, I would think of a reason to call and get her to leave.

'Nice artwork,' I said when Mel returned with the pot of tea I'd ordered. The little boy had followed her out and was nowhere to be seen. 'Are they of the area?' I wasn't particularly interested in art, not like Mattie, but it seemed important to make light conversation, especially after the oddness of our exchange the day before.

'Mostly.' Following my lead, Mel blew back a strand of fringe that had fallen across her eyes. 'They're by a local artist.' Her expression cooled. 'Well, not an artist as such. She illustrates children's books, but occasionally does landscape drawings in ink.'

My heart skidded. 'Illustrator?'

'Caitlin Garvey.' Mel's lips thinned when she said Caitlin's name. I guessed she was no longer a fan since Caitlin had dumped her brother. 'She lives nearby.'

'Oh, wow.' An idea began to form as I remembered scouring Caitlin's website for information. 'Didn't she do the series about the lonely hedgehog?'

Surprise flashed over Mel's face. 'I . . . yes, that's her,' she said. 'Unusual to remember the illustrator rather than the author.'

'My son was a fan of the books.' I poured milk in my coffee from a pottery jug, hand shaking slightly. 'He's too old now of course.'

I expected her to ask his age, but Mel was smiling in a preoccupied way as she inclined her head at the door. 'I'll go and fetch your breakfast.'

When she came back with a plate in one hand and a rack of toast I hadn't asked for in the other, I had decided on the perfect way to get Caitlin away from Sea View Cottage for a while.

Buoyed by breakfast and the thought of seeing Jack again, I headed out as soon as I'd eaten – taking care to lock the door to my room – making sure to ask Mel about local walks like any other tourist.

'There's a four-mile circular route, starting from the car park on the hilltop,' she said eagerly, no doubt relieved I hadn't accosted her about possible intruders again. 'It follows the disused Scarborough to Whitby railway line, takes you across the bridge to Boggle Hole, where you join the Cleveland Way, along the cliffs back to Robin Hood's Bay.'

I tried to look fascinated, while thinking it sounded exhausting. And Boggle Hole wasn't the most inviting name for a visitor attraction. 'Great,' I said, when I realised Mel had finished speaking and was looking at my feet.

'I could lend you some walking boots or wellies,' she said. Behind her, an older woman was bent over, loading a dishwasher in the kitchen. 'What size are you?'

'I've got some boots in the car.' The lie tripped off my tongue with frightening ease. 'I walk a lot when I'm not working.'

'I could make you a packed lunch.' Mel scrunched up the tea towel she was holding, her face open and friendly. 'Or you could stop at the Ravenscar Tearooms for refreshments. They do coffee and cakes, and you'll have a great view of the coast from there.' She glanced at the sky through the open front door, as if wishing she was outside. 'The forecast is good for a change.'

'I'll probably stop at the tearoom, but thanks for the offer.' I was careful to keep smiling as I gave her a wave and set off in the direction of the car park, imagining her watching, eyes narrowed with suspicion.

Once there, I got into the car and took out my phone.

I had wanted to ask Mel for Caitlin's mobile number but decided it was better not to involve her any more than necessary. I was already on her radar more than I'd wanted to be. Instead, I called the number of the cottage, catching my reflection in the rear view mirror as it connected. My eyes were wide and bright patches of colour stained my cheeks. Despite a strong sense that this wasn't really me, I had to try.

'Hello?' I spoke as soon as Caitlin answered – thank God it was her. 'Is that Caitlin Garvey?'

'It is.' She sounded surprised. Perhaps she'd expected silence again. 'How can I help you?'

'I'm writing a piece about illustrators past and present for . . .' I'd been about to mention one of the broadsheet newspapers but changed my mind. She could easily look me up and check me out. 'For a book I'm planning, and I wondered whether it would be possible to talk to you today, if you have an hour to spare.'

'Oh.' It was clearly the last thing she'd been expecting to hear. 'A book about illustrators?'

'I'm a lifelong fan of Quentin Blake's work,' I said, thankful Roald Dahl had been Mattie's favourite author, before he moved onto the Harry Potter series, wanting the glasses and a wand. 'And I confess that my son loved the lonely hedgehog series you illustrated. It's an area I think is overlooked in culture. People tend to focus on the author, don't you find? Anyway, I'm in the area and thought it would be great to meet you in person and ask some questions about your work.'

In the silence that followed, I imagined Jack overhearing and wondering who she was talking to, pictured Caitlin turning my question over. I was banking on appealing to her ego. The idea of being the subject of a book, rather than a contributor, would surely appeal.

'Couldn't you ask me some questions over the phone?'

'I'd much rather chat face to face.' I wished I was better at gushing. 'I was hoping for a photo too if you wouldn't mind.'

'I'm a bit busy today.'

I bet you are. 'Oh, that's a shame.' I poured a disappointed pout into my voice, picturing her creeping up to my room at the guesthouse, taking the lid off the tube of toothpaste. 'I'm leaving this evening and thought . . . it really would have made my day to meet you.' I didn't have to force the tears that swam unexpectedly to my eyes. If Caitlin didn't agree, I would have to think of something else. 'OK, well thanks for your time—'

'Just a minute.'

My heart leapt. There was a pause, and I held my breath. What if she invited me to the cottage? My brain was scrambling for a credible reason why I couldn't go there when she said, 'Where would you like to meet?'

'How about the Ravenscar Tearooms?' I mentally thanked Mel for the suggestion. 'I hear it has a wonderful view.'

'It does.' Her voice was strained, as if caving in was against her better judgement. Or maybe she was annoyed that vanity had got the better of her, outweighing the urge to stay at home with her newly returned husband, dreaming up new ways to scare off the woman who wanted him back. 'I'll take an early lunch break and meet you there at eleven.'

It didn't sound like a suggestion. 'Great!' The urge to cry was gone, my enthusiasm genuine. 'I can't wait to meet you.'

As she hung up, it struck me as arrogance on her part that she didn't ask if there was anything in particular she should wear, or about my credentials – not that I'd thought of any – but weren't most artists narcissists deep down, craving recognition and wrapped up in themselves? I was surprised by Jack's choice of wife if I was honest. I'd assumed his interest in Mattie's talent for drawing was to encourage him to work harder. He'd never hinted his wife was an artist of sorts, and I found myself wondering now whether the association had been painful, or he'd secretly liked having a link to her through my son. Not that drawing for toddlers was great art, and her line sketches at the guesthouse were pretty basic, now I thought about them.

Whenever I tried to imagine Jack and Caitlin talking to each other, the image dissolved, while the idea of them in bed together . . . I wouldn't let my mind go there. They weren't meant to be together, and soon Jack would be with me and Mattie, and none of this would matter.

I checked the time and directions by car to the tearoom. It was a twenty-minute drive, which meant Caitlin would have to leave around ten-thirty, maybe later if she didn't care about arriving on time. That gave me forty minutes to kill.

I got out of the car, wondering whether there was a different route to Sea View Cottage that would keep me out of sight of the guesthouse. It would be hard to explain why I was hanging around if Mel spotted me. Again, I wished I'd had the foresight to stay somewhere else. *That's your trouble, Lydia. You don't think things through properly.* As if my mother had any room to talk. She clearly hadn't thought anything through when she married Dad. There must have been signs, yet she'd chosen to ignore them, acted as though she was happy to be with him. *Love makes fools of us all*, she said once, when I asked why she stayed with him. *And I do love him, Lydia, just like you do.*

I set off along the coastal path that would bring me round the back of the cottage. No harm in being early. The more time I had alone with Jack the better. Once Caitlin arrived at the tearoom and realised I was a no-show, she wouldn't hang around.

Despite the sun it was bitterly cold, and my eyes watered. I stumbled a couple of times on the path and wondered why people did this for pleasure. If I wanted to look at great stretches of ocean I would rather do it from the deck of a cruise ship. The sooner Jack and I were back in London, the better.

Once more, I found myself on the other side of the shoulder-high wooden fence that bordered the cottage's garden, my heart a frantic drum in my chest. *This had to work.*

I risked a glance over the fence then heard a sound behind me. I turned my head so fast, I was sure I would have whiplash. No one there, but the feeling lingered that someone had slipped out of sight. Retracing my steps to the path, I caught sight of a figure hurrying away, something familiar about his movements. Broad-shouldered, wearing a hooded top so I couldn't see the colour of his hair. *Owen Whittaker?* Maybe I hadn't been wrong about him hanging around the cottage after all. At least he'd gone now, no doubt back to his store to charm some customers. *If only he'd been able to charm Caitlin.*

As though on cue, I heard the sound of a car engine revving and hurried back to peer around the fence, stomach lurching as I saw Caitlin at the wheel of the shabby black Fiesta. Shrinking back, I waited for her to pull away and for the tail-lights to vanish from view. My breathing was shallow, my senses heightened. *This was it.*

I made myself wait a few moments in case she'd forgotten something and returned. When it felt safe, I started to move, already rehearsing what I would say to Jack, imagining his response, and heard the shuffle of approaching footsteps behind me.

I stopped and wheeled around, expecting to see Owen Whittaker. My mouth fell open when I realised who was standing there. 'What are you doing?'

Caitlin gave me a pitying look as she grabbed my elbow. 'I'm giving you a chance to tell me what's going on,' she said, steering me away from the cottage. 'And when you're done, you're leaving.'

Chapter 18

Caitlin

'Let go of me.' The woman shook off my hand and stared at me, eyes wide with shock. Then she turned and ran.

'Wait!' I set off after her as she headed for the sloping path that led to the beach. 'Come back!'

Glancing over her shoulder, she tripped, arms flying out to the sides, but didn't stop. She was an incongruous figure in her suede ankle boots, knee-length puffer coat and knitted hat, small and slight but surprisingly fast. I was struggling to catch up, despite my daily runs on the beach, which I hadn't bothered with for the past few days.

Finally, down on the sand and hidden from view by the rock face, the woman stopped. She was panting, the tip of her nose bright red, the only spot of colour in a pale, narrow face.

This was the woman Jack had left behind. As soon as I'd heard her voice on the phone, my antennae had tingled, a spike of cortisol rushing through my body. It was *her*. The story she'd spun about book research hadn't rung true, the words too fast, her voice falsely bright. She didn't even tell me her name yet expected me to rush out and meet her.

'Don't come near me,' she warned, holding a hand out.

'I thought you wanted to talk to me.' I stepped closer, trying to get a clear look at the face that Jack had forgotten. She was in her late thirties at a guess, fine lines around her eyes, which were small and icy-blue beneath pale brows, her lips a thin, hard line. She was shorter than me by a couple of inches, with bony hands and skinny calves that gave her a fragile air, yet her glare was steely and determined.

'I wanted to get you away from the house.' Her voice sounded weak in the clear, bright air, the vowels short and precise. 'I didn't want him to see me.'

Him. 'You spoke to Jack yesterday.' The woman didn't deny or confirm it but took another step back. 'He doesn't remember you.'

'Not yet.'

'You sent me a card, a warning.'

'I shouldn't have done that.' Her gaze slid away. 'I didn't know then that he'd lost his memory.'

I swallowed, mind crowding with questions. 'How did you find us?'

'It wasn't hard, once I'd spoken to the hospital and they told me Jack's *wife* had picked him up. Your name and number is in the phone directory.'

'Why didn't you report him missing if you care so much?'

'You know nothing about me.'

'Jack is my *husband*.' It seemed important to make that clear. 'You knew he was still married?'

'He left you.'

This simple confirmation that she knew things about me, about my relationship with Jack, hit me like a kick to the chest. 'We're back together now and he doesn't remember you.' Questions fought for prominence – *How did you meet? What did he tell you about me? What did you do together? Why did he leave you?* – but already, I wanted our interaction to be over. 'There's nothing for you here.'

'You read my message?'

I thought of the card, which I'd torn up and thrown away. 'You're wrong,' I said, shaking my hair off my face. 'I know my husband, and he loves me.'

'You don't know him as well as you think.'

Her statement set off a tremor in my chest. 'What do you mean?' As I moved closer she stepped back, catching her heel on a half-buried stone. She toppled onto the sand and cowered, bringing her arm up to cover her face.

'Don't touch me!' She kicked out as I advanced, catching my shin with the toe of her boot.

I reeled away. 'I wasn't going to touch you.'

'I got your message too.' She struggled to her feet, brushing sand from the back of her coat. Her hat had slipped back, revealing an inch of dark-blonde hair, and silver studs in her earlobes. *Had Jack bought them for her?* 'But I'm not going anywhere.'

I had no idea what she was talking about but felt a ripple of danger like an approaching storm. 'Look, when Jack woke up in hospital, he wanted *me*.' It was a childish comment, as though Jack was a prize we were competing for. 'We were together for a long time. I know a lot more about him than you do.' *Except why he wanted to get away from London.*

'Then you know he hates liars more than anything?'

Something collapsed inside me. 'Why would you say that?'

'He believes they should be punished.'

'That's not the Jack I know.' *But hadn't he punished me by leaving?*

'Like I said, you don't know him as well as you think.'

My stomach was a knotted fist. 'And you do?'

'Better than you think.' She dashed a hand across her cheek, averting her eyes.

'People only stay in your life if they want to,' I said, pushing my hands in my pockets to disguise their trembling. 'That's why he's here.'

'He wanted *me*.' Suddenly, her eyes were swimming with tears. 'That's why this is so hard.'

141

I could normally read people quickly, but she was slippery; nervy one minute, hands flexing in and out of fists, then fearful and pleading. 'What's your name?'

She clearly didn't want me to know, small teeth gnawing her lower lip, before she grudgingly murmured, 'Lydia.'

Something about the name struck a chord. *Lydia.* The woman my husband had been . . . *in love with?*

'How long were you together?'

'A year.'

The urge to cry was overwhelming. *Almost since he'd left me.* 'He was in a bad place then,' I said. 'But he's back now and we're making it work.'

'I'm not just going away, Caitlin.'

I hated the sound of my name on her lips. 'You know he called me before?' I wanted to hurt her. 'He told me he wanted out and asked if we could meet.'

She jolted, as though hit by an electric shock. 'You're lying.' The pale sun had drifted overhead, casting a shadow across her face. 'He wouldn't—'

'Something was wrong,' I interrupted. 'I think he wanted to talk about us getting back together. He's made his choice, Lydia.' *Lids.* The memory slammed into me. The nonsensical word Jack had muttered in his sleep before lashing out. Had he been dreaming about *her? Lyds?*

'We were so happy.' Her voice gentled. 'He was good with my son.'

A shockwave rolled through me. 'You have a child?'

'He's a teenager now. I had him at twenty, married young.' She put a hand up to her hat and moved it to cover her hair. 'His father died when he was eleven and it led to some . . . problems. But Jack was amazing with him.' She looked right at me. 'He wants to be a dad more than anything.'

Sickness churned in my stomach. The sun dipped behind a cloud and a shiver racked my body. 'Please, just leave us alone.'

Suddenly a hand was clamped to her mouth, and she choked back a sob. 'It was going so well, but then . . .' Tears spilled down her cheeks. 'We were going to get counselling, talking about anger management, but—'

'Wait.' I held up my hands. 'What are you talking about?' She swiped her coat sleeve across her nose. 'I'm sorry if your son has anger issues, but that's not Jack's problem.' Was that the real reason she was here, sneaking about, trying to talk to me? She couldn't bear that she'd been left alone with her troubled son and needed his help?

Oh, Jack. He'd inserted himself at the heart of a family, where he felt needed, felt he could make a difference. It made sense somehow, after everything that had happened between us. Feeling raw and rejected when he left, he had sensed something in this woman – Lydia – that appealed to his instinct to protect and nurture. *That* was the Jack I knew, the man I loved. And Lydia must love him too, to have gone to these lengths. A wave of pity rose for her crumbled composure, but the fact remained that Jack was my husband and he had chosen to leave her, even before the call had come from the hospital. 'Do you have any family you can turn to, or someone at his school who could help?'

Lydia looked at me with pink-rimmed eyes that widened. 'I'm not talking about my son,' she spat. 'I'm talking about Jack.'

For a moment, all I could hear were the waves rolling in behind us, a screech of seagulls overhead, then I tuned back in to her voice.

'. . . and I wanted to tell you that you don't know what he's capable of.'

'I'm sorry, *what*?'

'I know all about how his mother died, and how it affected him. All that suppressed anger – I suppose it had to come out somehow.'

I remembered Jack's fist, punching the wall; his rage with his father for finding happiness again, with the doctor who had failed to diagnose his mother's illness until it was too late – anger disguising the helplessness he'd felt. *Or so I'd thought.* 'You're telling me that Jack . . .' I could hardly bring myself to utter the words. 'That he *hurt* you?'

I have to leave London, Caitlin. I made a terrible mistake that I can't put right. All I can do is get out.

Was that what his phone call had been about?

I looked at Lydia, trying to make sense of it. 'How do I know you're telling the truth? Jack has never been physically aggressive with me.' I thought of his fingers around my arm yesterday morning, the look on his face. The feeling that he'd wanted to hurt me. I hadn't checked for bruising – didn't want to see it.

As if reading my thoughts, Lydia gave a humourless smile. 'I think you do know.'

'I don't.'

'I had photos on my phone,' she said. 'I showed them to the police.'

'*What?*'

'I didn't press charges. I just wanted to shake him up.'

I couldn't believe what I was hearing. 'Where are they, these photos?'

She looked away. 'He took my phone, got rid of it. He even deleted all my pictures from the Cloud, so I have no proof.' While I was trying to process this information, she stuck out her arm, her palm in front of my face.

'See that?' My eyes were drawn to a long, uneven scar on her pale skin. 'That's where I snatched the knife off him.' Her voice was weaker now, words coming in bursts. 'But I grabbed the blade by mistake and cut my hand open. There was blood everywhere. I should have got it stitched but didn't want to go to the hospital to explain, so I patched it up as best I could and let it heal on its own. That's why the scar is jagged.' She paused. 'At least it was my left hand.'

I stared as though hypnotised, trying to picture the kind of incident I'd only ever read about, or seen in television dramas. 'Maybe this is why he doesn't remember you.' I was hardly aware of speaking the words out loud. 'Because he wants to forget.'

'That's why you have to let him go.'

I clamped my teeth to stop them chattering. The beach was empty, apart from a figure at the far end that I thought I recognised but couldn't focus on. 'I'm sorry for whatever's happened, and appreciate you letting me know, but I'm not going to throw him out if that's what you're expecting.'

She studied me for a moment, and I knew it was my imagination, but she seemed to grow taller. Her shoulders straightened, and just for a moment I was reminded of an animal scenting prey. 'Does he remember that you weren't together before his accident?'

'It wasn't an accident, it was a hit and run,' I said automatically, blindsided by the shock of what she was telling me.

She shook her head, looking at me with something close to pity. 'I can understand why you don't want him to know, but you're not doing yourself any favours.'

'I can live with it.'

Lydia's expression closed down, as though the effort of talking had sapped her strength. 'Don't say I didn't warn you.'

'I consider myself warned. Thank you.'

'You're one of those women.' Scorn curdled the words. 'He won't change. I've been with his type before.'

I tried to picture Jack with this woman, who seemed more adult than me; a woman who had given birth, lost a husband, and raised a child. Why would he hurt her? Jack, who literally wouldn't kill a fly, who hated injustice of any kind. Yet, she'd reported him to the police. She had scars, had taken photos, and I was behaving as though I didn't believe her – a response I would normally abhor. 'Maybe choose more wisely next time,' I heard myself say. 'For your son's sake as well as your own.'

Lydia was shaking her head, her eyes sharp and narrow. Her hands were tight fists by her sides, frustration and disappointment leaking from every pore. 'If you won't tell him to leave, I could give him a nudge.'

'What does that even mean?'

There was something vengeful in the smile that cracked her face. 'I could let him know that you haven't lived together for a year,' she said slowly. 'That you were in a relationship with someone else.'

'How . . . how do you know I haven't told him?' *How did she know about Owen?*

'Have you?'

I felt weak, as if my blood was draining away.

'And that phone call, before his accident?' Her smile dropped. 'He was going to ask you for a divorce.'

Chapter 19

Lydia

'I don't believe you.' Far from seeming upset, Caitlin's shoulders straightened. I wished I hadn't reacted so strongly to the news that Jack had called her. She might have been lying, but her words had rung with conviction.

'We spoke to a solicitor about it.' I flashed back to an old colleague of William's, looking awkward as he explained that Jack needn't go to court to get a divorce if both partners were in agreement. 'He doesn't love you.'

Caitlin was shaking her head, as if she knew more than I did. 'If you come near either of us, I'll call the police.'

A spark of hatred ignited. Couldn't she see I was trying to do her a favour? Their marriage was in name only. Jack had chosen me, and, for all his faults, I wanted him back, and I wanted my son back too.

I studied Caitlin's pale freckled face, framed by a cloud of dark hair, sickened that Jack had once vowed to love her forever in front of family and friends. This was why I had never pushed him to talk about her, or to reveal exactly why he'd left. I preferred it when she didn't exist. We were nothing alike – that much was obvious – though the air of quiet bookishness conveyed on her social media was missing. From the moment she'd materialised like a ghost, sending the blood hurtling around my body, I'd seen something desperate in her expression that had made me think she could do anything, even write a warning message in toothpaste, though she'd done a good job of pretending she didn't know what I was on about.

It was why I'd run; a primeval instinct to protect myself rearing up. Now, I understood. She was using Jack's amnesia to pretend they'd never split up and was terrified he would find out. *Which he would.* 'Let me talk to him.'

'No.' Seeming to harness her emotions, Caitlin was backing away. 'Leave us alone,' she said, intensifying her focus.

'Does he deserve to get away with what he's done?'

She turned without comment, walking back to the path.

'Don't you think you should tell him the truth?' My voice was raspy, as though I'd swallowed some of the sand beneath my feet. 'You're lying to him.'

She stopped and swivelled round. 'He's out of your life now, Lydia.' I caught the shimmer of tears in her blue eyes – our only similarity, though hers were round like a doll's with long dark lashes. 'I can look after myself,' she added. 'Go home to your son.'

I opened my mouth, but no words came out. There was nothing I could say without revealing my own truth: that I wasn't leaving here without Jack. He may have made promises to Caitlin in the eyes of the law, but he'd promised me things too. A baby, most importantly. A brother or sister for Mattie. It was what we needed, the thing that would bind us together and give new purpose and meaning to our lives.

It was true what I'd told Caitlin about counselling. Jack had reluctantly agreed to go, and I knew in my heart that whatever was broken could be fixed. A baby would be part of the healing process, and Caitlin had no part in that. There was nothing tying her and Jack together but her lies. Once they were exposed, Jack would remember why he'd left her.

The sight of her striding away, hair whipping behind her, as though out for a daily stroll, stoked my frustration. I would let her dwell for a while on what I'd said, on the fact of my presence in her home town, and the knowledge I held about her and Jack, and then call her. I had no doubt that in spite of her bravado, she would be brimming with doubts right now, recalling the sight of the scar on my palm – which burned and itched as though freshly cut – and scrolling through mental images of the bruises I'd catalogued and shown the police. She would look at her husband with fresh eyes, perhaps even wonder whether he was faking his memory loss as a reason to be back in her life, to make her pay for hurting him so deeply he couldn't shake her out of his system, despite his love for Mattie and me. Maybe it was even true. It would certainly explain some aspects of his recent behaviour.

Once Caitlin had vanished, I walked fast with furious energy in the opposite direction. Angry tears stung my cheeks and I brushed them away, kicking sand at a seagull swaggering past. *You could have handled that better, Lydia.* Mum had used those words once, after a disastrous parents' evening when I was ten. Mr Fleming had told her and Dad that I was struggling to grasp basic geography and I'd shouted that he was an idiot, before bursting into tears and running outside. *You need to learn to control your emotions.*

Not that my mother had room to criticise, considering what she put up with from my father. I wondered what she would say now if she knew the situation I was in. I had vowed to be different when I grew up, to never put myself in a similar position, but maybe our parents' behavioural patterns are embedded in our DNA. It was something I preferred not to think about.

I recalled Jack's face the day before, wondering again whether he *could* be faking his memory loss. I reran the scene for the hundredth time for clues, but his gaze had touched my face as though seeing it for the first time. Nothing had suggested he wasn't being honest. Despite being a closed book about his past – apart from the night he'd told me how his mother had died – Jack was open about his feelings, unable to hide his reactions, and anyway, if he'd remembered me, he wouldn't be here, living a cosy life with his wife again. He'd be somewhere far away.

Mel had seen someone close to the guesthouse, walking with a limp – *coincidence?* Or had Jack sensed something in our encounter, come looking for me with questions?

I shivered, recalling the words GO HOME scrawled on the mirror. Jack couldn't have been responsible; it wasn't his style. *But that was before his accident.* Perhaps I was the one who no longer knew what he was capable of.

Images inserted themselves in my head: Jack in Caitlin's bed, eating breakfast with her, touching her . . . I pushed the heels of my hands into my eyes, but the pictures replayed themselves over and over until I wanted to scream.

By the time I'd made my way back along the coastal path, my heartbeat had calmed, and the tears dried. The sun had reappeared, and people were milling around with rucksacks and walking poles; life carrying on as normal for everyone but me.

Feeling eyes on my back, I spun around, scanning the perimeter of the car park. There was a movement between two vehicles, one of them a white van with a florist's logo. The owner got out and pulled open the doors at the back, blocking my view. I walked over, fighting a suffocating feeling in my throat, but there was no one else there.

I returned to the guesthouse in time to see Owen Whittaker jogging round the side of the building, clothed in black. My heart skipped a beat. I looked back at the car park for his Land Rover, and spotted it at the far end, opposite my car. *His sister lives here*, I reminded myself, filling my lungs with oxygen. He had more right to be at the house than I did.

Inside the hallway, the older woman I'd seen in the kitchen was hoovering the stairs, bottom wavering in the air as she flattened the nozzle to the carpet. Not wanting to disturb her, I slipped into the communal living room on my right, a bright, comfortable-looking room with pale floorboards and a pair of cream sofas positioned either side of a long, glass-topped coffee table.

I let out a puff of air and sank onto one of the sofas, but my body hummed with tension, forcing me back to my feet. There was a window seat, with a view of the sea and I crossed to it and sat down, shedding my coat and hat, and shaking my hair loose. I took my phone from my pocket and called Harriet, desperate to check how Mattie was.

'Hello?' She sounded breathless as though I'd interrupted her hanging washing out, which seemed to be her preferred pastime when she was at home, regardless of the season.

'It's Lydia,' I said, with careful politeness, though she must have recognised my number.

'How are you, Lydia?'

'I'm well, thank you.' I yanked my thumbnail from between my teeth. 'How's Mattie?'

There was a moment's hesitation. 'Fine, as far as I know.'

'As far as you know?' Anxiety sharpened my voice. 'What does that mean?'

'He was perfectly fine yesterday,' she said quickly. 'He popped round before school and told me he's staying with his friend Callum until you get back.'

My breath shortened. 'How did he seem?'

'He's angry with you, Lydia.' I imagined the criss-cross of lines on Harriet's forehead deepening into a frown. 'He worries about you.'

'He's always angry; he's a teenager.' I tried to maintain a level tone, annoyed by her assumption. 'He understands that I need a little break after . . . everything.'

'It seems bad timing, I suppose.'

I chose to believe she was referring to Mattie's upcoming exams and forced some warmth into my words. 'You're absolutely right, Harriet, but I'll be home soon, and everything will be back to normal.'

In truth, I was relieved Mattie was at Callum's. His parents were the strict-but-fair variety with strong views about the importance of education, and they seemed fond of Mattie. I wished I'd suggested he go there in the first place instead of involving Harriet.

'Will you be coming back alone?'

Her question startled me back to the moment. 'Hopefully not,' I said without thinking, adding, 'I need your help, actually.'

'Oh?' The word was loaded with mistrust.

'It might sound silly, but I need you to find our passports and take a picture on your phone.'

'On my phone?' She sounded baffled, though she wasn't the sort of pensioner who knew nothing about technology. Mattie had helped her set up the shiny new mobile phone she had 'treated' herself to, that she listened to podcasts on, and used to post images on Instagram of the cakes she baked for her Women's Institute group. 'Why?'

'Please, Harriet. It's important.'

Perhaps she was worried I might ask Mattie if she said no or, more likely, she was curious to know what I was up to, but after a moment she gave an audible sigh and said, 'Right now?'

'Please. They're in a black shoebox underneath the bottom shelf in the wardrobe in the main bedroom.'

'I'm assuming it's *his* passport you really want a photo of?'

'Yes.' No point beating about the bush. She was going to disapprove of me one way or another and while – as with Shona – it was hurtful that her capitulation was somehow for Mattie's sake rather than mine, I was grateful when she said abruptly, 'Give me ten minutes,' and ended the call.

She'd had a spare key from back when William booked a surprise holiday to Cornwall, so she could water our plants, though I hadn't liked the idea of her snooping through our things.

When Mattie, Jack and I visited Center Parcs at Longleat for a long weekend for Mattie's birthday last year, I didn't bother telling her we were going, but had wondered afterwards whether she'd let herself in anyway and had a look around. I'd been tempted to ask for the key back after that but couldn't find a way to ask that wouldn't offend her.

Now, I was glad that I hadn't.

'You were at my store, yesterday.'

I leapt up, dropping my phone. Owen Whittaker had entered the room, the sound of his movements masked by the hum of the hoover. *How long had he been there?*

'You made me jump.' My heart drummed as I bent to retrieve my phone. When I straightened, Mel was behind him in the doorway.

'Don't mind my brother,' she said lightly. 'He likes to know what people are up to.'

He rested his forearms on the back of the sofa, not taking his eyes off me. They looked darker in the light from the window, the colour of seaweed.

'I did visit an outdoor clothing store yesterday.' I pulled my lips into a smile. 'I needed some comfortable socks to wear with my boots,' I said. 'The store is yours?'

'You know Caitlin Garvey.'

'Sorry?' Warmth spread up my neck to my face.

'I saw you talking to her on the beach.'

While I flailed for something to say, Mel stepped closer and flicked his arm with the tea towel she seemed to be perpetually holding. 'Why were you on the beach instead of at work?'

'I wasn't on the beach, I was out for a run.' He spoke mildly, but a vein pulsed in his forehead. 'I happened to see them while I was passing.'

Mel's face grew shuttered. I guessed she was working through the implications of him being in the same vicinity as his ex-girlfriend.

Thinking fast, I said, 'I was talking to Mel earlier about Caitlin's artwork and happened to bump into her as I was setting off on a walk this morning. We had a chat.'

Mel tore her gaze from Owen and looked at me. 'How did you know it was her?'

'I looked her up after we spoke.' I stretched my smile. 'I was excited about her living nearby but didn't dream I might run into her.' Hopefully, my blush would be mistaken for embarrassment at my gauche behaviour. 'She's *so* talented.' The gushing didn't sound convincing, but Mel's gathering frown was probably because she wanted the conversation over – the less said about Caitlin Garvey in her brother's presence, the better.

'I should get on,' she said vaguely, thumbing the hallway. The woman had finished hoovering and silence fell, only the beat of my heart audible to my own ears. 'Enjoy the rest of your day.'

When she'd gone, the silence seemed to swell, almost choking me. For a second, I considered blurting something out – telling Owen we were on the same side, that I wanted Jack and he wanted Caitlin and wasn't there some way we could make that happen? But I couldn't get past the image of his expression the day before; the idea he might see me as a threat, despite our goal being the same. That he might not see my side of things at all.

'Did she mention her husband?' he said unexpectedly, lowering his tone. 'Jack Garvey.'

My heart bumped. 'That's an odd question.' I locked my gaze to his. 'We spoke about her work as an illustrator.'

'She seemed upset.'

My mind raced. Had he watched our whole exchange? 'OK, well, as it happens, yes she did mention him. She said her husband had been hurt in an accident recently, and she was looking after him.'

'Right.' Owen's jaw set. 'Yet she was out *walking*.'

Was his derision directed at me, or her?

'She was on her way to the chemist's.' The words felt sticky in my mouth. 'I distracted her because I would love to feature her work in a book I'm planning, but then she got upset and said she had to get back and told me why.'

He nodded, lips compressed, as though what I had said made sense, even if he didn't like it. Finally, he stepped away from the sofa. 'She's got a lot on her plate,' he said, eyeing me narrowly.

Despite the implied criticism, there was a thawing sensation in my muscles. *He believed me.* 'I wouldn't have bothered her if I'd known.'

'Of course not.' He held up his hands as he retreated. 'I hope you enjoy your stay,' he said, flashing the smile he'd bestowed on me the day before. 'The weather's not great at this time of year, but at least the bay isn't crowded with tourists.'

If it had been, I might not have been so easily spotted with Caitlin.

'Luckily, I don't mind the cold,' I lied. 'Nice to meet you properly.'

As soon as he'd gone, I ran up to my room on legs that felt like overcooked spaghetti, making sure the door was locked behind me. The sooner I left this place, the better. Thoughts clashing, I jumped again when my phone buzzed in my hand. *Harriet.* True to her word, she had texted a slightly blurred image. The shoebox was on the floor with the lid off, alongside a pair of passports. Harriet's gnarled fingers were in shot, holding the passports open so mine and Mattie's faces were visible, his fresh, open expression a shock after growing used to his constant frown and attempts at facial hair. *Mattie.* But where was Jack's passport?

I scrolled down, looking for another image, gaze falling on a precisely written text message.

There were only two passports in the box. I checked the shelf and underneath but could not find another. Should I look elsewhere? Harriet.

Bile rose through my gullet.

No, that's fine, it's not a problem. Thank you for looking. Lydia.

I'd checked the box myself, worried Jack might have left the country. The passport had been there. I'd seen it with my own eyes. Yet there was no doubting the photo.

Jack's passport had gone.

Chapter 20

Caitlin

It was a shock to see Jack in the kitchen without his ankle brace on, fingers gripping the edge of the sink as he stared out of the window.

'What's happened?'

He turned, his injured foot pale and bare, held awkwardly a few inches from the floor. 'I wanted to take a shower without it on and try to walk without it.'

'You have to keep it on for a least a couple more weeks before you can do the exercises the doctor suggested.'

'I went outside.'

'Again?' His words set off a fresh ripple of nerves in my stomach. 'Where, outside?' *Had he seen me with Lydia on the beach?*

Misreading my expression he said, 'Don't worry, I didn't go further than the garden and used my crutch.'

'OK.' I tried to think but my mind was still reeling with everything Lydia had told me. *He wanted a divorce.* Was that true? Maybe they *had* talked to someone about it, but it wasn't why Jack had called me. Perhaps she'd said it in retaliation, clearly shocked to learn he'd spoken to me before he ended up in hospital. *She has a son.* It had been harder to hear that than anything else, knowing how much Jack longed to be a father. It was so easy to picture how brilliantly he would have fulfilled that role.

Walking back from the beach, Lydia's words bouncing around my head – *what had she meant about getting my message?* – it had struck me that Jack must have forged a relationship with her son, yet he'd forgotten him as completely as he had Lydia. Had the boy seen Jack's supposed treatment of her, and why was I having such trouble believing it? *Because it wasn't the Jack I knew.* But then ... wasn't that what women said all the time? *He would never hurt anyone. He's not like that ... he's not like that with me.* My mind flickered back to the morning before, his fingers digging into my flesh, arm twisted over my head. *I have to get away*, he'd said in his phone call. If only I'd asked what he meant.

Jack looked shaken, paler than he'd been when I left. He inclined his head towards the kitchen table. 'I found my passport in the hall.'

'Sorry?' For a second, I couldn't compute what he was saying.

'Remember, I thought it was lost?'

My gaze slid to the crimson rectangle. 'That's ... where was it?'

'In the hall, by the mat. It must have been there all this time.' His smile didn't reach his eyes. 'I won't need a new one now.'

His words were obviously meant to reassure, but all I could think was *How did it get there?* I imagined Lydia scurrying up to our front door and sliding it through the letterbox, but it didn't make sense. If she'd had Jack's passport, she would have held on to it for dear life. 'Well, that's great,' I managed. Maybe it got caught up with his things at the hospital after all and slipped out of the carrier bag the day I brought him home, though it was odd I hadn't spotted it when I picked up the post yesterday morning.

'How did your meeting go?' Jack's voice was flat. 'You weren't gone long.'

I blinked, pulling my gaze from the passport. 'Waste of time,' I said quickly, removing my coat, surprised he couldn't see my heart pumping through my jumper. 'She wanted me to look at some illustrations, introduce her to my agent, that kind of thing.'

'That's sneaky. I'm sorry.'

I looked at him more closely, shaken out of the paralysing fear I'd felt since my exchange with Lydia. He was holding himself at an odd angle, his shoulders stiff, as if he might fall apart with the slightest movement. 'What's wrong?' *He knows.*

'I saw your friend again.'

'Friend?' For some reason, I thought of Dee, recalling her warning me to be careful.

'He was on the path, just staring into space.'

'You mean Owen?' My stomach plunged.

'When he saw me, he came over and asked whether he'd left his watch here.'

'What?'

'He said he left his watch here, just before Christmas.'

I felt as if I'd stood up too quickly, even though I hadn't moved. 'I . . . didn't even know he even wore a watch, let alone left one here.' At least that much was true. It was obviously Owen's way of letting Jack know he'd been a visitor to the cottage. 'Why wouldn't he have asked me before now?'

'He said he doesn't wear it often, and only just noticed.' Jack's face seemed weirdly unfamiliar, reminding me horribly of the day he left.

'Well, of course it's not here.' I was gripped by a sudden headache. 'I think I would have seen it.'

'He said he remembered putting it on the windowsill in the bedroom, next to the silver jewellery box that used to belong to your grandmother.'

Panic began to circle. 'Well, if he wants to ask me himself I can tell him it's not there and never was.'

'He mentioned the view from the bedroom, said how we were lucky to be able to see all the way to Ravenscar on a clear day.'

I tried to steady my breathing, keep my face unclenched. Though wouldn't it be natural to look worried? 'That's weird.'

'He talked about your grandfather, said he vaguely remembered your gran and that you were lucky you'd had a good relationship with them.'

'And what did you say?' I was buying time, wondering whether to just tell him the truth. Whatever the fallout, it couldn't be worse than feeling like this – like a molecule of something nasty being examined under a microscope.

'That I was close to my grandparents too, that they were married for sixty years and the only thing they ever argued about was the monarchy.'

My granddad is against the institution, but my gran loves the queen, thinks she's an asset to the country. She's started to look a lot like her.

All old ladies look like the queen eventually.

It was one of the random topics of conversation we'd covered in the pub, the day we met.

'Sounds like you had quite a chat.'

'How would he know what the view from our bedroom window looks like?'

'It wouldn't be too hard to guess.' My palms were hot. 'I never slept with Owen if that's what you're wondering.' *Not for want of him trying.* 'I told you he helped me move in. He used the toilet upstairs, so maybe he saw the view then.' Also true. 'He's trying to stir up trouble.' All my dry-mouthed answers sounded unconvincing, fanning the flames of panic licking through me. My heart thumped as I imagined Owen watching the exchange between Lydia and me on the beach, no doubt thrilled when Jack appeared. *Had he planned to call at the cottage again?* 'Don't listen to him, Jack.'

He swung himself across to the table and rested his palms

on the surface, lowering his head. 'The thing is, I . . . I think I remembered something.'

'To do with Owen?' It felt as if all my blood had pooled in my feet. 'What do you mean, remembered something?'

He ran a hand over his hair. 'It was a kind of flashback, to the night I was hit by that car.'

Still, I couldn't move, my nails digging into my palms, my breathing shallow. 'Go on.'

'I'm pretty certain it was him.' His forehead creased above horrified eyes. 'I think Owen was the one driving the car that hit me.'

'Oh my God.' Owen had guessed that Jack was the 'friend' on the phone the night I ushered him out of the cottage. Could he have tracked him down? Perhaps he'd followed me to Brighton the other night, knowing Jack was in hospital, perhaps even hoping he wouldn't recover? *He had his heart broken once before and it didn't end well.* Perhaps he'd been watching me ever since I broke up with him, suspecting Jack was the reason. 'Are you sure?' All the things I hadn't told him were stacking up, tight bands around my chest, but it felt too late to backtrack now.

'It makes sense if he wants you to himself.' Jack looked at me across the table. 'Maybe he wants to finish what he started.'

A chill trickled down my back. Owen had promised he wasn't giving up on me. He'd turned up the night I brought Jack home, and there had been something off about his manner then. What if he'd intended to kill Jack and was furious he'd survived?

It was too much on top of this morning's revelations. Another thought shunted into my brain. *If Jack had been flashing back to that night, how long would it be before he remembered Lydia?*

'We need to tell the police in Brighton,' I said. 'They have to hear this.' Sucking in a breath I finally moved, taking out my phone, but Jack was quicker. He came round the table and grasped my wrist.

'Are you sure you want to get them involved?'

161

I stared at his fingers, the bones of the knuckles white. 'What are you saying?'

'Just . . .' He let go of me and hopped backwards, bumping into a chair. 'We have to live around here,' he said. 'It'll create bad feeling if Owen ends up being arrested—'

'Which he *should* be,' I burst out. 'Jack, if you think he was driving the car that hit you, we have to report it.'

'But what if I'm wrong?' His face was wrung with pain. 'Maybe I can't trust my own memory and I'm getting mixed up because he's been around here so much.'

'Let the police decide once they've interviewed him.' I could hardly believe the words coming out of my mouth. A month ago, I was convinced that if I tried hard enough, I might be able to love Owen one day. 'I'll go and talk to his sister first,' I said when Jack shook his head. 'She might know where he was that night or let something slip.'

'I'm not sure that's a good idea.' Jack reached for his crutch. 'What if he's there?'

'He'll be at work.'

'He wasn't earlier.'

'Look, the guesthouse isn't far, and it's broad daylight.' Battling the urge to cry or scream, I reached for my coat. 'Come with me,' I said, hating the way my mind was working. *He wouldn't be here to answer the phone if Lydia called.* 'You can wait in the car.'

He nodded. 'I'll put my brace back on.'

Five minutes later, I was knocking on the door at Hill Top guesthouse, aware that the last time I was here, Owen and I were together.

'Caitlin, hi!' Mel couldn't hide her surprise as she stood aside. 'Come in.'

I didn't dare glance back to Jack in the car in case Mel spotted him too.

'If you're not back in ten minutes, I'll call the police,' he'd warned, unhappy about me confronting her alone. 'I really don't like this, Caitlin.'

162

'Well, I don't like the thought of Owen getting away with hurting you,' I retorted. Or the way he was insinuating himself in our lives. 'If he doesn't have an alibi for that night, we have to do something.'

Mel's face was set in a smile that made her look younger. I wondered whether she thought I was there to say I had changed my mind and wanted to be with her brother after all.

'Can we talk for a moment?'

'Of course.' She led me through to the kitchen, which was long and bright with a large range oven, granite worktops, and shelves stacked with crockery. The air was scented with cinnamon, the atmosphere cosy. 'I'm making a cake for Dad's eightieth tomorrow.'

'It smells good.' Ignoring a stab of guilt that I was about to spoil her day, I said quickly, 'I wanted to ask you about Owen.'

Sliding her hand into an oven glove, Mel shot me a guarded look. 'What about him?'

'You said the other day that his last relationship break-up didn't end well.'

She released a sigh and squatted in front of the oven, jeans straining around her thighs. 'I shouldn't have said that.'

'What did you mean?'

I had the feeling she was putting off telling me as she opened the oven door and peered inside. I thought of Jack, waiting for me, time ticking down. 'Please, Mel. It's important.'

She rose, pushing her fringe back. 'It was nothing really, a long time ago.' Her cheeks were tinged red. 'He had a hard time taking no for an answer,' she said, defensively. 'Kept texting her, stuff like that.'

My pulse accelerated. 'Is that all?'

Mel threw down the oven glove and fixed me with a hard stare. 'She took out a restraining order, OK? It gave Owen a scare and he kept his head down after that, concentrated on his business. He stayed away from relationships until . . .' She gave a frustrated shake of her head. 'Until *you*.'

163

Anger flared in my chest. 'It might have been good to know that before we started seeing each other. I had no idea.'

Mel had the grace to look ashamed. 'It's not something he's proud of. He asked me not to say anything, because he didn't want to frighten you off.'

'I had a right to know.'

'I agree, he should have told you, but I don't think he'll ever behave like that again, in spite of what I said.' Her gaze held a plea. 'I was wrong to be angry with you, Caitlin. I'm sorry.'

'He came to the cottage yesterday.' My voice wavered. 'He was acting as though Jack was holding me there against my will, and this morning Jack saw him hanging about on the coastal path and he was asking about a watch he'd supposedly left at the cottage.'

'He usually goes for a run along there.' Mel's face was tense even as her shoulders slumped. 'As for talking to Jack, he's worried about you, that's all.'

'It doesn't sound as if he's worried. It sounds like he's making up excuses to get Jack away from me.'

'He wouldn't do that, Caitlin.'

I wondered how she could be sure. 'Mel, do you know where Owen was on the fourteenth?'

Her eyes – so like Owen's, it was as if he was looking at me – fired with annoyance. 'Why do you want to know?'

'Please, Mel, it's important.'

'Why don't you ask him yourself?'

'Because he won't be honest with me.' He had harassed a woman into taking legal action, and I hadn't known – maybe because I hadn't looked deeply enough. *Secrets will always come out with all their repercussions.* Hadn't I learned that already? Except . . . I wasn't being honest either, at least not with the person who mattered the most.

Mel looked at me a moment longer, her expression a blend of wariness and dislike. 'I'll check if you tell me why.'

I bit my lip, knowing there was no taking back what I was

about to say. 'Jack's accident . . . he's certain that Owen was driving the car that hit him.'

'*What?*' Mel's face stretched with incredulity. 'You've got to be kidding.'

'I was going to call the police but—'

'The police?' Mel's voice rose in alarm. 'Please, Caitlin, don't do that. He's worked so hard to shake off what happened in the past.'

'So, help me.'

'Hang on.' She came a fraction closer, her brow creased. 'You seriously think that my brother tried to run over your ex . . . your husband . . . whatever he is?' I recoiled from the choked fury in her voice. 'He's made mistakes, but Owen isn't a *murderer.*'

'I'm not saying he wanted Jack to die.' I thought of Owen's face in the car the night I brought Jack home, the darkness behind his gaze, and wasn't so sure. 'Jack can't remember what happened, but he had a flashback earlier, after seeing Owen.'

'Oh, and that's your proof, is it?' She closed the gap between us, so close I could smell coffee on her breath. 'Owen loved – *loves* – you, but he wouldn't go as far as hurting someone to keep you.'

I stood my ground. 'If you could just check, please, Mel. That's all I'm asking. I won't call the police until I know.'

She folded her arms, thrusting her chin out. 'How do you know I won't make something up to give him an alibi?'

She was right. I wouldn't know. Sinking under the weight of her stony stare, I said shakily, 'I guess I'll leave it to the police then.' I turned, unable to hold her gaze any longer, my heart beating sluggishly in my chest. I wasn't equipped for this sort of confrontation, should never have come.

'There won't be any need for that.'

I looked up, breath catching in my throat at the sight of Owen in the hallway, outlined by the light coming through the glass above the door.

'I didn't hear you come in.' Behind me, Mel sounded almost afraid. 'How long have you been there?'

'Long enough.' He didn't move yet seemed to fill the space, feet planted wide apart, arms clamped by his sides. 'I came to ask if you wanted me to pick up anything for Dad's birthday party tomorrow night.'

A frustrated groan emerged from Mel. 'Owen, I'm sorry you had to hear that.'

'Please understand why I'm asking,' I appealed, wishing he would move so I could read his face. *Had Jack seen him come in?* 'I know how you feel about Jack and me being back together, and he's convinced—'

'I was at the Taverner Inn until eleven. You can check with the landlord,' he said in a monotone. 'Thursday is quiz night, and I was on the winning team for a change. I wasn't tired afterwards, so went to the gym, did a workout, then got on with some paperwork in the office. There's CCTV there, which should prove I wouldn't have had time to drive to wherever I was supposed to be and get back to open the store the following morning. My assistant Jay will confirm it, as will the security cameras should the police want to take a look.'

My scalp prickled. Something about his speech sounded rehearsed, as though he'd gone over it before. 'And you're certain it was the fourteenth?'

'Caitlin, for God's sake,' Mel exploded, pushing past me to stand with Owen, the pair of them blocking my way out. 'You're lucky *we're* not calling the police.'

'As it happens,' Owen said, stepping forward so his face came into view, his green eyes full of sorrow and something I couldn't make out. 'The fourteenth sticks in my mind because the landlord called to remind me about the quiz and asked me to make up a team as someone had dropped out. Like I said, you can check with him.'

'OK, fine,' I stuttered. 'I'm sorry.'

'Please go.' Mel stiffly opened the door. 'And don't come back.'

Owen caught my fingers as I passed. 'Caitlin, be careful,' he said, holding me for a moment in the mesmerising glow of his gaze. 'You're not safe.'

It sounded more like a warning than a caution. 'I'm fine.' I snatched my hand away, fingers tingling. 'Goodbye, Owen.'

I hurried back to the car, blinking away tears. Jack was leaning against the passenger door, his face strained. 'I was about to call the police,' he said, waving the phone I'd given him. 'I just need to press one more nine.'

'It wasn't him,' I said dully. 'Let's go.'

As I opened the driver's door, I looked at the house once more and glimpsed a face moving out of sight in one of the upstairs windows. I could have sworn it was Lydia.

Beverley was outside the cottage when we got back, dressed in a swingy grey poncho, and holding a casserole dish.

Jack peered through the windscreen. 'Who's that?' He'd barely spoken since I left the guesthouse and explained that he didn't need to call the police, because Owen had a solid alibi, other than to say, miserably, 'Maybe I'm losing my marbles.'

'It's Beverley Evans.' My blood was pumping, alive to a new threat. 'She owns the grocery store.'

'That's right.' His tone warmed up and some of the tension left his face. 'I think I recognise her.'

I leapt out of the car before he could move, keen to head her off. Despite her promise not to refer to Jack's accident, or us being back together, I was worried something might slip out. 'Hi, Bev!'

She came over, a smile creasing her face, holding out the earthenware dish like a peace offering. 'It's my morning off and I was doing some cooking. I made far too much and thought you might like some. It's chicken and leek.'

'That's kind of you.' As I took the dish, which warmed my icy hands, she peered round me at the car, probably checking Jack was really back and not a figment of my imagination.

'I was a bit surprised you weren't in, what with his leg being injured.'

'Only his ankle.' I forced out a smile. 'It's much better.'

Jack unfolded himself from the passenger seat and climbed out, holding the rim of the car door for support.

'Hi, Beverley.' He sounded pleased to see her, no doubt relieved to meet someone who didn't present a risk. *If only he knew.* 'Something smells good.'

It was true that the aroma from under the foil was fragrant and enticing but I felt sick, my stomach tight with nerves. 'Could you take it inside, please, Jack?' I thrust the dish towards him, but Beverley intercepted it.

'He can't do that when he can barely walk,' she scolded, shaking her head. 'You give your husband a helping hand.' She gave me a wink and I hoped Jack wouldn't read anything into it.

'I can manage,' he said with a smile, limping ahead, leaving his crutch in the car as if to prove a point. I couldn't help a flash of pride as I watched him go.

There was a moment of awkwardness as we crowded into the hallway before Beverley headed to the kitchen. She'd been a regular visitor when my grandfather was alive, happy to play chess with him for hours. He'd tried to teach me, but I'd never been a worthy opponent.

'Sorry,' I whispered to Jack.

He shook his head. 'She's nice.' He looked brighter than he had ten minutes ago, as though lifted by the sight of an innocent, friendly face. 'I'm starving.'

'It's chicken,' I said, thinking how keen he would have been a year ago to tuck in.

'My favourite.'

I stared in surprise as he hobbled after Beverley and asked her how business was doing. *Had he forgotten he was vegetarian now?* A thread of hope curled around my heart that this subconscious link to Lydia might have broken – until everything she'd told me about him rushed back.

'I'm hoping to pick up some gardening work, once my ankle is better,' he was saying.

'You're definitely staying around here then?'

'Well . . . yes.'

'Why do you ask?'

Jack and I spoke at the same time.

Beverley flapped a hand. 'Oh, it was just that Owen Whittaker came in the shop and was saying he didn't think you'd be here long—'

'Owen Whittaker?' Jack's voice was taut.

'He's got a quite a thing for our Caitlin,' Beverly continued, seeming not to notice the frantic semaphoring of my eyebrows, no doubt caught up in the romance of a possible 'love triangle'. 'You'll have to watch that one, unless . . .' She swung round from the worktop to pass a knowing look from me to Jack, a gleam in her eyes. 'You two *are*—'

I leapt forward and grabbed her arm before she could continue. 'Actually, Bev, there's something I'd like to talk to you about in private.' Seeing Jack's confused and angry expression, I lightened my tone. 'Nothing serious, but not for male ears.' I tried desperately to think of something convincing. 'Back in a few minutes.'

Seeming keen to be the recipient of some gossip, Beverley accompanied me out of the cottage, tapping the side of her nose as she passed Jack.

He raised his eyebrows. 'Will my ears be burning?'

'Probably.' I kept up the jokey tone, threading elbows with Beverley until we were out of sight of the cottage, fighting the urge to yell at her, knowing it wasn't her fault. 'Sorry about that,' I said, letting go of her solid arm. 'I didn't want to say in front of Jack, but he's vegetarian now and gets upset at the thought of anyone cooking or eating meat.' I wanted to steer her away from the topic of Owen. She obviously knew we'd been seeing each other and assumed I would have told Jack. 'I thought once you whipped off the foil, it might get tricky.'

'Why didn't you mention it straight away?' Beverley's features collapsed into a frown. 'I wouldn't have been offended,' she said.

'Lots of people are veggie these days, or vegan.' She shook her head and carried on walking, leaning into the hill as we began the incline. 'I don't understand it myself, as long as the meat is organic and not pumped full of hormones.'

'I know, but . . . it's more of an ethical thing. Jack prefers a plant-based diet. In fact, he's planning to grow vegetables once the weather improves.' I had no idea whether this was true, and the realisation brought a swell of emotion to my throat.

'You don't seem very happy, if you don't mind me saying so.' Pausing, Beverley turned to face me, her cheeks ruddy with exertion. 'Is everything OK?'

I tried not to shrink from her direct gaze. 'We're working through a few things,' I admitted, deciding there and then that I had to come clean to Jack – tell him the truth, regardless of the consequences. I couldn't go on like this.

Chapter 21

Lydia

I moved back to the window, wondering whether Caitlin had seen me earlier, when she left.

Hearing her turn up, I'd thought she must have followed me back to the guesthouse, but it was Mel she wanted to talk to.

I'd leant over the banister to listen to their exchange through the open kitchen door, their words sinking through me, setting my pulse racing.

When I heard the click of the front door and Owen had entered the hallway, I disappeared back to my room and searched his name on my phone, curious about how serious his past offence had been. It took some scrolling before I found a link to a local newspaper report, dated almost ten years ago.

A Whitby resident who sent unsolicited messages to his former girlfriend has been issued with a restraining order for harassment.

Owen Whittaker, 24, of Robin Hood's Bay, originally denied harassment, then changed his plea. Prosecutor, James Harrow, *told the court that Whittaker and his victim had been in a short relationship, which subsequently ended. He said the harassment had taken place during a short period, during which time Whittaker sent the victim a high volume of texts, emails, and voicemails, and later visited her address.*

In a statement, read out in court, the victim described how she had been bombarded by threatening messages from Whittaker and felt scared for her safety. Victoria Hartwell, 23, waived her anonymity to say in an interview, 'I should be allowed to end a relationship without being made to suffer and fear for my life. Let this be a warning to all men who think they're entitled to frighten women into submission.'

Whittaker apologised for any distress caused, saying his behaviour was out of character and promising it wouldn't be repeated.

He'd clearly kept his promise – until now. Caitlin must have unleashed something inside him that had perhaps been lying dormant all this time. He must have believed he'd found the woman he wanted to spend the rest of his life with and couldn't cope with her rejection.

I understood that feeling of powerlessness, of not being in control of your own destiny, and the overwhelming fear and insecurity it created. I'd experienced it strongly after William died, more so because him returning to me was impossible – no amount of messaging, pleading, and promising would ever bring him back – but harassment wasn't the answer, would surely repel the recipient. *Isn't that what you're doing?* I dismissed Shona's voice in my head. I wasn't harassing anyone. I needed the man I loved back in mine and Mattie's lives; it was as simple as that. It would be so much easier if Caitlin was out of the picture, but as things stood, I couldn't see a way of wiping her from Jack's mind; not now he'd forgotten the past year of his life – *our* life together – and the reason he'd left her in the first place. I couldn't even attempt to get Caitlin away from the cottage again, so I could talk to him. I'd had my chance and blown it.

Frustration tore through me as I paced the room, sawing my thumbnail between my bottom teeth. My thoughts were sharp-edged fragments, and it was difficult to catch my breath. On impulse, I found the number for Callum's mum, stored in my phone, and fired off a text. **Thank you for looking after Mattie. Lydia.** She probably thought I was a terrible mother, was always brisk when our paths crossed, a coolness in her gaze. She knew nothing about being a single parent – a widow. She immediately replied: **He's always welcome!** Not *You're welcome* and I felt a flash of resentment that Mattie preferred being at Callum's again. Another reason to bring Jack home.

I pushed open the window to draw in some air. The view was shrouded in low-lying cloud, the sun casting weak rays onto the sea. Coldness pinched my cheeks and stung my eyes. I hated it here. I tried to picture being at home without Jack, reshaping my life without him, but all I could see was an empty space that stretched for miles, my son becoming a virtual stranger, and waves of anger beat inside my brain.

As I went to slam the window shut, I noticed a heavyset woman halfway down the hill, wearing a voluminous charcoal cape that made her look like a giant moth. She was talking to a figure in a purple coat. I angled myself further out. It was Caitlin. *Why wasn't she at home?*

An idea dropped into my head. After snapping the window shut, I snatched my phone off the bed and called the cottage, fingers slipping across the screen in my haste.

No answer. I called again. Once more, it rang out. *Third time lucky?* Jack had to be there if Caitlin was out on her own.

'Come on, come on,' I urged, nipping at the skin around my knuckle. I imagined Jack moving slowly to the phone, hindered by his painful ankle. 'Please, pick up.'

I shot back to the window in time to see Caitlin waving to

the woman as she turned and headed quickly in the direction of the cottage.

'Hello?'

His voice in my ear at last, like a familiar song. Tears sprang to my eyes. 'Jack.' It came out in an anguished burst before I could stop it. 'Jack, it's . . . you don't remember me, but it's Lydia.'

In the brief silence that followed, I pictured the crease of his brow and the slight narrowing of his eyes that happened when he was thinking, as clearly as if he was in front of me. 'Jack, please don't hang up. This is important and I don't have much time.'

'I don't understand.' His voice was low and guarded. 'Who did you say you were?'

Trying to ignore the stab of hurt in my chest, I said, 'Please, just listen, Jack.' I was pacing again, stumbling over my words. 'I know you've lost your memory and you don't remember that we – you and I – are . . . *were* . . . in a relationship for a year before your . . . before you were injured.' I swallowed. 'Your wife, Caitlin, she isn't being honest with you, Jack. She's lying to you.' It was important to stress the dishonesty – the thing he hated most. 'She hasn't told you about me because she's worried you'll leave her, like you did before. Please believe me, Jack. I—'

'You're the woman who came here yesterday.'

The woman. My throat was beginning to seize up, but I managed to rasp out, 'Jack, don't say anything to Caitlin about me, or tell her I called. You could be in danger.'

'Danger?' Bemusement, overlaid with something else. *Fear?* Was he starting to remember?

'Meet me at midnight tonight,' I pushed on, a pulse twitching under my eye. 'I'll come round the back of the cottage and meet you by the gate, so you won't have far to walk. Don't bring anything with you.'

Silence. I strained but couldn't hear him breathing, or anything else, other than a cacophony of seagulls outside the window.

My nerves were taut, my own breath high in my chest. 'Trust me, Jack.' I wanted to tell him I loved him but didn't dare. *Not yet*. 'I'll explain everything when I see you, I promise.' *Mattie*. I would tell him about Mattie, try to get him to talk to Jack on the phone once we were on our way to London. But not now. I wanted to be there with Jack when his memory returned, or even if it didn't. If he really couldn't remember . . . in a way it didn't matter. It was a chance for a fresh start, without the problems that had dogged our time together. Now I knew the trigger points, I could make sure there were no more explosions. 'But you mustn't let her know,' I continued when he didn't speak. 'I mean it, Jack. It's vital you carry on as normal.'

If he told Caitlin, she would have the opportunity to talk him round, to persuade him not to leave. Even after everything I told her, I knew she wouldn't let him go.

'Jack?' I was waiting for him to ask me to verify who I was to him, but the silence stretched to breaking point. Perhaps he was in shock. At least he hadn't slammed the phone down on me. That had to mean something. 'Jack?'

'You say your name is Lydia?'

'That's right.' A thrill of excitement ran down my spine. 'I'll tell you everything later.' I paused in front of the door, certain I'd heard a floorboard creaking. I headed across the room, keeping my eyes on the door handle. 'Midnight, but I'll wait,' I said quietly. 'However long it takes.' It took a moment to realise the buzzing in my ear was the dialling tone. He'd gone.

I waited a few seconds, heart beating fast. Should I call back and extract a promise to meet me? *No*. He would need time to process my call, but I was as certain as I could be that curiosity would get the better of him. He would be there.

Clutching my phone to my chest, I crept towards the door and whipped it open.

Mel was outside, a small stack of white towels in her arms. 'Oh,' she said, eyes widening. 'You *are* there.'

'You knew I was.' *Had she been listening?* 'You saw me come up earlier.'

'I thought you might have gone out again.' She was a bad liar, her gaze darting about as if unsure where to settle. 'I was going to leave fresh towels.'

'And clean the toothpaste off the mirror in the bathroom?' I didn't know why I said it. She was hardly going to blush crimson and say, *Oh God, I'm sorry about that horrible message. It was my brother/Caitlin/Jack Garvey/my mother. You're not wanted here, you see.*

'I thought you didn't want—'

'It's fine, I was joking,' I said. 'You could have knocked.'

'I was about to.' A hint of indignation entered her tone, as if she wasn't used to being challenged. 'You might have been asleep.'

'Well, as you can see, I'm wide awake.' My lips twisted into an irritated smile as I held out my hand for the towels. 'Thanks,' I said, when Mel relinquished them with obvious reluctance. 'I appreciate it.'

'Listen, about earlier . . .' She hooked her thumbs in the pockets of her jeans and glanced over her shoulder. 'My brother can be a bit full on sometimes when it comes to people he cares about.' Her voice dropped lower, as if worried he could overhear. 'He's a good person but shouldn't have questioned a guest like that.'

'Don't worry about it.' I was prepared to be generous in the face of her apology. Owen's offence had led to a court case, the results published in the local paper, which couldn't have been easy for his family to deal with. I guessed it still cast a shadow. Perhaps Mel was constantly on edge, worried he might be doomed to repeat his behaviour one day – which seemed to be exactly what was happening. She must be as annoyed as her brother was that Caitlin had reunited with Jack. I felt a momentary blast of pleasure that soon Owen would have Caitlin to himself once more and Mel would be able to relax. She looked like she needed a break. 'Families can be difficult,' I added, tucking the towels under my arm.

'How old is your son?' Her mouth curved into a smile. 'You said he was a teenager?'

'Doing A levels soon.' I didn't want to talk about Mattie and give away more details about our lives. I'd been in the spotlight too much already.

The doorbell pealed, making us both jump.

'That'll be the Carlsons,' Mel said with a laugh, pressing a palm to her chest and rolling her eyes. 'Lovely couple, from Manchester. His mother's in a care home in Whitby so they come here every few months to visit and make a holiday of it.'

'Shame about the weather,' I said politely, grateful to the Carlsons for providing a welcome distraction. Hopefully, Mel would push me out of her mind now.

'You're welcome to join us for dinner later.'

'Actually, I'm eating out, but thank you for asking.'

I didn't want to enter another situation where I would be forced to make up a reason for being at the guesthouse, alone.

I watched Mel jog down the stairs, the overhead light picking out grey strands in her parting and wondered whether Caitlin would be crying on her shoulder once Jack left. Would she confess to Mel that she'd known Jack was living in London with another woman and hadn't told him? And with me gone too, would Mel realise that woman had been me?

Chapter 22

Caitlin

After saying goodbye to Beverley, I called Dee, hoping she wasn't in the middle of a class.

'Everything's going wrong,' I said the minute she answered.

'Tell me.'

The words poured out while she listened in silence, as I made my way back to the cottage. Feeling a tickle along the back of my neck, I looked around in case Owen was following, but there was no one around. 'I know I've brought this on myself, Dee.' I stopped by the car and brushed tears from under my eyes. 'I've taken advantage of Jack losing his memory and hate myself for it. I can't carry on, not with Lydia hanging about, waiting for me to tell him the truth, and Owen turning up and dropping hints.'

'I suppose it was inevitable that Jack met someone else,' she said grimly once I'd run out of steam. 'It's hard to imagine him hurting anyone though. But what would this Lydia have to gain by lying?'

'She wants him back.' I sniffed. 'They were going to have counselling, apparently. Jack had become a father figure to her son.'

'Really?' Dee sounded cynical. 'Not much of a role model if he was hurting the boy's mother.'

Hearing her say it made my stomach curdle. 'He has been ... different,' I said, choosing my words carefully. 'It's like, he's so happy to be here, to be with me, and he says he loves me, but then there are these gaps, I suppose where he's trying to remember things, or having flashbacks, and I feel as though I can't reach him, that I don't know him as well as I thought I did.' I couldn't bring myself to tell her how he'd pinned me down while dreaming, knowing she would urge me to throw him out. I would have said the same to Dee if it was the other way round, but she hadn't seen the look on his face when he saw me cowering on the floor, the self-loathing he'd felt about frightening me. 'I want to tell him the truth, but don't think I should be on my own with him when I do. Not after last time.'

'But he doesn't remember that?'

'No, but what if it all comes back?' My head was pounding. 'It'll be a double shock, hearing I've kept something this important from him again.'

'You seriously think he might fly into a rage?'

'I don't know, Dee.' I shivered in spite of my coat. The air was like a cold flannel on my face. 'I don't trust Lydia, though. There's something off about her.' I explained how she'd tried to trick me into meeting her. 'But I can't deny that scar on her hand, and she definitely said he'd taken her phone and deleted pictures of her with bruises.'

'Listen, why don't we meet up,' Dee said. 'I can be there when you talk to Jack, if you like, preferably somewhere public.' The sound of children shrieking and laughing filtered through the phone. She must be on playground duty. 'That way, he can't cause a scene or hurt you.'

Her words felt like tiny claws, burrowing into me. I wanted to say *Jack would never hurt me*, but said instead, 'It's a five-hour drive to Brighton.'

'We can meet halfway, say . . . Leicester services.' Dee waited, but I couldn't speak. 'It's not far from my brother's place. I can pop in for a visit afterwards. Tell Jack I suggested we meet while I'm there because I miss you. Which I do,' she added firmly.

'When?'

'The sooner the better.' She paused, as if thinking. 'I've got the day off tomorrow.'

'I just spoke to Dee,' I said back at the cottage, after removing my coat and checking I didn't look too much like I'd been crying. 'She'd like to meet up tomorrow.'

'That's short notice.' Jack was sitting on a footstool in the living room, stoking the fire with the poker. 'It's a bit of a trek to Brighton.' He glanced over his shoulder. 'We're still settling in here.'

'She suggested halfway. Leicester services.' I tugged the cuffs of my jumper over my hands. 'She's going to visit her brother.'

Jack hunched forward, returning his gaze to the leaping flames. 'I don't know, Cait.' His tone sounded wrong, as though he was making an effort to be polite. *Was he going over what Beverley had said about Owen, and starting to build a picture?*

'It'll be nice to see her.' And to get away, I didn't add – from Owen, and Lydia, their words tattooed on my brain. *He took my phone, got rid of it. He deleted the pictures from the Cloud.* I kept seeing the scar on Lydia's palm, deep and jagged. *That's from when I snatched the knife off him.*

And Owen's warning, his sombre face. *Be careful, Caitlin. You're not safe.*

My throat began to close up, the familiar signs of panic taking over my body.

'Do we both have to go?' Jack was very still now, as though my answer was of the utmost importance. Something about his rigid posture made me shiver. There was a time I would have known without words what he was thinking, but his face was turned away, and I couldn't bring myself to ask.

'Of course,' I said, the words catching on an involuntary in-breath. 'You get on well with Dee, and you said that you're feeling much better.'

'OK.' He didn't sound enthusiastic, but at least he hadn't refused. If Lydia decided to phone in the meantime, I would ignore it. Better still . . .

'I'll make us some coffee.' I hurried through to the kitchen and unplugged the phone, tucking the cord behind a jar of pasta so Jack wouldn't notice. There was no other way she could make contact without coming to the cottage. Hopefully she would hold off until after we'd left in the morning.

I stood for a moment, nose fizzing with tears, trying to impose logic on the actions that had led me to this. The cottage – our haven – no longer felt safe, and I had only myself to blame.

'Are you phoning the Taverner Inn?'

I let out a blurt of fright. Jack had entered the kitchen behind me, without his crutch. I'd got used to the sound of it heralding his movements, but remembered he'd left it in the car and the second one was still somewhere in the living room.

'I'll make the coffee first, then call, if you want me to, but I'm sure Owen was telling the truth.' I felt a flush on my cheeks. 'There wouldn't be much point in him lying when he could easily be found out.'

'I guess not.' I saw in Jack's eyes the hardening of a doubt already there.

'Maybe whoever was driving the car looked a bit like him and that's why he came into your head.' His face twitched with a flicker of frustration. 'Should we contact the police and ask for an update?' I added, head pulsing with the speed of my thoughts. 'There might be some new information.'

'They said they would call if there was any news.' Jack gave a sigh heavy with resignation. 'Maybe it's better if I never find out.'

I was desperate now to lighten the atmosphere, to make the most of whatever time we had left before everything changed forever. 'Listen, why don't you work on those flyers?' It hit me as I said it that there was probably no point – not once Jack knew the truth. 'There's a good printers in Whitby, not too expensive.'

'Are we OK, financially?'

'Fine, we're fine.' I grabbed a cloth and began wiping round the sink, the tips of my ears burning. We'd always had separate accounts. After Jack left I used my savings to pay the rent and bills until I left Brighton but had no idea how much money Jack had spent or earned during the past year. Once he had access to his account, there were bound to be questions. He could have a new one, for all I knew, and earned a fortune – or spent all his money on Lydia and her son.

How had I expected to get away with this?

'I might have some of that casserole if you don't mind.'

'Of course.' I decided not to remind him he no longer ate meat. 'I'll bring some through.'

He searched my face, as if looking for clues, stoking a panicky fear inside me. What was he looking for? Something about him had changed, or maybe it was me, my head now full of Lydia, seeing him in a different light.

I was filled with a sudden, deep despair. *Why couldn't she have stayed away?*

My shoulders dropped when Jack silently left the kitchen, his limp pronounced.

I took out a plate with shaking hands, pausing as I noticed a glass on its side in the sink, as though dropped there in a hurry. Jack must have used it, after I'd gone outside with Beverley. He usually put things away, but maybe the fact that he'd left the glass there was indicative of his state of mind.

Turning to grab a serving spoon, I froze. The back door wasn't shut. I'd taken a bin bag out the day before and must not have dropped the latch when I came back in.

After Owen's visit, and Jack's early departure to bed – me

following soon after to lie aching and tense in the dark – checking the place was secure had slipped my mind.

I glanced at the floor, as if a boot print might be evident, but if someone had slipped into the cottage while we were out, they would have probably wiped their feet on the bristled mat or removed their boots. *Owen?* Who else – unless Lydia had been watching the place and had let herself in.

Fresh panic ticked in my chest. Could she have left something here for Jack to find as proof of their relationship – something to trigger his memory? I thought again of the passport turning up but couldn't link it to her. I scanned the kitchen, but nothing – apart from the glass in the sink – seemed out of place or to have been touched, although . . . I couldn't remember leaving my phone charger plugged in by the toaster, but maybe Jack had used it.

I locked the door and checked the window was fastened shut before dishing up a plateful of lukewarm casserole and taking it through to Jack, who was looking out of the window with a melancholy expression.

'You're not having any?' He turned but didn't meet my eyes.
'Maybe later.'

Hit with the face-slapping truth that I no longer felt comfortable in his company, I said, 'I think I'll get on with some work in a bit.' When he didn't protest, I wondered whether he felt the same way.

Upstairs, I looked around for signs someone had been there, scouring the spare room and then Jack's side of the bed, checking under the pillow as if Lydia might have slipped a necklace, or her earrings, there for him to find – gifts, perhaps, that he'd bought her.

My insides burned at the thought of Jack seeking out something special for Lydia, as he once had for me, yet the image didn't square with Lydia's description of him being angry enough to wield a knife. What had gone so wrong between them? And why hadn't I seen even a hint of that side of Jack while we were together?

Back in the kitchen, I opened my laptop, yearning briefly for my ordinary, quiet life of just a week ago, when work dominated my days, my guilt and grief shrinking to something manageable, and my biggest concern – other than getting the fire to stay lit – was persuading Owen to accept we were better off as friends.

I replied to an email from my agent, who had a couple of branding projects she hoped I would be interested in – one for an up-and-coming musician that I immediately wanted to tell Jack about.

I poked my head around the living room door to find him slumped in the wing-backed chair apparently asleep, the television on low and flickering in the corner of the room.

I watched him for a few seconds, a flame of worry igniting when I realised I couldn't see his chest moving.

'Jack?'

I ran in, practically tripping on the rug, and touched his wrist. It was cold. I held the back of my hand beneath his nose, overcome with relief when a huff of breath warmed my skin. His head rested against the wing of the chair, his expression peaceful. The purple bruising around his eye was fading and he looked more like himself. Leaning closer, I felt a treacherous surge of love, and when his eyes snapped open, I jumped. For a second his stare was completely blank, then his arms shot out and he pushed me. I staggered, knocking against the coffee table, cracking my elbow as I toppled over, narrowly missing hitting my head on the hearth.

'Why did you do that?' Breathless with shock, I scrambled to my knees, shrinking back as Jack lumbered to his feet and towered over me. His face was a hard, unreadable mask. 'Jack?'

He stared for a moment longer. I shunted backwards, watching as he returned from wherever he'd been in his mind, inhabiting his body once more, his face transforming into a puzzled frown. 'Caitlin!' Then, more urgently: 'What are you doing down there?'

'I . . . you were sleeping.' I rose slowly to my feet, careful to keep some distance between us, cradling my throbbing elbow. 'I disturbed you and you pushed me away.'

'What?' He stepped back, hitting the chair with the backs of his legs, and dropping heavily onto the cushion. 'Why would I do that?'

'I don't know, Jack.'

His face fell into his hands. I stared at his nails, neat and cleaner than I'd ever seen them. 'I was dreaming again,' he said. 'That's no excuse, but—'

'What were you dreaming about?' I circled the sofa to the door, my pulse drumming in my ears. 'It must have been more like a nightmare.'

'It was, I . . .' He raised his eyes, glassy and dark. 'There was a boy, but I don't know who he was. He was crying.'

'A boy?' Immediately, I thought of Lydia's son. 'Maybe . . . do you think . . . I don't know, that he represents you, when you were younger, I mean?' It was a long shot – he'd never had bad dreams when we were together – but he nodded slowly, drawing his hands down his face.

'Maybe,' he said slowly. 'There was . . . I was fighting, gripping hold of someone—'

'The boy?' I couldn't bear for him to say it was a woman, or anything that would confirm what Lydia had told me. Not that fighting with a boy was any better. *It was only a dream* I told myself. *Or was it a memory?*

'I don't think so.' He scribbled his fingers through his hair and winced. 'I don't know, Cait.'

I felt profoundly wrung out, incapable of deciphering what it all meant. 'I'm going for a shower.'

'Caitlin, I'm so sorry I pushed you.' I ignored his wretched cry as I left the room and ran upstairs, close to tears, only one question swirling through my mind: had bringing Jack home been the biggest mistake of my life?

Chapter 23

Lydia

Filled with a jittery energy after Mel had left to attend to her new guests, I packed my few belongings and decided that, to pass some time, I would complete the walk to the oddly named Boggle Hole that she'd recommended.

The air felt chilled, but the sky was a pale, cloudless blue, and the sea shimmered as I strode along, arms swinging. It was hard not to admire the view now the rain had finally stopped. The golden arc of sand, glistening rock pools and craggy outcrops looked like a film set, but I wasn't in the mood for taking photos as I began constructing sentences in my head. I needed to find the right words to convince Jack to return to London with me and I couldn't afford to get it wrong. I might not get another opportunity.

I'd warmed up and felt almost cheerful by the time I reached the café where I'd arranged to meet Caitlin earlier. I sat by the window and drank a mug of strong tea with a slice of lemon cake that took me back to my grandmother's kitchen in Huddersfield. She'd tried to teach me to bake on the odd occasion we'd visited, but I hadn't the patience, or skill.

Harriet baked; great slabs of flour, butter and raisins that stuck to your teeth, but Mattie loved her cakes, often slipping round there after school when he was younger, coming back too full to eat his dinner.

Out of nowhere, I became annoyed with Harriet. If I asked her, I knew she would refuse to speak to Jack on the phone to confirm we were a couple, believing we were better off apart. *She would be in for a shock when we returned.*

At least I had the counselling appointment as proof – a confirmation email that came through after Jack left – though I was starting to hope we might not need it; that a brand-new start was all we required. We could even move away, far from Harriet's prying gaze, perhaps even go abroad once Mattie had finished his exams. He'd no doubt kick up a fuss about leaving Callum behind, but would make new friends, more easily, perhaps, somewhere different.

Lost in thought, I started when a figure loomed in front of me at the table. Chair legs scraped across the floor and Owen positioned himself opposite, clasping his large hands on the gingham cloth in front of him.

'What are you doing here?' I pushed my crumb-scattered plate aside, trying not to show how rattled I was to see him.

'I was going to ask you the same thing.' His tone was deceptively mild, his eyes stone-hard as they drilled into me. 'What are you up to, Lydia *Fielding*?'

The sound of my surname – William's surname – gave me a jolt. 'I don't know what you mean.' I flashed him the friendliest smile I could muster. 'I went for a walk and I'm having refreshments. Would you like a drink?'

'No, thank you.' His lip curled into a sneer. 'And that's not all you're doing.'

I resisted a nervous impulse to fiddle with my hair, flattened by the woolly hat I'd taken off. 'You're not making any sense.'

Owen sat back, looking at ease as he threaded a hand through his own, wind-tousled, hair. A pair of red-cheeked women at the next table were darting him admiring looks and one bent forward to say something that made her friend laugh.

'Something's going on between you, Caitlin, and Jack.' Owen spoke calmly, as though discussing the menu. 'She's been on edge since he came back, all over the place, and worse since you appeared.' I bundled my hands into my lap so he couldn't see them shaking. 'I didn't buy your story about being a fan of her work,' he continued, head on one side in the manner of a lion appraising a gazelle. 'I looked at your booking details at the guesthouse—'

'How dare you?' My angry tone provoked a startled stare from his pair of fans. 'That's against the law,' I hissed. 'Haven't you heard of data protection?'

'Feel free to call the police.' He folded his arms, so his biceps bulged under his jacket, a flash of dark amusement crossing his face. 'There wasn't anything incriminating about you online, I checked, but I had a friendly chat with your lovely neighbour, and she gave me a bit of an insight into why you're here.'

Harriet? I briefly closed my eyes, imagining her telling this charming man, who must have fed her God knows what story about why he was calling, all about her neighbour's troubled relationships, and how she'd gone tearing off on a fool's errand – just the sort of phrase Harriet would use – leaving her son behind.

'You don't have much luck with men, do you, Lydia?'

My eyes sprang open.

Owen was angled towards me, all humour stripped from his chiselled features. 'Look, I care about Caitlin, a lot. I wish she wasn't with Jack again, but she is. He's made his choice and I think you should leave them—'

'Did she tell you he has amnesia?'

I felt the electrification of his shock. 'Amnesia?'

'Jack lost his memory after his accident and doesn't remember me.'

188

The satisfaction I felt, watching the certainty slide from Owen's face, gave me a surge of strength. 'Caitlin hasn't told him they were separated.' I fidgeted on the hard, wooden chair. 'She's pretending they've been together all along.'

Owen's colour had drained. 'That's crazy.' He looked at me for a moment, then rubbed a hand over his face as if to rearrange his features. '*Shit*,' he said softly.

'You believe me?'

'It makes sense of a few things.' Though still defensive, the look he gave me was fractionally less hostile. 'What if his memory comes back?'

'I don't think she's thought that far ahead.' I tried to keep my tone neutral. 'The doctor said he might never recover his memories. Apparently it's not uncommon after a head injury, or traumatic incident.' I thought of the car, flying out of nowhere, Jack spinning through the air like a rag doll. 'He gave the hospital her number when he came round, and she picked him up as though they'd only seen each other the day before.'

'Wow.' Above his collar, Owen's neck muscles were taut. 'I knew something was off, but never guessed . . .' He gave a twisted laugh. 'No wonder she didn't want me anywhere near her, giving things away.'

'I'm sorry.' I assumed an expression of sympathy. 'I would have said something sooner, but I didn't know you two had been in a relationship,' I lied. 'I overheard a conversation at the guesthouse, when she came to see your sister.'

His breath exhaled in a blast. 'So . . .' He refocused. 'You found out he was here with Caitlin, and you want him back?'

'That's why I was talking to her on the beach. I wanted to give her a heads up, a chance to come clean with him.' A partial truth, but it seemed to satisfy him.

'And he definitely doesn't know they'd broken up?'

'Not unless he's pretending he's lost his memory, and I don't think he is.'

'How can you be certain?'

'I've spoken to him already. He didn't recognise me.' I tried to ignore the sting of rejection, and the suspicion that he might have come to the guesthouse looking for me – that his injuries might not be as bad as he was making out. 'I couldn't bring myself to tell him who I was there and then, but I can't go home without talking to him.' I nearly told him I'd arranged to meet Jack later on, but something stopped me. Knowledge was power, and Owen had too much of that already.

The women at the next table were leaving, fiddling with coats and scarves while casting us covert glances.

'What's the plan?' Owen's eyes tightened. 'You're going to go over there and break the news if Caitlin doesn't tell him first?'

'Something like that.' I couldn't read his expression. 'When he leaves, Caitlin will need someone to turn to.'

He gave an exasperated snort. 'You think it's that simple?'

A flush threaded across my skin. 'It could be,' I said. 'We'll both benefit from Jack leaving.'

'Caitlin loves him.' He bowed his head between tense shoulders. 'She won't give him up without a fight.'

'Neither will I.'

He raised his eyes, and I saw the strain in them. 'Your neighbour seemed to think you were making a big mistake, and it's better for you and your son that he stays away.'

I was desperate to know exactly what Harriet had said but wouldn't ask. 'It's none of her business,' I said icily. 'She doesn't know what she's talking about.' *Bloody Harriet.* My resolve to move away strengthened, the sooner the better.

'Do you think he's a danger to Caitlin?'

Startled out of my repressed fury, I managed a cautious, 'Maybe.' *Tread carefully, Lydia. Don't go saying the first thing that springs to mind.* My mum seemed to be taking up residence in my head. 'Once he finds out she's lied to him.'

'That's what I'm worried about.' Owen's words were quiet,

almost as if he was speaking to himself. 'Especially as it's not the first time.'

The silence that fell was underscored by the distant rush of the sea. Cold air pushed through the door as the women left the café.

'He told me he couldn't forgive her. He felt let down.' It was a risky statement, when I hadn't a clue what Owen was talking about, but he nodded.

'That's why it was a shock when she told me they were back together,' he said, as if temporarily forgetting I was the enemy. 'He wanted a family and finding out she'd had a termination without telling him . . .' He gave a slow shake of his head, eyes distant. 'It broke them. Caitlin said there was no coming back from that.'

For some reason, it surprised me that Caitlin had confided in Owen Whittaker, but maybe she'd believed they had a future together and didn't want any secrets coming out later. 'Sounds like it was serious between the two of you.' I was desperate to steer him away from his revelation in case he guessed I hadn't known. *Poor Jack.* So upright and honest – and keen to be a father. Discovering Caitlin's betrayal must have destroyed him.

'I thought it was.' A chill settled in Owen's voice. 'I thought it could be again if he wasn't on the scene.' A frown darkened his brow. 'You think if you jog his memory, he'll leave her just like that?'

'He hates being lied to.'

Owen's eyes hardened. 'Why do you care so much? It sounds like you were in an abusive relationship, and it's not your first.'

I felt like throttling Harriet. 'You wouldn't understand.'

'Let me guess.' Seeming more in control, he rested his forearms on the table, giving an imperceptible shake of his head as the waitress approached. 'You seek out men who are damaged, or have emotional baggage, and think you can fix them.'

It wasn't a question. 'No one understands other people's relationships.'

'I know when a relationship isn't healthy.'

His words stoked a flicker of anger. When the waitress had retreated, I tipped towards him, almost knocking over my empty mug. 'Like when you stalked your ex-girlfriend and she had to take out a restraining order?' I pushed my chair back, grabbing my coat off the back. 'You're not the only one rooting about for information on the internet, Owen *Whittaker*.'

Braced for an angry response, I was surprised when he grimaced, as though I'd aimed a punch at his stomach. 'That was a long time ago.' His voice was pained. 'She lied to the police because I asked for the engagement ring back that belonged to my grandmother, but even so, I should have let it go. I learnt a lot from that experience.'

He sounded so sincere, I wondered for a moment whether I'd read him wrong.

It wouldn't be the first time, Lydia. Mum was starting to get on my nerves.

'Well done for victim blaming.' I didn't bother hiding my scorn. 'Typical male bullshit.'

Owen's eyebrows rose, but he didn't respond. He didn't look away either and my eyelid flickered with nerves. 'Anyway, I'll be gone tomorrow.' I pushed my arms into the sleeves of my coat. 'You won't see us again.'

'You're very sure of yourself.'

I pulled my hat out of my pocket. 'What are you going to do?'

He considered for a moment, perhaps weighing up how the situation might benefit him. *He should be thanking me.* He would be there for Caitlin, picking up the pieces when Jack left her again.

'I'll see how things play out,' he said, and although I wanted to extract something more – a promise that he wouldn't do anything to jeopardise my plan – I had the sense not to say anything. Instead I gave a tight-lipped smile before heading into the late afternoon, where storm clouds were gathering above the grey and squally sea. As I headed back to the guesthouse with the wind pushing at my back, I felt a rush of elation. Knowing the truth about Jack and Caitlin's separation would make it so much easier to prise them apart again.

To keep up the pretence that I was eating out, I left the guest-house just after seven and stashed my overnight bag in the car, grateful to leave after mindlessly watching television and checking the time every five minutes, going over and over in my head the likely outcomes of tonight. There was only one I could accept: driving away with Jack.

I left my room key in the lock inside for Mel to find in the morning. She was unlikely to check I was there tonight and would assume I'd left before breakfast.

I wondered whether Owen would tell her why I'd really been staying in Robin Hood's Bay. I thought of the look on his face when I mentioned the restraining order. If I'd misjudged him and he'd changed, perhaps he would be good for Caitlin. She'd opened up to him about her past, after all – which was more than she'd done with her husband.

I was desperate for midnight to arrive, wondering how I was going to fill the remaining time. Outside, the temperature had dipped as darkness fell and an icy breeze worked its way inside my coat. A salt and vinegar tang in the air drew me across the car park to the Fish Box at the top of the hill. Inside, the seating area was busy with customers despite the weather and time of year.

I bought a portion of cod and chips and took it outside, sitting on a low wall to eat, warmth from the carton seeping into my fingers. For a moment, I gave myself over to the pleasure of hot, fluffy potato and crispy batter, until I remembered the last time I'd eaten fish and chips, on holiday in Cornwall with William and Mattie, when a seagull had swooped down, and William dropped his chips and was annoyed when I couldn't stop laughing. Remembering that evening had ended with shouts and slaps, I stood abruptly and dropped the half-full carton in a waste bin before trudging back to the car. Inside, I closed my eyes, holding my hands in front of the heater and rehearsing my lines once more.

You love me, Jack. And you love my son. He misses you. We both do.

I called Mattie, but it went to voicemail. I didn't know what to say, so texted instead: **I love you. Home soon xx**

I imagined his face when Jack walked in, and how he would forgive me for everything, his face melting into the ready smile he'd worn as a toddler. He'd been so much easier than during his baby months when he'd cried constantly, and I'd struggled with breastfeeding and postnatal depression and William had taken the reins.

I turned on the radio and one of Jack's favourite songs snaked around me, a soppy ballad by Westlife that I'd teased him about. Pain spread through me as I remembered our first date; walking over Westminster Bridge, stopping so I could take a photo of him pinching Big Ben between his finger and thumb, like a proper tourist, the Thames spread either side of the bridge, rippling under the sunshine. We'd been happy – happier than I'd felt in a long time.

My eyes closed, tiredness rolling in like a wave I couldn't fight. When I woke with a start, my limbs were cold and stiff, my neck muscles tight, but my brain felt clear and receptive.

It was gone eleven. Flooded with energy and unable to wait any longer, I got out of the car and stretched. I would walk down the hill, past the steep maze of dimly lit alleys and tightly packed houses, to the slipway to look at the one-time smuggler's tunnel that Jack had mentioned – had probably explored in the past with Caitlin.

As I made my way there, it was easy to picture the place as it had been a couple of centuries ago, huge waves crashing into the sea wall at high tide, ships heading close to the jagged rocks, sailors disembarking in the shadow of darkness.

The entrance to the tunnel was beneath the hotel above, accessed from the beach. The tide was out tonight, the rolling water glinting under moonlight. It was quiet, apart from the lapping of waves. I shuddered, glancing around, feeling as if I was the only person alive.

Boots sinking into damp sand, I moved inside, shining the torch on my phone around. It smelt dank, the sides of the tunnel damp and green with moss. A smaller shaft opened up on my right, wooden timbers above my head that looked like the floor-boards of houses above.

The area's smuggling past felt suddenly close and I didn't like it. I imagined pirates snaking along the tunnels looking for places to store their contraband, the bar overhead filled with locals swigging beer and singing sea shanties.

Turning to leave, my phone light caught a movement at the mouth of the tunnel.

'Who's there?' Ice swept over my chest. 'Hello?'

I hurried forward, cursing myself for coming down here alone, slipping a little as I emerged, peering out to see a figure disappearing with a lopsided gait.

'Wait!'

In my hurry to follow Jack – it had to be him – I dropped my phone, swearing as I wasted precious seconds stooping and scrabbling around to retrieve it.

By the time I looked up, he'd gone.

Panting, my heart jumping with nerves, I followed the now familiar path to Sea View Cottage, braced for Jack to jump out any second. But everywhere was quiet again, no sign that anyone was about. As my heartbeat slowed, I began to wonder whether I'd conjured him up, my fevered imagination getting the better of me, fired by the idea of smugglers sneaking about underground.

Perhaps Jack was on the lookout at the cottage. I pictured him upstairs, glancing through the bedroom window and seeing me arrive.

For a split second I allowed myself to wonder whether he'd told Caitlin I'd called him, but some sixth sense told me he hadn't. Her car was outside the cottage, lit by a lantern on the front wall. The downstairs windows were dark, a curl of smoke hanging in the air above the chimney. It reminded me of a child's drawing of a home and for a moment, I felt a savage desire to kick down the door, force my way in and grab hold of Jack, pulling him away from his cosy set-up.

Hearing a sound, I spun around, my face numb with cold. The sea was an oily black swell, lit by a shimmering trail of moonlight, the cliffs a jagged outline against the sky.

'Hello?' I said for the second time that night, my voice barely more than a whisper, carried away on the wind. A strand of hair worked free and blew in front of my eyes, almost obscuring a stirring of activity further down the path. *I hadn't been imagining someone was there, after all.* I edged closer to the fence, glancing up at the cottage. No lights on upstairs. Hopefully, Caitlin was in bed, asleep. Another sound, closer, made my pulse leap. Fear kicked in as I realised that no one knew I was here. Unless . . . I looked around again, eyes straining through the darkness. Could Owen be there, keeping an eye on me? Oddly, the thought wasn't as frightening as it should be. He was looking out for Caitlin – that was all. She was lucky, really. *But what about the limp?* I hadn't imagined that earlier – unless Owen was impersonating Jack.

I risked a glimpse at my phone. *Not long until midnight.* Would Jack be on time, or was he waiting to make sure that Caitlin wouldn't be disturbed by him leaving? Perhaps he would make an excuse about needing some air. *Or maybe he was out here already.*

My breath shortened, confusion prickling over me like a rash. I paced up and down, soles slipping on the muddy track. 'Come on, come on,' I muttered, my breath filming the air, stomach cramping with nerves.

'I'm over here.'

My head whipped round at the sound of the loud whisper. 'Jack?'

196

'I'll meet you on the beach.' His voice sounded different, angry almost. He must be terrified of Caitlin discovering he'd gone. The thought – that he cared about her reaction – brought a rush of rage. I could see the figure again, ahead, moving in the direction I'd walked with Caitlin before that led down to the beach.

'Jack, wait!' I began to hurry, fiddling with my phone to find the torch once more.

I glanced up but could no longer make out the shape of him in the dark. 'Jack?'

Cold fingers of fright touched the back of my neck. I stopped, hearing nothing but the ceaseless sound of the sea and the blood pounding my ears. 'Jack!'

Sensing movement, I began to turn, in time to see a figure right behind me, holding something aloft, moonlight glinting off metal. Before I could scream, a jarring pain exploded across the back of my skull. With a hollow cry, I staggered forwards and lost my footing, tumbling down the slippery path onto sand, smacking my head on a boulder. There was a moment of terror and searing, red-hot agony before everything went black.

Chapter 24

Caitlin

I was pitching on the edge of sleep when a noise filtered into my mind, like a latch turning. Used to the sounds of the cottage I recognised the faint creak of the back door. I grabbed my phone off the bedside table. *Nearly midnight.*

Lurching out of bed, I reached for the cardigan I'd thrown off earlier and pulled it over my pyjamas. The pillow next to mine looked cold and empty in a strip of moonlight. Jack hadn't come to bed.

After his lengthy afternoon snooze – though I wasn't convinced he'd been asleep the whole time – he'd claimed he wasn't tired, despite the hooded appearance of his eyes that signalled exhaustion.

The atmosphere had been strained all evening. I hadn't known how to chat naturally, knowing I was on the verge of blowing our relationship apart yet again. Jack had seemed equally uncertain, absorbing himself first in a book, then a TV quiz show while we ate the rest of Beverley's casserole – he picked around the meat as if he'd remembered he was vegetarian – before asking if he could use my laptop to check out a few things. I couldn't think of a way to say no but felt weak with relief when the Wi-Fi signal failed, and he couldn't get online.

'What do you want to look up?

'I thought I might see what Dad's been up to, maybe message him and let him know . . .' for a heart-stopping moment, I'd had the oddest sensation he was going to say *that we're back together*, but he continued, '. . . about the accident and moving here.' He gave me a narrow look I barely recognised. 'I take it you haven't told him we've left Brighton?'

'It wasn't my place,' I said, flushed and panicky. 'Remember at the hospital, I said I would call him for you when you're ready.'

'I was going to check out his Facebook page, see what he's been up to.'

Rosita had set up the page so she and Neil could post snippets about their life in Italy in the hope Jack wouldn't be able to resist looking, but he never had when we'd been together.

When I'd accepted her friend request, giving access to a string of posts about their new puppy, dinners out with friends, photos of her and Neil on the beach, and not-so-subtle invites for 'loved ones' to come and visit alongside heartfelt 'missing family in the UK' messages, Jack refused to look.

If they're happy, good, but I don't want them rubbing it in my face.

So why look now? It had felt as though he was testing me, but I couldn't work out why. Unless he'd remembered something that went further back than Lydia.

All at once, my mind had tumbled back to the terrible day he walked out. It had started with him bursting into the apartment on a Thursday lunchtime a few days after Christmas, bits of compost and moss clinging to his gardening clothes, a wild look on his face I'd never seen before.

'What is it?' I leapt off the sofa where I'd been nursing a cold, feeling sorry for myself because a commission had fallen through.

'Is it true?'

199

Instantly, I knew what he was talking about. It was the moment I'd been dreading for years on some level. I didn't bother pretending. 'Jack, I'm so sorry—'

He doubled over as though I'd kicked him, hands plunging into his hair. 'I didn't want to believe it.'

For a moment, I thought I was going to be sick and managed to whisper, 'Who told you?'

He straightened, eyes wide and dazed with disbelief. 'That gardening job, this morning. Carol Trainor?' I closed my eyes, swaying slightly. 'Her daughter was there, visiting from New Zealand.' His voice sounded raw, as though he'd been shouting. 'You remember your friend Louise?'

Of course I remembered Louise. She'd been the third side of the friendship triangle with Dee and me – the baker of the lumpy cakes – through university and beyond, before we lost touch after she went to New Zealand with her dad when her parents divorced.

Dee had been on holiday with her boyfriend the weekend I discovered I was pregnant. I'd told Louise first, breaking down because I was terrified; too young, I wasn't ready to be a parent. I'd only been seeing Jack for two months, and he'd gone travelling for the summer with friends. I wasn't even sure we had a future at that point, or whether I was ready to settle down, and my career was just taking off.

I don't know what to do, Lou.

It's up to you, Caitlin. Your body, your future.

I'd recently begun taking the Pill and could only think it hadn't started working properly. My periods were normally so regular, I'd known even before taking a test why I'd missed one.

I don't want him to feel forced into staying with me and I don't want to be a single mum.

You're only a couple of weeks along, Caitlin. There are options.

It was an option I'd never thought myself capable of taking, had never considered I would have to, yet when it was over – after an initial storm of tears and sadness – I felt relieved.

Louise – and Dee, when she returned and heard the news – had been at pains to reassure me it meant I'd made the right decision, that it hadn't been the right time.

When Jack came back a month later and gathered me into his arms, burying his face in my hair and saying how much he'd missed me, more than he'd thought possible, and could we please be together – *properly, if you'll have me, Caitlin, and I'm talking 'meet your parents' properly* – I couldn't find the words to tell him what I'd done. The moment to come clean had passed and I'd resigned myself to carrying my secret forever if I wanted us to stay together. It was a decision I wasn't proud of, and had fretted over with Dee, but in the end had agreed there was no point risking losing the man I loved over a choice I'd had every right to make. But I'd known it was more than that. I didn't want him to think less of me.

Only when faced with his absolute devastation did I truly understand what a terrible mistake I'd made in keeping it from him.

'I don't know why Louise chose to tell you now,' I managed, swallowing tears I had no right to cry. 'I couldn't tell you, Jack . . . I just . . . It wasn't the right time. We weren't ready to be parents—'

'We could have made it work,' he cut in, tears shining in his eyes, the sight of them worse than hearing the anger and loathing in his voice, and I didn't dare tell him that, lately, I'd found myself picturing what our child would have looked like; whether it would have been a boy or a girl; what sort of parents we'd have been. He might tell me what I already knew – that I wasn't worthy of being a mother. 'You didn't give me a choice, Caitlin.' He dropped onto the arm of the sofa like a puppet whose strings had been cut. 'And it wasn't Louise who told me. Carol made me some coffee and was asking after you, and whether we were planning to start a family, and she turned to Louise and said, "Was it Caitlin who got rid of a baby years ago? It would have been nearly seven now," and the look on Lou's face . . .' He huffed out a bitter, disbelieving laugh through bloodless lips, while the words *nearly seven now* tore through me. 'She just said, "Mum, for God's sake," and couldn't meet my eyes, so I knew it had happened when we were together. Her mum must have thought I knew, or that it happened with someone else.'

Tears blocked my throat. Of course Louise had told her mum. They'd always been close, Lou used to tell her everything before she emigrated with her dad and broke her mother's heart. Carol – a big, warm-hearted, gossipy woman – tended to say whatever came into her head, so I shouldn't have been surprised she blurted it out like that. 'It was a horrible, thoughtless thing to say.'

'Well, I'm glad she did,' Jack said, twisting the knife. 'Or I would never have known what you're really like.'

I found out later that Louise had tried calling me to apologise, leaving a frantic voicemail after Jack left her mum's house, but my phone had been charging in the bedroom and I hadn't heard it. Not that it made any difference. The damage was done and there was no one to blame but myself.

When Jack had thundered upstairs to throw some things in a rucksack, I'd followed, my heart burning and breaking, knowing that pleading, crying, and begging for forgiveness wouldn't work. In Jack's eyes, we were done.

And here I was now, deceiving him again, so desperate to be with him that it hadn't occurred to me to be honest at the hospital before grabbing my second chance. Perhaps it was in my nature to try to get what I wanted by any means. *Had I learnt nothing?*

As Jack watched me over the laptop, I forced down the rising tide of emotion mottling my face and waited for him to say it: *I've remembered everything, Caitlin.* But instead, he dropped his gaze back to the screen and said flatly, 'Maybe it's as well I can't get online, but I would like to speak to Dad.'

Instead of relief, a coil of tension fastened around my ribs.

'Maybe once we've seen Dee.'

'Maybe.'

It had been my turn to plead a headache before heading upstairs where I messaged Dee that we would be leaving first thing in the morning.

Sure you don't want me to come up there tonight, babe? I can leave now. X

No, I'm fine, but thanks X

I jumped when another text arrived, this time from Owen.

Spoke to Lydia today. I know what's going on. My legs trembled and my head began to swim. I sank onto the bed, fighting an overwhelming nausea. **You should come clean before someone else does.** Did he mean her, or was he planning on telling Jack the truth himself?

It took several goes to get my reply out: **I'm going to tell him.**

Falling back onto the pillow, tears trickling into my ears, feeling as if bits of my heart were breaking off once more, I willed morning to come quickly as I laid wide-eyed in the dark, my stomach churning with dread at what was to come – until the click of the door downstairs jolted me into action.

Now, I stood at the window and looked out, expecting to see Jack lit by the moon, perhaps getting some air in the garden, working through whatever was on his mind.

I darted my gaze around, trying to make out a person in the darkness. Across the bay, the sea glittered, water rippling in the rock pools on the beach, stars glittering in the velvet-black sky above.

I longed to feel Jack's arms around my waist, and the gentle weight of his chin in the dip of my shoulder, the way I had the first time he came to the cottage when we'd slept in the room next door, being quiet so as not to wake my grandfather.

I caught my breath and pressed closer to the window, glimpsing a sudden change in the shadows beyond the fence. My breath misted the glass and I swiped it clear, but if Jack had been there, he'd gone now, merging with the darkness.

My gaze switched to the outline of the car. I tensed,

half-expecting it to start and Jack to drive off, but of course he wouldn't be able to drive with his injured ankle.

I edged out of the bedroom and paused on the landing. Maybe I'd misheard and Jack hadn't gone outside at all. I held my breath, trying to sense his presence, wondering why I wasn't rushing down to check that he was OK. He could have fallen, but would surely have cried out, or made more noise if he had. Unless he was unconscious. Though he hadn't complained of a headache today, he hadn't been himself – the self I thought I knew – and it had only been a few days since his release from hospital.

About to run downstairs, another sound reached me, like someone closing the back door. There was movement in the kitchen and a muffled curse in a familiar tone. My lungs emptied. It was Jack, not an intruder. It sounded as though he'd bumped into something. The kitchen door squeaked open, and he came into the hall. I darted back into the bedroom and pulled the door to as his lopsided tread came up the stairs.

Through the gap, I watched him head into the spare room where he clicked on the light, a strip of yellow spilling onto the landing. I was trembling all over and drew my cardigan tightly around me. Boxes were being shifted and drawers pulled open. I felt his frustration winding under the door.

Unable to stand it any longer, knowing it would seem odd if I pretended to be undisturbed, I forced myself forward and into the room, blinking in the glare.

'What are you looking for?'

Jack looked up from the dresser drawer he'd been rifling through, seeming surprised to see me. He looked dishevelled and smelt of cold air, panting as though he'd been hurrying. 'I can't find my leather jacket.' My heart sank at his new, accusatory tone. 'The one I got for my eighteenth birthday.'

'I know which one you mean.' He'd been wearing it the day he left, and I realised with a new wrench of anguish that Lydia must have it. 'I . . . I guess it must have—'

'Got lost in the move?' The sarcastic tint to his voice was also new. Jack had always preferred a more direct and positive approach, partly a result of the therapy he'd had after his mother's death. *What had happened to the Jack I brought home from hospital, grateful to be here, loving our time together, keen to look forward? Had I done this to him?*

He held something up, deep suspicion in his gaze. 'I found this though.'

Nausea crept up to my throat when I recognised the Christmas card he was waving. He'd obviously seen the message inside but opened the card and read aloud: '"Here's to a better year, Caitlin. You've got this. All my love, Dee." What does she mean, and why is it made out to you and not both of us?'

Why had I kept it? Hardly anyone sent me cards, apart from my parents, but Dee and I had a tradition of picking something funny or quirky at Christmas, and hers, depicting a row of miserable elves and the caption, *The Most Wonderful Time of the Year – allegedly*, had made me smile. My first Christmas without Jack, spent with my parents, congratulating myself on getting through the year intact while trying not to think about Christmases past – the little presents we couldn't resist opening on Christmas Eve; drinking Buck's Fizz in bed on Christmas morning, carols playing in the background because they made us feel festive. Jack's face, a mix of love and pride when he opened his card from me, an illustration I'd work on for several days, the last one depicting him wearing a Santa hat, holding a spade, a heap of dug-up parcels by his feet, the words inside: *You're the only gift I need.*

I'd resolved to try harder with Owen when I got home. He'd asked what the card from Dee meant too, spotting it when he called round with a badly wrapped present – a fruit bowl made of sea-glass that I'd accidentally smashed a few days later – and in a moment of weakness I'd told him why Jack had left me, perhaps seeing it as a chance to get closer. He'd barely responded, beyond a nod, before drawing me into his arms and kissing my hair, and never referred to it again.

Jack was waiting, eyebrows lowered, his mouth a thin line.

'I was worried about work, that's all. I'd finished the illustrations for Emma's books and didn't have any new stuff.' My voice was weak, but it wasn't a lie. It just wasn't why Dee had sent me a card without Jack's name inside. 'She was trying to cheer me up.' I hugged myself, fear circling my body and making me shiver more violently. 'You know Dee's sense of humour.'

His expression shuffled between relief and doubt. 'It's silly how not remembering little things is starting to get to me,' he said at last, dropping the card back in the drawer. 'I can picture us putting up the tree at the flat and lifting you up so you could stick that angel thing on the top that you dragged out every year.' The one that had sat on top of the tree at my parents' house during all the Christmases of my childhood. 'Your dad set the pudding alight as usual, but didn't blow out the match before putting it down and the tablecloth nearly caught fire.'

A lump crept into my throat, emotions rising. 'It wasn't last Christmas,' I whispered, wondering for the first time how he and Lydia and her son had spent the day. 'I'm sorry, Jack.'

There was a touch of defensiveness in his frown. 'It's not your fault.' When I dropped my gaze to the faded pink carpet that had been there as long as I could remember, his tone changed. 'Cait, is there something I should know?'

Not now. Please, not now. 'I'm just really tired,' I said, a dragging feeling in my bones. 'We should get some sleep.'

He came closer and, before I could move, wrapped me in a hug so tight I could barely breathe. 'I love you, Caitlin.'

Tears filled my eyes. I tried to move away, but his grip strengthened even though it must be hurting his ribs. A bubble of panic expanded in my chest.

'Jack . . .'

He let go, saying, 'Let's go to bed.'

I felt as if I was floating. 'I'll check the place is locked up first.' I sidled past him and ran downstairs, heart thumping my chest. The back door was secure, but the mat had shifted slightly, suggesting it had recently been stood on. The kitchen felt cold and unfamiliar, a faint smell of casserole lingering. For a second, I longed for the reassuring presence of Toby, whose gruff bark had belied his friendly nature, certain to scare off unwanted visitors.

I hurried into the living room, where the fire had almost burnt out. My laptop was open on the sofa as though Jack had abandoned it before going outside. Hearing the bathroom light come on upstairs, I hurried over and sat down, pressing the enter key on the laptop. A gallery of photos sprang up: holidays, Christmases, our wedding day, Mum and Dad on their thirtieth wedding anniversary, our friends at various gatherings, images of Jack and me on a road trip we'd taken through Scotland in a camper van, stopping by lochs and forests, cooking on a camping stove, our faces tanned and happy. I'd done lots of sketching on that trip, and Jack had tried his hand – unsuccessfully – at fishing. *I'm glad I was useless, because when you think about it, it's cruel.*

Had he been taking a trip down memory lane, or looking for something in particular? More recent pictures, perhaps, of me with Owen? I'd deleted the few I had from my phone after I ended our relationship, and as far as I knew, he didn't have any on his.

My head was starting to pound, and my palms were damp. I checked the search history in case the Wi-Fi had leapt into action, pulse skittering as I read the most recently closed page: *Symptoms of amnesia.*

'You're not working, are you?'

A scream flew out. 'God, Jack! You scared me.'

'You always were jumpy.' There was a snap in his voice that I didn't like.

'I was just switching it off.' I slammed the lid of the laptop, wondering how long he'd been standing there and whether he'd seen what I was looking at. 'I'm coming up now.'

Chapter 25

Lydia

'I'd like to leave now, please.'

The nurse looked faintly alarmed to see me out of bed and struggling with my coat. 'Wait a minute, Lydia.'

'I'm absolutely fine.'

'Of course you're free to go, but why not wait to see the doctor first.'

'I've been here all night. There's nothing wrong with me.' Filled with panic, I looked around the quiet ward, feeling afresh the horror of waking up in hospital.

When I had opened my eyes on the beach last night to see flashing blue lights burning through the darkness, I'd thought the police were there. I lashed out at the paramedic bent over me, trying to shine a light in my eyes, then almost fainted when pain lanced through my skull.

I was carried into the back of the waiting ambulance on a stretcher, unable to do more than feebly protest, pushing away hands that tried to examine me, barely able to concentrate on the questions being gently but persistently asked.

Yes, I knew my name and where I was. *I slipped and fell while out walking and hit my head.*

I'd felt something warm and sticky by my eye, and when I touched it my fingers came away bloody.

Yes, I can see how many fingers you're holding up. Three.

No, I don't need you to call anyone. I'm here on holiday, alone.

I had no intention of telling them what actually happened, still unable to believe it myself.

'You were lucky, Lydia,' the female paramedic had said slowly, as though addressing a child. 'Someone saw you take a tumble and called 999.'

My assailant? It seemed unlikely anyone else would have been out that late.

'Did they see what happened?' I'd longed to leap up and out of the speeding ambulance, but even speaking was an effort, my words slurring a little. *Jack.* I flinched, recalling the weapon that had struck me, not wanting to acknowledge the image lodged in my mind. It had looked like a crutch. *But if Jack was responsible, why call for help?*

It was more likely Caitlin. She'd found out – or he had told her – we'd arranged to meet and wanted to warn me off. Not kill me, hence her calling an ambulance, but to send a clear message to me that she wasn't letting Jack go. Or maybe she *had* intended me to die, but Owen had been there, saw what happened and decided to do the right thing.

Answering the paramedic's questions on autopilot, while fighting waves of sickness and pain, I'd struggled to make sense of it all, insisting I was fine to go home before sliding into exhausted semi-consciousness.

On waking, there had been a few seconds of terror as I tried to work out where I was, until everything rushed back in gaudy technicolour. *I couldn't be here.* I had to talk to Jack.

The pain in my head had dulled to a throbbing ache, and a couple of butterfly stitches had stopped the bleeding near my

210

temple. The nurse who spotted I was awake had taken my blood pressure and told me again that I was at the Whitby Urgent Care Centre, as if she thought I might have lost my memory. The irony almost made me laugh.

'If you start being sick, or feel dizzy, or the pain worsens, you must get someone to take you straight to hospital, but apart from a sore head, I think you'll be fine.' I'd thought of Jack then, coming round in a hospital bed. A cold chill clasped my throat as the urge to laugh died away.

As soon as the nurse had moved down the ward, I rolled out of bed and pulled on my clothes, which were draped over a chair, gritting my teeth through a wave of agony.

'Lydia, sit down for a moment.' Jolting me back to the moment, the nurse cupped my elbow and steered me back to the bed. 'While you were being examined, it was noted you had some . . . injuries.' She turned my palm over as if to show me the scar there. 'Some old bruises up your arm.'

I snatched my hand away, making an attempt at a smile, but my lips had stuck to my teeth. There was a horrible taste in my mouth and my tongue felt swollen. 'I'm actually on holiday, would you believe?' I tried to do up the zip on my coat, but my hands were trembling too much. My head felt like the inside of a washing machine. 'I couldn't sleep and decided to go for a walk, which was silly after all the rain, and I took a tumble.' Tumble was such an innocent word. I wished it was true.

'These were old injuries.' The nurse's voice was unbearably kind. I fought an urge to throw myself into her arms and cry. 'There are people you can talk to—'

'Honestly, I'm very clumsy.' The little laugh I tried didn't come off, emerging as a hiccup. 'I know what you're thinking, but you're wrong.'

Her look said, *That's what they all say*, but she didn't press it, reaching past me to the unit by the bed. 'This was found next to you on the beach.'

211

She unfolded a crumpled sheet of paper and held it up, a few grains of sand slipping to the floor. As the words reached my brain, sweat broke out on my upper lip. **GO HOME** was written in bold capitals, in thick black ink.

'Lydia?' The nurse leant over and placed an arm around my shoulders. 'Did someone deliberately hurt you last night?'

Yes. I pulled in a breath and breathed out slowly, waiting for the sickness to subside. 'Of course not.' I looked away from the instruction – because that's what it was. The same two words that someone had left for me at the guesthouse. *Caitlin?* She must use pens like that for her artwork. Probably not toothpaste though. 'I already told you what happened. I've no idea what that even means.' In spite of everything, the last thing I wanted was to get the police involved. 'It could have blown onto the beach from anywhere. It wasn't intended for me.' I was overcome with an intense wave of exhaustion. 'Like I said, I'm visiting the area. I'm staying at a guesthouse in Robin Hood's Bay.' I wondered whether Mel had realised I wasn't there. 'I have to get back, or they'll wonder where I am.'

I dug in my coat pocket, thankful to feel my phone, and pulled it out, only to find the battery was dead. 'What time is it?'

'Just after seven,' the nurse said with an air of resignation, crumpling the piece of paper into a ball. She knew she wouldn't get any more information out of me. I hoped she would leave it at that. 'I can call you a taxi if you insist on leaving.'

'I do, thank you.'

On the journey back to the guesthouse, I stared out at the gloomy scenery, barely lit by a heavy grey sky that looked swollen with rain, avoiding the curious glances of the taxi driver and his attempts at conversation.

Not really holiday weather, is it, love? What happened to you, then?

A glance at my reflection in the window showed a thin, ghostly pale face, and ratty hair that hid the painful lump on the back of my scalp, thankfully overlooked at the hospital, the focus on the bleeding gash by my temple, where bruising had started to bloom. *What would Jack make of it?*

The thought of Jack made my mind fuzzy, and my breathing quicken. It would have taken strength to wield that crutch, but he was wiry from his years of gardening. And I'd definitely heard him call me away from the cottage last night, and was sure he'd followed me to the tunnel, earlier.

How can you be certain? Owen had asked when I told him Jack couldn't remember me. The truth was, I couldn't. I'd assumed he was no good at pretending, had seen for myself how easily he reacted in the moment, had flinched from the raw honesty in his eyes, but . . . maybe I was wrong.

I began to shake in the back seat, anger and frustration boiling in my stomach. It wasn't supposed to be like this, everyone getting in the way – Caitlin, Owen, Harriet . . . Fury fizzled whenever I thought of Harriet spilling my secrets to Owen over the phone – even Jack himself.

I thought of Mattie, and how light he'd been after Jack came into our lives, and the way that darkness had descended once he'd gone. I badly wanted to call my son and hear his voice, but remembered my phone was dead. How would he feel, if he knew about all this; if the worst had happened last night and he'd received a call to say I was dead? The thought was unbearable, and resolve hardened like concrete in my chest. Jack had to come back to London with me and give our relationship another chance. I still had my trump card – the one I desperately didn't want to play but would if I had to. *I could have him arrested any time I chose.*

After paying the driver with the debit card I kept in my phone case, I slipped into the guesthouse and up the stairs before I was seen. Chatter floated out of the dining room – the guests who had turned up the day before, no doubt early risers – and smells of cooking drifted from the kitchen. My stomach growled, but I knew if I tried to eat anything I would throw it back up.

My room was as I'd left it but, too late, I remembered my bag was now stowed in the car.

I made a drink, using the last teabag, then threw myself under the shower, running the water as hot as I could stand, steam billowing as I scrubbed myself clean with the hand soap from the basin, then emptied the complimentary bottle of shampoo on my hair and worked up a lather, grinding my teeth as my fingers dodged the bump on the back of my head. If I was going to claim Jack, I didn't want to turn up looking like someone he would cross the road to avoid, let alone have a child with one day.

Wrapped in a towel, I blow-dried my hair with the dryer I found in the drawer of the bedside table, running my fingers through the silky strands in lieu of a comb, arranging it to fall across the stitch-tape at the side of my head. There wasn't much I could do to disguise the deepening bruise forming. I didn't use make-up and considered for a moment asking Mel if she had some I could borrow, but it would mean explaining – involving her further in the drama my visit had turned into – and I couldn't bear it.

Instead, I pulled on my woolly hat, tugging it low but keeping some hair down to frame my face. I tried out a smile, to make my eyes twinkle, but something was off. The nerve that twitched in my eyelid – I wished I could turn it off – and that I was the sort of person who naturally had some colour in their cheeks. It struck me I'd lost too much weight; that I wasn't the person Jack had fallen in love with, but that was easily resolved. Once he was home, I would start cooking healthy meals, and Mattie would help like he used to, chopping onions while he chatted about his day.

Fired with enthusiasm, a spark finally entered my eyes, so I looked more like the me I wanted to be, even if my clothes looked like they'd been slept in.

In the car – thankfully unseen as I left the guesthouse for the final time – I rummaged through my bag and pulled out the top I'd worn the day I arrived. I slipped it on, then brushed the worst of the sand and dirt from my coat. My boots were fit for the rubbish bin but would have to do for now.

As I turned on the engine, attaching my phone to the in-car charger before switching up the heaters to banish the chill, Mel materialised on the doorstep.

Gritting my teeth, aware of a faint pounding behind my eyes, I buzzed the window down. 'Morning!' It came out sounding strangled.

'No breakfast before you go?' Mel wrapped her arms around herself, clearly unwilling to step into the rain that had started falling like needles.

'I wanted to make an early start,' I called in my chattiest voice. Owen obviously hadn't mentioned my real reason for being here. *Yet.* 'Long drive home.'

'OK, well, I hope you enjoyed your stay.'

Recalling the toothpaste message daubed on the bathroom mirror, I doubted I would be putting a five-star review on TripAdvisor, but I nodded, regretting the movement when my vision began to swim. 'Thank you for having me.'

Mel waved and retreated, firmly shutting the door. It felt oddly like a snub – as if she was glad to see the back of me and rush back to her nice, normal guests, who appreciated her hospitality. Resisting the urge to go over and kick the door – I didn't have the energy and the rain was hammering down – I swung the car round, wondering whether I could drive down the track to Sea View Cottage, or park further down the road, out of Mel's view, and wait for the rain to ease before making my way there on foot.

I didn't want to risk the car tyres getting stuck in mud, so decided to wait it out, wishing I'd thought to bring some pain-killers. Whatever I'd been given at the hospital was wearing off, as was the caffeine rush from the strong tea I'd drunk in my room. My temple was throbbing, and pain radiated from the back of my head to my neck.

When my phone rang, I snatched it up, hoping it was Mattie, but it was Shona's voice I heard.

'Lyddie, thank God. I was worried about you,' she said in response to my curt *Hello*. 'I tried to call you last night and you didn't reply or answer my texts.'

'My battery died. I only just realised,' I said, rubbing my fingers across my forehead. 'Why were you calling?' A burst of adrenaline cleared my vision. 'Is it Mattie? What's happened?'

'No, it's nothing to do with Mattie. Well, only in as much as I'm not going to lie to him if he calls.' Shona sounded defensive. I imagined her telling her husband what I was up to and him, disapproving as ever, saying she shouldn't get involved, that it wasn't fair to Mattie. As if it had anything to do with Connor.

'You don't have to,' I said frostily. 'I'm going home today, anyway.'

'Oh, Lydia, that's great.' Her tone warmed up once more. 'Did you manage to talk to Jack?'

'I did. He's coming with me.'

Silence swelled at the other end. I wondered whether, like Harriet, Shona had thought I was on a fool's errand, that there was no way I wouldn't be returning alone.

'I just . . . I don't understand why you're doing this, Lydia.'

'I love him, and so does Mattie. It was all one big misunderstanding, that's all.'

'It wasn't though, was it?'

Despair curled through me. I knew she'd seen too much. That time with William, when she'd been staying with us, before she met Connor. She must have overheard the argument, got up to go to the loo, not realising we were in the bathroom.

Despite me whipping a towel off the rail, she'd seen the gouges, the blood, old bruises and scars, her wide eyes reflecting the horror that must have been in mine.

'It's a pattern, Lydia.' Her tone was careful now, like someone trying to calm a nervous animal. 'You can't keep going like this. It's not fair on Mattie—'

'He loves Jack.'

Her sigh was filled with all the things she had said before and knew better than to say again. 'We're going for counselling,' I added, eager to give her a crumb, an affirmation that there would be positive changes in my life. 'Mattie can come too; it will help him understand.'

'Oh, Lydia,' Shona said softly. 'Why not be on your own for a while? You don't need a man.'

'Easy for you to say with Connor, the perfect husband.'

Ignoring my tear-laced sarcasm, she said, 'He's not perfect. No one is. You could talk to someone on your own about changing the way you think about relationships.'

'OK, well, like I said, Jack and I will be home sometime today, so if you've nothing nice to say, I might as well go.'

'Lydia, wait—'

I ended the call and sat for a moment, waiting for the storm of emotion inside me to settle. Who did Shona think she was, telling me how to live my life? Had she always been like that, and I hadn't noticed? Bossy, wrapped in softness. *Bitch.*

Mattie would be thanking me later. I *had* to hold on to that.

As I put my phone back on charge, prepared to get out of the car now the downpour had stopped, leaving glistening puddles on the tarmac, I saw a black Fiesta approaching from the direction of Sea View Cottage.

Pulling my hat low and shrinking down, I stared through the side window as Caitlin drove slowly past, with Jack in the passenger seat. His gaze was angled towards her, and he was smiling at something she'd said. They looked like the perfect couple.

A fuse of anger sizzled, a tornado starting in my head. I stared at the vanishing car in my rear-view mirror, my fingers tightening around the steering wheel. I revved the engine, before spinning the car around, tyres squealing on the wet road as I pulled away.

Wherever they were going, so was I.

Chapter 26

Caitlin

'Did you go outside last night?' It felt safer asking Jack in the car as we headed away from the cottage, gazes fixed on the rain-slicked road. 'I'm sure I heard the back door closing.'

'Why didn't you say something?' His tone was mild, and he gave a faint smile when I glanced at him. 'I heard something, or someone, outside,' he said. 'Or I thought I did. It might have been on the TV.'

'You didn't mention it.'

'There was no one there, so I didn't see the point.'

'Did you think it might be Owen?'

I wasn't sure why I was pursuing it when I wanted to keep things light until we got to Leicester, especially while the air between us felt fraught.

Over a mostly silent breakfast, which we'd struggled to eat, I'd caught a look in his eyes as he watched me, as if I was a puzzle he couldn't solve. It wasn't until I jumped up from the table to rinse my plate that it struck me I was probably looking at him the same way.

'I didn't think sneaking around would be Owen's style,' Jack said. 'But I don't know him as well as you do.'

Nerves prickled over my body. 'I don't know him that well.'

'Don't you?'

'Jack, what is this?' It was as almost as though Lydia had got to him and tipped him off, but the old Jack would have said something instead of tiptoeing around. And how would she have contacted him, anyway?

An image flashed into my head: Jack standing over her with a knife, Lydia cowering in fright before snatching it off him, blood dripping from her palm.

'Careful,' Jack warned, a hand reaching for the steering wheel as I veered across the white lines. A driver coming the other way blasted his horn, headlights flashing.

'Sorry, I'm sorry.' I slowed so abruptly the car behind skidded to a halt, tyres screeching. Expecting another angry toot, or the driver to get out, I was relieved when they didn't react but waited for me to continue.

'You're jumpy this morning,' Jack said.

'I didn't sleep well.'

At least that much was true. I'd finally dropped off around dawn, waking with a start when my phone alarm went off under my pillow. Seeing the screen as I fumbled to switch off the persistent trill – the two nines waiting for a third – I'd felt vaguely ridiculous, closing it down before Jack could see it and ask why I'd been on the verge of phoning the police.

'We don't have to go to see Dee,' he said.

'I want to,' I lied. What I really wanted was to have my marriage back the way it had been before he discovered my lie; for me to have not deceived him in the first place. For him to forgive me. For him to never have met Lydia and treated her badly. 'Dee's expecting us.' On cue, my phone rang. 'That's her now,' I said, connecting through the hands-free system. 'Hi, Dee, we're just leaving Robin Hood's Bay.' I caught Jack's look of surprise. Maybe my jaunty tone hadn't hit the right note.

'What's the weather like up there?'

'Cold and wet.' I tried to imitate the voice I'd always used on the phone with my friend, and not give away that the call had been prearranged.

With the atmosphere so tense over breakfast, and unable to gauge what was going on in Jack's head, I'd quickly messaged Dee from the downstairs toilet. **Call me around eight a.m. Act normally. Jack's being weird.**

Caitlin, I'm worried X

It's fine. You'll be on speaker, so he'll be able to hear you.

I deleted the messages, trying not to react when I opened the door to find Jack standing outside, saying brightly, 'Ready to go?' his ankle boot firmly in place.

'Sorry to hear about your accident, Jack.'

As Dee's bright voice filtered into the car, I risked a glance at his face for signs of anger. I hadn't had a chance to tell him before he left that Dee had known about my pregnancy, but he would have assumed if Louise knew, Dee did too. As Dee had been a party to my deception, Jack would be cold at best if he had any memory of that time, but instead, his face relaxed a little. 'I suppose you've heard I can't remember what happened?'

'Pity,' Dee said. 'Someone out there has got away with dangerous driving, not to mention they could have killed you. Can't you remember anything?'

In my peripheral vision, Jack flinched and brought a hand up to cover his eyes. *Was he having a flashback?* 'I thought I did, but ended up accusing one of the locals,' he said, flashing me a sideways look. 'Owen Whittaker.'

To my relief, Dee didn't bite, saying instead, 'I miss you guys. I'm looking forward to seeing you both.'

'Can't wait,' I said, wishing it was as simple as visiting an old friend. 'We should be there by eleven, so send out a search party if we're late.'

I caught Jack's eye and smiled, hoping it wasn't too much.

'Give me a call ten minutes before you get here, and I'll order drinks.'

'You need that much notice?' Jack's tone was as teasing as it had always been around Dee before that awful day. For a moment, I wondered why I was still doubting him. Why was I making sure that our journey and estimated time of arrival was being logged in case . . . *what*? Jack forced us off the road; took the wheel and demanded to know what I was keeping from him? *Tried to hurt me, like he had Lydia?* My brain hissed with confusion. 'See you soon,' I chirped, ending the call.

'I'm assuming she and Sebastian have broken up?' Jack sounded puzzled, and I remembered that before he'd left, Dee was seeing an old boyfriend she met at a school reunion. It fizzled out soon after and she'd had another short-lived relationship since but was happily single now.

'She prefers being on her own,' I said, my stomach folding over when I realised I would be single too after today. Even if Jack forgave me for hiding the truth, how could we carry on when I knew how he'd treated Lydia? *How could I still love him when he was capable of that?*

As I turned onto the road that took us through the North Yorkshire moors, a faint noise reached me from the back of the car.

'Did you hear that?'

Jack, who had seemed hypnotised by the rhythm of light and shadow flickering past the car window, turned to me with a frown, clearly emerging from some deep thought I couldn't begin to guess at.

'What?'

'Did you hear that scraping noise?'

'Where?' His frown deepened as he turned to look in the back. 'Have you had the car serviced recently?'

I nodded, heat flooding my face as I recalled Owen recommending a garage, where a friend of his gave me a discount. 'It passed its MOT too.'

'Maybe it was something on the road.'

As he shifted, adjusting his seat belt, something struck me. 'Where's your crutch?'

'Sorry?'

'You left your crutch in here yesterday when Beverley turned up.' I adjusted the rear-view mirror, expecting to see it lying across the back seat, but there was only a woollen scarf that had lain there for months, alongside a couple of bags for life. 'I was sure it was still in the car.'

'That's where I left it.' Jack was craning his neck and bent forward as though the crutch might have slid under the seat. 'Weird.'

I tried to focus on the long, straight road, which was thankfully empty in front, only the white car from earlier still behind us. On either side, the moors stretched dramatically under a canvas of pewter sky, the colours muted – unlike previous trips made in summertime, when sunlight picked out the myriad shades of green in the rolling scenery.

'You didn't bring it inside and forgot?'

'My short-term memory is fine,' Jack said drily. 'I think I would have remembered.'

'Maybe it fell out and rolled under the car and we didn't notice.' I wasn't sure why I was bothered, but not knowing the crutch's whereabouts felt wrong. 'You might need it.'

'I'll be fine.' Jack sounded terse. 'It's not like we're going for a five-mile trek. I'll be sitting down for most of the day.'

Aware of my heartbeat all of a sudden, cold washed over my body. I hadn't thought beyond what would happen once I'd told Jack everything. Would I drive back alone and leave him to it? *Where would he go?* He'd been running away the night he was hit by the car, so resuming his relationship with Lydia seemed unlikely, despite her grand plans.

222

Perhaps Dee would end up driving him back to Brighton. The thought was somehow unbearable, but so was the alternative, Jack confused and distraught, memory still lost, not understanding what was happening, pleading to come back to Robin Hood's Bay, promising I'd got it all wrong.

I wondered whether Lydia would pitch up at the cottage today. Once she realised we weren't there, perhaps she would return to London and put the whole episode behind her. Then I remembered the look of grim determination that belied her frail appearance and shuddered. She seemed hellbent on being with Jack, no matter what.

I tried to picture myself saying to him, *Don't contact me again or I'll go to the police and tell them everything I know*, but couldn't make it stick. It sounded like something from a movie, and I knew I would never say it. Did that mean I was complicit in his abuse of Lydia? *Abuse.* The word brought bile to my throat. She must really believe he could change, but was she fooling herself? Did men who hurt women ever change? Should they even be given the chance to? Another sound jerked me out of my dismal thoughts. A thud, as if something had hit the back of the car.

'What the hell?' Jack swivelled round. 'You heard that, right?'

I nodded, slowing the car, a nagging suspicion circling my brain. 'It's coming from the boot.' There was another thump, this time accompanied by a muffled voice.

I felt Jack's stare, saw his mouth drop open. 'You'd better pull over.' He unclicked his seat belt as if preparing to jump out, a feverish tint to his cheeks.

Panic clawed my insides. I swerved into a lay-by next to a thicket of waterlogged shrubs. The car behind shot past, narrowly missing a motorbike roaring the other way.

I left the engine running and listened, senses heightened. Jack was as alert as a meerkat beside me, neither of us breathing.

'There,' we said at the same time, hearing another bang, like a fist hitting metal, followed by a stifled cry. Our eyes met in mutual horror.

'There's someone in the boot.' Jack shoved open the door and almost fell out of the car.

'Wait!' I cried, hardly able to comprehend what was happening, let alone mobilise myself. What if it was a trap? *Was it Lydia?*

I stumbled into a biting wind that pulled at my hair. 'Jack, be careful!'

He'd rounded the back of the car and was fumbling for the catch that would open the boot. Imagining someone springing out with a knife, I hurried to join him, elbowing him out of the way.

'Let me do it.' With frozen fingers, I found the lever and pressed it, then jumped back, pulling Jack with me so we practically fell over. As I steadied myself, I was fleetingly aware that the car that had overtaken was backing up, tail-lights flaring. We must look as though we'd got engine trouble.

Jack was gripping my arm, his hair thrashing back from his face which was a stark, sickly white against his dark beard. I followed his gaze as if in slow motion, to see a man dressed in black, unfurling himself from the depths of the car, then crawling, gasping, and retching to the verge where he threw up. 'What . . . ?'

Not a man. As he peered fearfully over his shoulder, drawing the back of his hand across his mouth, I saw a teenage boy with a flop of brown hair and spots circling his jaw, barely hidden by patchy stubble. 'I'm sorry,' he said, voice cracking into a sob. 'I'm so sorry.'

Jack stared, as though at an apparition, T-shirt rippling against his chest in the wind. His eyes were glassy voids while his mouth worked silently, a muscle spasming in his cheek.

'Who is this?' My voice was pitched high with fright, yet I had no idea who I was more frightened of. 'What's going on?' I looked at the boy. 'Who are you?'

An engine whirred and the driver of the white car pulled up in front ours.

The boy turned at the sound, then scrambled to his feet. Lurching forward, he reached into the boot and snatched up a rucksack, his movements jerky and panicked. The action dislodged something as he jerked away that fell back with a clatter: Jack's crutch. I looked at Jack in dismay, but he was staring at the figure by the car, arms clamped to his sides.

'I was trying to help,' the boy said, and then he was pushing awkwardly through the shrubs and onto the moor.

Fear was starting to claim me, seizing my limbs, my throat, and I almost screamed when Jack leapt into action as though a switch had been flicked.

'Wait!' he bellowed. He was moving after the boy as fast as his limp would allow and after a second's stunned silence, broken by the hard slam of a car door, I grabbed the crutch from the boot and set off after them. The ground was boggy in places, icy water seeping through my leather boots. Ahead, Jack was struggling, favouring his uninjured foot, which gave him an uneven gait.

Twice he pitched forward, and my breath snagged as I imagined him falling face first into the prickly gorse, but he righted himself and kept going, occasionally calling *Stop!*

In the distance, the boy was slowing, as if it had dawned on him there was nowhere to run – just an endless stretch of soggy, purple-and-brown heather moorland leading to hills, and pine forests he would get lost in. In his jeans, trainers and hoodie, the rucksack slung over his shoulder, he clearly wasn't used to this kind of terrain – but neither was Jack.

I screamed his name, but the wind snatched it away. I heaved a breath into my burning lungs. 'Jack!'

The sky pressed down, the light ebbing as rain approached, giving the moors a dystopian feel. The air felt alive, creating an eerie soundtrack as wind pushed through cracks and crevices in the surrounding sandstone crags.

The boy had reached a drystone wall and clambered over, disappearing from view for a moment, before his head bobbed up again.

As I caught up with Jack, he stumbled and crashed to his

knees, head hanging between his arms. 'Jack!' I squatted beside him. 'Are you OK?' He was shivering, his teeth clattering. When he looked up his eyes were filled with torment. 'Jack, what is it?' I dropped the crutch and struggled out of my coat. 'Here, you're freezing.' I draped it around his shaking shoulders.

'Tell him to come back,' he managed, making no move to stand up. 'I have to talk to him.'

I raised my eyes to see a veil of rain sweeping across the moors, the boy emerging through the mist like a photo coming into focus. He was running awkwardly, rucksack bouncing, slipping as the ground became soaked and spongy, one hand clutching the hood he'd pulled over his hair.

'Is he OK?' Panting, he dropped to his knees in front of Jack, rosettes of colour staining his cheeks. There was something familiar about the shape of his eyes, his cheekbones, that I couldn't pin down.

'I'm fine,' Jack said, shaking his head as he stared at the boy like he'd never seen another human being before. 'What are you doing here?'

'You know who I am?'

I stared from Jack to the boy, water seeping through the knees of my jeans, feeling as if I'd slipped into a parallel universe. I uncurled my fingers and reached along the springy heather for the crutch I'd dropped, pulling it towards me. 'Is someone going to tell me what's going on?'

Jack was smiling, eyes shining with tears, and the sight was as unsettling as the cluster of sheep that had gathered nearby to stare. 'Caitlin, this is Matt,' he said. 'He's Lydia's son.'

Chapter 27

Lydia

'Get away from him!'

Heads whipped around as I approached Jack and Caitlin, both crouched on the carpet of brown and purple with Mattie. The fact of my son's presence had barely begun to penetrate. *Mattie.* Here, in this godforsaken part of the world, among a landscape so desolate it looked like the end of the world. Fine rain that seemed to envelop everything dripped down my face and pain lanced through my head. I had to force my legs to keep moving, to keep my eyes pinned on my son. 'What are you doing here?'

It was all I could think to say, while they looked at me in varying degrees of disbelief, like players on a saturated stage.

'You followed us?' Caitlin was the first to straighten, sweeping her hair off her face as she squared her shoulders.

'I warned you.' I jabbed the air near her rain-speckled face with a shaking finger. 'You were supposed to tell Jack the truth.'

I was still reeling from seeing them drive past me, for all the world like a couple embarking on a shopping trip. I'd almost bashed into the back of their car when Caitlin executed an emergency stop out of nowhere. For a wild second, I thought Jack must have spotted me and regained his memory, perhaps yanked on the handbrake, but they carried on driving so I had no choice but to follow, but they didn't notice, too wrapped up in each other. After the trouble I'd gone to, warning Caitlin, giving her the chance to come clean.

The burn of anger and humiliation had propelled me on, fingers rigid with determination around the steering wheel, but they'd suddenly swerved off the road as though a tyre had blown and I'd veered past, slowing further along the empty road to see what was happening.

What I hadn't expected in a million years was a figure to emerge from the back of their car, on hands and knees like a child – *my child* – the sight of him pushing my heart into my throat.

'I don't understand,' I said, switching my attention to Mattie before Caitlin had a chance to speak. 'I thought you were staying at Callum's.'

'I knew where you were going, Mum.' Far from the apologies, the flurried explanations I'd expected, Mattie's voice was sullen, a throwback to the boy he'd become after William died. 'You must think I'm pretty stupid.'

'How did you know where I was?' If Shona had told him, I would never forgive her.

'I checked your phone when you were asleep the other night.' He finally got to his feet, but reluctantly, as though kneeling in soggy countryside was preferable. His fringe was soaked, but he either didn't notice or didn't care. 'I saw you'd booked into that guesthouse here and knew straight away what you were up to.'

'What I was *up* to, Mattie, was trying to bring Jack home.'

'He doesn't want to come home, Mum!' His voice rose, cracking a little. 'Why can't you get that into your head?'

Shocked tears flew to my eyes. 'Don't talk to me like that.'

'This is your son?' Caitlin's voice had a bemused quality, as though she'd found herself in the middle of a peculiar dream. Her

228

long-sleeved top was soaked and clung to her breasts. I had an overwhelming urge to slap her. 'I thought he would be younger, thirteen maybe.'

'He might look like a man, but he's still my boy.'

I could see Mattie hated that, as if I wasn't letting him grow up, but I missed so much the boy he used to be. Jack had brought him back, but I'd let him get away again.

'Wait . . . you've spoken to her?' Jack's voice, the voice I'd missed like a favourite tune and constructed so many memories around, was jagged with emotion. He pulled himself upright as I turned to look at him and my heart overflowed with love.

'You remember me.' I could see it now, as clear as my reflection in his pupils as I took a step closer, the sky a bright sphere behind me. 'You recognised Mattie.'

When Jack switched his gaze to Caitlin, it was as if a light had been switched off inside me. 'As soon as I saw him, it all came back.' He addressed the words to *her*, not me. Not the woman he'd agreed to father a baby with, to attend counselling sessions with; the woman whose son he'd promised to teach to sail like his father taught him as a boy; the woman who loved him more than Caitlin ever could.

'Don't speak to her.' Darting forward, I grabbed the sleeve of the coat that was slung across his shoulders – too small like a child's. It slipped, puddling in the heather at his feet. 'She's been lying to you, Jack. She knew all along that you'd been in a relationship with me and didn't tell you.' I was stabbing my finger at her again when all I really wanted was to grab Jack and Mattie and run. 'She took advantage of your memory loss to bring you here, but I know you don't love her anymore – you told me—'

'Actually, I never told you that.' His voice, stripped of warmth, was like a punch. 'You wanted to believe it, but the truth is, I never stopped loving Caitlin.'

Anger threatened to engulf me. 'That's not true, Jack. You wanted a divorce.'

'You were the one who went to see a solicitor about it.'

'It's true, Mum.' When I dared to look at Mattie, his eyes were wide, frightened pools, like a little boy again. 'He doesn't want you.'

'What the hell were you doing in that car, Mattie?' I hadn't meant it to come out so aggressive, but Jack's ridiculous claim that he still loved his wife cut deeply and I wanted to lash out. 'I could have sorted this out on my own, without you interfering.'

'Why are *you* here?' he shot back, seeming to gather some strength from somewhere. In that moment, I saw William in the pout of his lips and the raised arch of his brows and realised how like his father he really was. 'You were supposed to be in hospital.'

For a second, I thought I hadn't heard him properly. 'You knew I was there?'

'Hospital?' Caitlin said at the same time, scanning my face with those doll-blue eyes, no doubt seeing the bruise near my eye that was pulsing with a life of its own. 'What happened?' When she flicked a look at Jack, I felt a sick pinch of triumph that she'd begun to doubt him after our meeting; to wonder exactly what he was capable of.

She was loosely holding his crutch, and I remembered the note the paramedics had found next to me on the beach. **GO HOME.** A louder, bolder echo of the toothpaste message at the guesthouse. 'It was you, wasn't it?' I pushed my face to Caitlin's, so close I could see the scattergun freckles across her nose and smell the salted scent of the sea in her hair – the scent Jack had been sniffing around.

She reeled back, and he shot out his arms to steady her.

'Leave her alone, Lydia.'

He was defending *her*, now? As if everything revolved around her existence.

Seized by rage, I spat, 'She pretended to be you last night, coming out to meet me like we'd arranged, then whacked me over the head with that thing.' I nodded to the crutch, the movement causing a starburst of pain in my temples. 'I fell and hit my head, passed out. Luckily, someone saw me and called an ambulance, or I might have died.'

'She didn't hit you.' The almost weary intonation in Jack's voice inflamed my anger further – not even a sliver of shock had crossed his features at the news that I'd been injured. 'Caitlin was in bed by midnight.'

'Wait . . . you arranged to meet her?' Caitlin looked from Jack to me, her expression almost comically confused. 'What . . . ? That's where you went, last night?'

'I didn't go anywhere.' Jack gave her the earnest look I knew so well, had seen many times over the past year when he was trying to make a point. 'She called the cottage yesterday morning while you were out, told me we'd been in a relationship and that you were lying to me, said I was in danger.' He'd grown intense and his mouth twitched, as if the words wouldn't come fast enough – words that ripped at my heart. 'She wanted us to meet so she could explain, and asked me to trust her, and to not tell you.'

The rain had stopped as suddenly as it had started, the sky brightening further so that I had to shield my eyes.

'I admit, I was tempted to go,' Jack continued, as though he and Caitlin were the only people present, Mattie appearing to hang on his every word, his mouth gaping slightly. 'I was curious to know what she meant, and everything between us two felt so . . .' He made a helpless gesture with his hand, while Caitlin stared at him as though he was Heathcliff, arms belted around her waist. Even with her hair in rat's tails, smudges of purple under her eyes contrasting with her milk-white skin, she looked more together than I felt. I wanted to retch, to scream, to push her over, but kept on listening, as rapt as Caitlin and Mattie. 'I had this feeling you were hiding something, Cait. I thought it was about him . . . Owen Whittaker. You'd seemed so happy to have me home but then you got all edgy.' She was leaning towards him, as if to absorb his words more easily. 'I couldn't work it out, so when it got close to midnight, I decided I would go and see what she had to say, but when I got past the fence, there was no one there.

'I *was* there,' I protested, close to a toddler's whine. 'I heard you call out my name.'

'It wasn't me.' Jack's voice was spiked with conviction, the way it always had been – good old Jack, who hated any implication that he wasn't upstanding and honest. 'I waited a couple of minutes then went to go back inside. I thought I heard a noise near the car, but couldn't see anything—' his gaze swung from a statue-like Mattie, pale-faced apart from the livid line-up of spots beneath a coating of fluff, back to me '—so I went indoors.' He looked at Caitlin, his eyelashes wet, with rain or tears it was hard to tell. Jack was a crier, had wept more than I could have imagined during our time together. 'For some reason, it got to me that I couldn't find my leather jacket. It seemed to tie in somehow with her phone call—' his gaze flicked to me and away '—and then that card I found from Dee.'

Who the hell was Dee?

'I understand now,' he said softly, and where was the outrage, the horror at realising he had been duped, misled, lied to, deceived by a woman who claimed to love him – a wife he'd left once before because he hated liars? 'The thing is, I was coming back to you anyway, Cait. At least . . .' His Adam's apple slid up and down. 'I wanted to talk, to see whether you would consider having me back. If not, I was going to get a new passport and leave the country, start over.' Another glance in my direction, eyes piercing mine like tiny, poison darts. 'I never wanted to see her again.'

My furious reply was cut short by a passing car tooting its horn, the driver no doubt confounded by the sight of the four of us on the moors, playing our scene to an audience of shaggy sheep.

'I told her about you, about what you did.' Desperation oozed from my voice as I stuck out my hand. 'She knows what you're like, Jack, but I explained that we're going to see a counsellor.' My outstretched palm seemed to glow like a beacon, their gazes drawn as if hypnotised. 'You know I can go to the police, any time I choose. You would be arrested, just like that.' I snapped my fingers, and the gesture broke the moment of awful silence.

'She told me she had photos and you destroyed them.' Caitlin's voice was juddery. She was shivering, perhaps cold, maybe from fear and shock. Mattie's hand seemed glued to the strap of his rucksack, his gaze now locked on mine. I read a plea in their depths that I had to look away from. He hadn't run to me, hadn't hugged me, hadn't seemed pleased to see me at all. What was he here for if not to protect me, or to ensure I made it home safely?

'She did have photos, that's true,' Jack said, cutting eye contact. 'I took her phone and deleted them from everywhere I could, then I threw her phone away.' I heard Caitlin's intake of breath. 'I couldn't have her going to the police again.'

'She told me she'd reported you.' Caitlin's voice shook.

My mind scrabbled for a distraction and found one. 'Wait.' I looked from Caitlin to Jack, a band of pain tightening around my head. 'If neither of you were there last night, who did this to me?' I pressed a palm against my temple, pushing my damp hair aside. 'It was a warning,' I said. 'Someone left a written message, telling me to go home, the same as they did in my room at the guesthouse.'

'Maybe it was Owen.' Caitlin had taken her coat, which Jack had plucked off the ground, and was wrapping it around her shoulders. She looked haunted, as if unsure what to think or who to believe. 'He's been behaving weirdly. He told me I wasn't safe.'

'Why would *he* want me to go home? If anything, he'd want me to leave with Jack and have Caitlin to himself.' I looked at Jack through a wave of tears. His face looked wiped clean, as if he'd taken off the mask that made him familiar. 'You know they were together before you came back?'

Caitlin's expression twisted as she reached a hand towards him. 'Jack, I—'

233

Chapter 28

Caitlin

The impact of the boy's words was electrifying.

Lydia hands flew to her mouth and her watery eyes stretched wide. With a guttural cry, she dropped to her knees as though shot.

Jack grabbed hold of Matt's shoulders, bringing his face close to the boy's.

'Is it true?' Though taut, his voice was laced with a kind of sympathy I didn't understand. 'Did you hurt your mother?'

'I wanted her to go home.' The boy was crying, terrible snuffling sounds that, despite everything, made me want to hug him. *Why was Lydia looking at him like that?* He was her son, yet she'd made no move to go to him since appearing wild-eyed, yelling at him to get away from us. It had felt surreal, a nightmare, seeing her there, like a shadow, a ghost, who wouldn't leave us alone, though I'd known deep down she wasn't going to leave quietly.

I looked back at Matt – Jack had called him that, the boy's appearance forcing open the door to his buried memories – and their close relationship was evident in every movement, a father-son bond. But it didn't take away from the fact that the boy had followed his mother here and hurt her badly enough that she'd been hospitalised – *her own child.*

My brain was on spin cycle, churning thoughts that wouldn't settle, images flashing kaleidoscopically, making no sense. Jack had admitted deleting photos of Lydia's injuries and throwing her phone away. I couldn't understand it. Were he and Matt in some sick game together, or was Matt trying to protect Jack: a man who came into his life when he was vulnerable, taking the place of the father who had tragically died?

Jack had been on his way back to me the night he phoned if what he'd said was true. Had he intended to tell me the truth or hoped I would never find out? And where did the boy fit in? *What had happened in London?*

I couldn't get warm, in spite of my coat, great shivers rippling through me. The sun had slid out through a gap in the clouds but held no warmth. My soaking wet top felt frozen to my skin.

A part of my brain was waiting for Jack to turn on me now he'd remembered Lydia and Mattie, the crucial missing pieces slotting together – his break-up with me and his new relationship – and the fact I'd kept them from him. Not to mention that I'd been seeing Owen as more than a friend. But in the face of everything else, did that even matter?

I pictured Dee on her way to Leicester, expecting to see Jack and me. My phone was in the car. I couldn't even call her, or anyone else.

'I didn't mean for Mum to fall or hurt her head. I called an ambulance and waited to see that she was OK.' Matt wasn't looking at Lydia, but talking to Jack, words gushing out like a river breaking its banks. 'I told her to leave things alone, said it was better that you weren't around anymore, but she was obsessed. I knew she was lying about going to stay with Aunt Shona, and once I found out she was coming up here, that she knew where your wife lived, I guessed she was coming after you. I pretended I was staying at Cal's, and I took your passport out of the box in the wardrobe—'

'It was you who pushed it through our door . . .'

As if I hadn't spoken, Matt carried on speaking, looking into Jack's eyes as though they were holding him up and without that connection he wouldn't be able to function. 'I didn't know what to do after that. I managed to get inside the guesthouse the other morning while some woman was taking her shopping in, and I found Mum's room—'

'You're the one who left that horrible message?' Lydia's voice cracked with shock. 'You were in the room downstairs, weren't you?'

'I thought I could hide there for a while but got scared of being caught and ran out. I slipped down the stairs and twisted my ankle.'

'That's why you were limping. Mel saw you.'

I could barely drag my gaze from Lydia's face, which looked wrenched out of shape with shock.

'I thought it was Jack,' she said, shrilly. 'And all the time it . . . it was *you*?'

Matt kept talking, eyes flicking from me to Jack as though his mother wasn't standing right there. 'I had nowhere else to stay, and I'm sorry, but I let myself into your cottage while you were out, and I charged up my phone and had a drink of water.'

I remembered the sense I'd had that someone had been there, the glass lying in the sink, the back door ajar – the figure I thought I'd seen in the garden.

'I hid outside when you came back. That old woman was there with the casserole, and then I heard your wife on the phone to her friend, and that's when I realised you'd lost your memory, that you couldn't even remember us.' He scrunched his eyes shut for a moment, lips compressed as though holding back more tears. Jack's knuckles were white on Matt's shoulders. He gave him a gentle shake, urging him on. Now, I couldn't take my eyes off the pair of them and daren't look around for Lydia.

'I thought if Mum would just go home, everything would be

237

OK and you could get on with your life, but then she came out late last night—'

'You followed me to the tunnel.'

It wasn't a question and Matt continued as if Lydia hadn't spoken. 'She came up to the cottage again and I didn't know what she had planned. I thought she might break in and hurt your wife, or . . . I knew she would say anything to get you to come back, then I found your stick in the car – it wasn't locked – and I took it to give her a fright.' He gulped in air. 'I swear I didn't mean to hit her that hard, or for her to fall.' A sob erupted. 'When she went off in the ambulance, I was frightened. It was cold, I didn't know what to do or where to go, so I climbed in the boot of the car and left it open a bit, thinking it would be warmer there and I would figure things out in the morning. I fell asleep and when I woke up the car was moving. You know I get really carsick. I tried to hang on but couldn't. I'm sorry, I'm sorry. I've messed up, I'm so sorry.'

'Matt, it's OK, mate.' Jack pulled the boy's head onto his shoulder and the act was so tender, a side of him I hadn't had a chance to witness – a father comforting his child – that I simply couldn't reconcile the scene with ones of him hurting Lydia.

'Get off him, you bastard.'

Suddenly she was there, attempting to wrestle her son from Jack's grasp, pulling at his hoodie, snatching at his rucksack with grasping fingers while Jack tried to hold her off.

Her hair flew around in limp strands, the bruise by her temple staining her skin, giving her a bloodied, broken appearance. I thought of the other bruises on her body, saw how small and thin she was, how close to losing her grip on reality.

'Did you hurt her?' My words, directed at Jack, created a freeze-frame effect. He became motionless, shielding Matt with outstretched arms while Lydia paused in a half-turn, her eyes laser beams of fury. '*Why*, Jack?' He looked like a scarecrow in his damp, baggy T-shirt and loose jeans, hair made wild by the wind,

238

eyes hollow and red-rimmed, yet I couldn't switch off the love surging through me. 'How could you?' I started to cry, because he wasn't saying anything, and Lydia's mouth had curled into a smirk, and the boy was lowering his head, swinging it back and forth, and still Jack wasn't speaking. I couldn't bear that after everything, this was it – the end of my marriage. The end of Jack and me, here on the moors in the middle of nowhere, because there was no coming back from this. I couldn't stay with a man who had hurt another woman.

'No!' Matt came to life, shouldering past Jack, who shot out a hand and grabbed his wrist.

'Don't.' His voice was a warning that made the hairs on my neck stand up. 'It's OK, Matt. You don't have to say anything.'

'That's right, Mattie.' Lydia grew coaxing as she crept closer to her son, hands out as though to take hold of his. 'You don't have to say anything, sweetheart.' Reaching up, she gently swept his fringe away from his forehead. 'We should get you home. You've got exams, remember?'

Matt cringed away. 'Get off me.'

'Mattie!' Lydia sounded crushed and in spite of myself, my heart went out to her. To be physically hurt, then rejected, by your child after what she'd been through must be the worst feeling in the world.

'I keep telling you, my name's Matt.' The boy's head was pulled back, one hand fiddling with the zip on his hoodie.

Lydia touched her fingers to the back of her head. 'I understand why you did it,' she said softly, but her gaze had slid to Jack. 'I forgive you.'

'Just stop it.' Matt positioned himself between Jack and his mother. 'I hate you,' he said, his face transforming into a snarl. 'You're a bitch.'

I couldn't contain a gasp when Lydia slapped him so hard, his head jerked down to his shoulder. 'You ungrateful brat.'

'Lydia!' I felt as if I'd missed several pages of a story and no longer knew whose side I was supposed to be on. Matt had hurt his mother, yet he seemed so . . . *lost*. 'I'm sure he didn't mean it.'

'Yes I did.'

Lydia raised her hand again, but Jack caught hold of her skinny arm. 'Leave him alone.' Something in the pitch of his voice made me do a double take. It sounded like a precursor to violence, a tone I'd never heard him use in all the time I'd known him. 'If you hit him again, I'll call the police.'

'Don't tell me what to do.' Lydia's body language changed. Wrenching free, she pulled herself up to her full height and stabbed a finger at Jack's chest. 'I'm not scared of you.'

'Is it revenge?' I said, wanting her to stop looking at Jack like that, and for his hands to uncurl from the fists they'd made as he let go of her. 'Is that why you're really here?' Lydia turned, her expression oddly blank. 'You don't want him back at all, do you?' I went on. 'All that stuff about counselling. You want him to pay for what he did to you. Isn't that right?'

'He didn't do anything.' For the first time, Matt met my eyes with a look that was filled with shame and anxiety. 'Jack never hurt Mum, not once.'

'Mattie!' Lydia's voice was a threatening growl. 'Don't talk rubbish.'

'Just stop it, Mum.'

I inched closer to him, thinking at last that I understood, because things were making sense now. 'Was it you?' I said quietly because I didn't want to provoke him. He'd already put Lydia in hospital. He was tall and strong, unpredictable. Clearly capable of inflicting pain. '*You* were the one hurting your mum and Jack is trying to protect you.' Even as I spoke, a looping thread in my mind said it didn't make sense. Jack wouldn't have stood for that; he hated seeing anyone hurt. And why would Lydia be up here telling me she'd reported Jack to the police, that he'd threatened her with a knife, that she had photos of her injuries if it had been her son all along? Unless she couldn't forgive Jack for leaving a situation he could no longer bear and wanted *him* to suffer instead of the real culprit. 'Just be honest,' I said to Matt, the irony hitting home. How could I preach about honesty after the part I'd played? 'This can all be sorted out.'

'He's done nothing wrong.' Jack seemed to have come to a decision. He briefly met Matt's eyes and curled a hand over his shoulder.

'Shut up!' Lydia flew at Jack in a ball of fury. The force of her, and the unexpectedness of it, threw him off balance and he staggered backwards, shooting out a hand to break his fall. Somehow, the crutch that I'd dropped at some point was in Lydia's hands, raised high above Jack's head.

'No!' I lunged for her, knocking her sideways.

She lost her grip on the crutch, which Matt grabbed hold of and threw so it sailed through the air and landed out of sight.

I scrabbled to Jack, gulping air like a dying fish. 'Are you OK?'

He flung himself onto his side and pushed awkwardly to his feet, his face contorted with pain, but before I could move, Lydia was on her feet too. I watched with almost detached disbelief as she raised her hand and raked her nails down the side of Jack's face. He didn't take his eyes off her but didn't move either, his back ramrod straight.

'You promised we could have a baby.'

'I never said that, Lydia.'

As though enraged by his response, she let out an animal cry and brought her fist smashing into the side of his face, then battered his chest with both fists. Like a tree weathering a storm, Jack swayed, then bowed his head, but didn't retaliate or attempt to move away.

Fighting waves of dizziness and lack of breath as panic surged through my body, I lunged forward and threw my arms around Lydia's knees, bringing her crashing down.

She wriggled and squirmed, kicking out and trying to bite me, before landing a punch on my jaw that made my teeth clatter. 'You stupid cow.' Her lips pulled back in a snarl, her face made ugly with rage. 'Why are you defending him? He's pathetic.'

241

Suddenly, she was straddling me, the springy moss a mattress beneath my back. Her hands closed around my throat, surprisingly strong. Black dots began to dance in front of my eyes as I fought to unlatch her fingers. Then a figure swung into view and Matt hauled her off me. Gulping in air, I struggled upright, the scene in front of me wavering. Jack had Lydia in a restraining hold, and she'd gone limp in his arms.

'This is what she does.' Matt was breathless, face blotchy with tears and snot. 'She was like this with Dad too.' He brushed his sleeve across his face. 'Aunt Shona knew. She saw Dad's cuts and bruises once, when she was staying with us. I saw them too. Mum always tried to make it better afterwards, but we were scared of her. That's why Dad went out running every day, to get away from her. He wouldn't have died if it wasn't for *her*.' Another sob erupted. 'She *killed* him.'

'Mattie, don't say that.' Lydia raised her head and pulled free from Jack's hold, flashing him a look of hatred as she rubbed her arms. 'Your dad was weak; he couldn't stand up to me,' she said. 'I thought Jack was different – he *is*,' she added, doubt clouding her face. 'I want to be too,' she amended, voice catching. 'I don't want it to be like this.' She began to cry, face screwed up like a child's. 'That's why I booked us some counselling.'

'*You* need counselling,' Jack said. I could hardly look at him, understanding now what he'd been through with Lydia. My gentle Jack, who I'd known in my bones wouldn't hurt anyone, had become enmeshed in a situation he must have felt trapped in, probably not believing it could be happening to him, perhaps staying for the boy's sake. 'I just need to be here now, with Caitlin.'

'She hid his passport,' Matt said to me, rubbing his nose with his knuckles. 'Jack didn't know where it was. And his driving licence. She drove him everywhere because she didn't like him doing anything on his own. That's why I took it, so he could have it back and get away if he wanted to.'

I nodded, unable to speak. My heart felt as though it was breaking.

'You know I was going to get in touch with you, once I was settled somewhere,' Jack said to Matt, and it was as if it was just the two of them now on the moor. 'I didn't want you to think I'd abandoned you.'

Matt nodded, lips compressed as though holding back more tears.

Lydia covered her face, her shoulders heaving with sobs. 'I'm so sorry,' she said, tears dripping through her fingers. 'I'm sorry for everything.'

I could still feel the imprint of her fingers on my throat. Seeing the scratches on Jack's cheek where she'd dragged her nails down made me want to be sick. I joined him, wrapping my arms around his waist.

'I'm so sorry I didn't tell you the truth,' I said, guilt rising hot and fast. 'I'm so sorry, Jack.'

'You've nothing to apologise for.' He rested his cheek on my hair. 'I understand why you didn't.'

Over his shoulder, blue lights flashed in the distance. Two figures were moving towards us, one tripping on the uneven ground. *Police officers.*

'I would have been in touch sooner,' Jack said to Matt over my head. 'I didn't plan on losing my memory.'

'You know that was her fault too?'

'No, Mattie, no.' Lydia's voice was a despairing wail.

I turned in Jack's arms to face Matt. 'What do you mean?'

He was looking at Lydia. 'Why did you hire a car to come up here?'

'You know I don't like driving.' She wiped her face with her hands, her voice an appeal. 'I took the train to York.'

Matt's wide, scared eyes met Jack's. 'She didn't want to use her car because she's scared the police might be on the lookout.' Jack's body stiffened. 'She went looking for you,' Matt went on, and I suddenly knew what was coming. 'She's the hit-and-run driver.'

Chapter 29

Lydia

Being accused by my own son, then turned over to the police like a stranger was my lowest moment, and there had been plenty of those.

Seeing my father hit my mother for the first time was probably the worst, then understanding that, however sorry he was afterwards, however much he cried and begged for forgiveness and made excuses, it would happen again. And again. He never directed his anger at me; he loved me. We had happy times together, the two of us. He doted on me; everyone said so. I'd basked in his adoration.

I couldn't understand why Mum let him treat her like that. Her scurrying about and trying to please him somehow made him angrier, but the one time she threatened to leave, he begged her so hard to stay, saying he would change and that everything would be different, she caved in. She was clever with foundation and concealer, though Dad was mostly careful about not leaving bruises where they showed.

I grew to despise my mother for being so weak, and to

understand what it was about her craven need for my father's love and approval that made him turn on her time and time again. I knew from about the age of ten that I would never grow up to be that kind of woman. No man would ever push me around. I was strong, like my father.

I was like my father.

That realisation was another low moment. The first time I punched William hard enough to leave a bruise and got away with it.

God, he was a wimp. Anything for a quiet life. A yes-man, easily flattered, easily pleased, gentle to the point of being taken advantage of – traits I'd mistaken for solidity, maturity, and reliability when I met him on a night out with Shona.

I'd felt powerless to control the rage that engulfed me when he meekly put up with my demands and requests, my insistence on things being done a certain way – a way I didn't even care about, infuriated that he went along with it anyway, keen to keep the peace and to avoid the pinches and scrapes I couldn't help inflicting, even when he obeyed me.

If he'd stood up to me, I might have respected him more.

Back in my car now, shaking and sobbing, the scene in front of the police officers played over and over in my head; Mattie telling them I'd been *stalking* Jack, that I wouldn't leave him alone and had chased them across the moors.

'He left me,' I'd screamed, incensed that the officer was taking handcuffs from his belt, as though I was a dangerous criminal.

First William, out running whatever the weather, and totally wrapped up in Mattie whenever he was home, until I had to remind him I existed, and now Jack – younger, more attractive, and everything I had thought I wanted – had *left* me.

It had taken me a while to acknowledge that his vulnerability – being fresh from a marriage break-up and clearly heartbroken – had been part of what drew me to him. He'd been so keen to escape and be with someone different, somewhere new, a man I could mould into the kind of husband and father I craved. Not a weak character, like William, but gentle and kind. Except . . . something about Jack's instant attachment to Mattie, which had seemed more heartfelt, more *real* than his feelings for me, had begun to twist the curl of love I'd felt growing, bending it into something misshapen and familiar, the old need to control someone's feelings starting to overwhelm me. I knew it was wrong; I wasn't stupid. That's why I'd agreed straight away when Jack suggested counselling, promising to do better, to *be* better – not just for his sake and my son's sake, but my own.

The knowledge that all along Jack had been planning his escape, as if a few slaps and scratches from a woman smaller and slighter than him was the worst thing he would ever encounter, had made my blood boil, burning me from the inside out. I would *not* let him get away. I'd had no choice with William – though I wasn't convinced he hadn't willed himself to have a heart attack on purpose – but it wasn't too late for Jack and me. If I could get him back, I would show him things would be different, something Dad had never managed to do, dying of a stroke when I was seventeen, leaving Mum bereft – as though she actually missed him after the way he'd treated her. I couldn't look at her afterwards, had never visited my old home, where I presumed she still lived.

She'd never met Mattie and probably never would.

I'd known Jack wouldn't get far without his passport, or a driver's licence – though he could easily apply for new ones – which gave me time to track him down.

Driving to Brighton that day had been a long shot. I honestly hadn't expected him to run back to his wife with his tail between his legs, but there he was outside their flat, clearly bemused that she no longer lived there. He was wearing the pricey weatherproof jacket I'd insisted he wore instead of that awful leather one, which he must have left behind with everything else, to fool me into thinking he was coming back.

I followed him on foot to the seafront, where he sat on a bench in the freezing cold, looking at the boiling sea and occasionally tilting his head back, as if seeking inspiration in the clouds. At one point, he dropped his head in his hands, and it had taken all my strength to not run over and comfort him. I knew if I did, he would run. He'd been so desperate to get away, he'd left without telling Mattie. It would take something special to bring him back.

I'd tried to clear space in my head, sifting through the anger to make a plan, but then he got up and walked back to the flat.

He spoke to a passer-by, perhaps asking if the person knew Caitlin and where she'd gone but was given a shake of the head and a wide berth. He couldn't look at his phone for information because he'd left that behind too, to fool me.

Despite the expensive jacket, he looked homeless – he *was* homeless – an air of desperation to his movements that made people look twice and avoid him.

I expected him to look up an old friend at least – apparently, he'd had plenty in Brighton – but he didn't seem inclined to leave the area, pacing up and down the pavement with his hands in his pockets, skinny shoulders hunched up around his ears. I hadn't realised until then just how much weight he'd lost.

It's stress, he said abruptly, when I told him he was starting to look unattractive.

Why had I said that? Jack was the most attractive man I'd ever met, and more, the kindest. Or so I'd thought. Leaving me in the lurch with Mattie wasn't very kind.

It was February, and darkness had fallen early. Watching from the car, I waited to see where he would go next, fingering one of my earrings, remembering how, at Christmas, I'd turned my nose up at them, telling him what I really wanted was a baby. He and Mattie had exchanged a look, but he'd nodded – probably to keep the peace and not ruin the day.

Perhaps he would go to a B&B if he had any money on him. Or maybe he would regret coming to Brighton after all and go back to London. I would have forgiven him – eventually.

When he started walking, I followed him round the streets, hanging back in case he recognised the car he hadn't been allowed to drive because I didn't trust anyone but myself behind the wheel.

It had never been my intention to hurt Jack. I only wanted him to choose to go home, or to maybe get out and talk to him, but when he finally slowed on a quiet, unlit street, as though alerted by the steady engine noise behind him, and turned, shielding his eyes against the glare of headlights, I panicked.

Instead of hitting the brake, I pressed the accelerator and the car shot forward at speed. I tried to swerve, but he leapt the same way, right into the path of the car. He flew quite a distance on impact, head bouncing off the kerb as he landed, one leg twisted awkwardly underneath him.

I flung the door open and leapt out, whimpering with fear, certain he was dead, a feeling like fireworks fizzing in my head. But then he stirred, groaned, and somehow I was back in the car, pulling away and driving past, keeping my eyes on the pool of light on the empty road in front, peeping up at the rear-view mirror to check there was no one behind me.

I drove until I reached the motorway, then the familiar roads that led home, shutting the car in the garage before rushing indoors to throw up, minutes before Mattie came home and looked at me suspiciously, asking what I'd been doing.

For a while, I expected the police to arrive with the news that Jack was dead, to announce I'd been seen fleeing the scene of a crime, I'd been caught on CCTV, that I was under arrest, but when nothing happened it was worse. If Jack was dead, it would have made the news – if he wasn't, he must have seen me behind the wheel, or read the number plate and guessed it was me, so I still feared a knock on the door. I couldn't settle or sleep, waiting for the axe to fall. And most of all, I wanted Jack with me, telling me not to be silly, that everything was going to be fine.

Endless questions had circled my brain. *Was he dead or alive? Would he come back, or had he gone for good? Did he know* what I'd done and was going to exact his revenge? Hardly Jack's modus operandi, but I couldn't bear not knowing.

That's when I had the idea of going to the police to report him missing but couldn't go through with it, knowing it would lead to more questions, especially as I'd been there before, as insurance, to report the cut on my hand, and the bruises on my arms where Jack had fended me off, letting them believe he'd inflicted them deliberately.

In the end, there was only one way to know for sure what had happened, and that was to try the hospitals in Brighton, where he was bound to have been taken, assuming he he'd been found alive.

The discovery that he *had* been in hospital and was now 'at home' with his wife had sent a dagger of poison straight to my heart. I'd known I couldn't let her keep him. Finding out Jack had amnesia was like being given a loaded gun I could hold to his head.

It was just a shame I hadn't managed to pull the trigger.

I'd fully expected to feel those handcuffs around my wrists once the full story came out about how I'd hit Jack with my car and driven away, but to my astonishment no one told the police officers.

Knowing Jack, he kept quiet to protect Matt, based on some idea that his mother shouldn't be sent to prison, and maybe Mattie loved me after all and couldn't bear to turn me in. Caitlin could have said something. I was sure Jack would back her up as he seemed to think he couldn't live without her, but she'd looked at me steadily, perhaps daring me to confess, holding tightly to Jack's hand as though one of them might be about to fall over.

Stalking was a serious offence, the older officer had informed me, as if I didn't know, but when asked if he wanted to press charges, Jack had silently shaken his head. I knew what he was doing: being the 'better person', or perhaps he wanted to impress Mattie with his generosity of spirit, something my son seemed to think I was lacking, not understanding the whole point of my being there had been to bring Jack home. Or maybe Jack was proving to his wife what a good person he was – the sort who would never leave a woman because she'd chosen not to keep his baby and hadn't told him. *Hah*.

I supposed I should be grateful, but I was driving home to an empty house feeling dizzy and alone – the opposite of what I wanted to be – without Jack or my son. Harriet would be gleeful. At first, I'd had the impression she thought *I* was the one in trouble, when she heard through the walls the shouts and the items being thrown about, but she stopped us in the street one day and asked William outright about the cut on his lip, and although he lied and said something about a cupboard door – an excuse that wasn't even believable in the Seventies – I could tell by her cutting glare that she wasn't fooled.

Still, Mattie would come round eventually, even if he'd refused to get in the car with me today. He was angry, that was natural, but he was no angel. When I thought of him cutting school to come up here and spy on me, creeping into my room to daub toothpaste on the mirror, hiding out and following me, then whacking me with that crutch, it was like a giant hand was squeezing all the love for him out of my heart. And Callum's mother had let me think he was with them – unless she thought I was thanking her for all the times he'd stayed over. Well, that was going to stop, until he'd proved he could be trusted.

At least he'd called an ambulance so I could be saved. *Poor Mattie*. And he'd twisted his ankle running away from the guesthouse. No wonder I'd thought he was Jack, though it hadn't bothered him that much when he was charging across the moor like a fugitive.

I wanted to be better, for him. I really did. I had to try harder and grab this chance I'd been given, try to repair our relationship before it was too late. I thought of Jack's face before the officers escorted me back to my car across that horrible, spongy moorland, sheep scattering out of sight, and knew I'd lost him forever – if I'd ever had him. But my son . . . we were bound by blood. He would be back. I knew it.

Chapter 30

Caitlin

'Can you really forgive me?'

'I already have.' Jack stroked my hair, his touch gentle. 'If I hadn't left you like I did in the first place, none of it would have happened.'

We were on the sofa at the cottage in front of the fire, my head resting on his chest, listening to the steady beat of his heart. 'I should have told you straight away. I honestly don't know what I was thinking,' I said. 'It was instinctive, but that doesn't make it right.'

There was a moment's silence when I thought I'd read everything wrong, and then he said, 'I haven't been entirely honest with you either.'

I sat up and turned to face him, part of me marvelling that he was here, his memory intact at last. 'What do you mean?'

'As soon as I woke up in hospital, I remembered the argument we had before I stormed out of the flat.' He cupped my cheek in his palm, eyes scanning mine. 'It was there, at the front of my mind, like it had only happened the day before.'

I stared, absorbing his words. 'But you didn't say anything.'

'I was mortified.' He kept looking at me, nothing hidden. 'I couldn't believe I'd walked out on you like that. It was a totally idiot move on my part.' His eyes grew bright. 'It was like I could suddenly see the situation clearly. There I was, lucky to be alive, but you weren't there because I'd gone all holier than thou over something that happened years ago that I had no right to be so furious about.'

'You had every right.' My voice broke, the deep and grinding shame I'd felt at the time rising inside me like steam. 'Of course I should have told you. That's on me.'

'We all make mistakes, Cait. I wasn't even around at the time it happened.'

'I didn't want you staying with me just because I was pregnant.'

'I would have stayed with you because I loved you. *Love* you.'

'I thought you'd hate me. To be honest, I hated myself for being that person, the sort who would . . . do what I did because it wasn't convenient to have a baby back then.'

'Don't.' He pulled me close. 'It's in the past,' he said, breath warm against my ear. 'Now is what matters.'

We were silent for a moment, lost in thought and regret. The saddest thing was, he would have been a brilliant dad – a thought I hadn't allowed myself to acknowledge until after he'd gone.

'I was so happy to be here with you,' he said moments later. 'I felt . . . reborn, I suppose, though I know it sounds silly. I wanted to put the past behind us, where it belongs, and move on. To be honest—'

'Ha,' I said, pulling back, and he smiled a wry acknowledgement.

'Now we're being honest,' he continued, 'I thought you might bring it up at some point, but when you didn't, it felt OK. I was just grateful you were giving me another chance. I couldn't believe my luck.'

I tightened my arm across him, reliving what he'd told me on the drive home, about the bad dreams he'd been having, where he saw a boy's face he now knew was Matt's, based on a photo of him as a young boy, and in the dream he was running and running, feeling a sense of danger, then would see his own hands gripping a woman's arms, but couldn't work out why. 'I would do that at first, to hold her off when she started lashing out,' he said quietly, while Matt dozed in the back of the car. 'That's where her bruises came from, and it's why I grabbed you the other morning, and why I pushed you over when I woke up yesterday. I was dreaming about her but didn't realise.' His face had worked with the memory. 'I didn't intend to hurt her, Cait, I promise. I was trying to defend myself, but when she told me she'd taken photos, shown them to the police and would take it further if I told anyone, or tried to leave . . . after that, I just let her get it out of her system. I tried to work out what set her off and to avoid doing it, but there didn't seem to be any kind of pattern.'

He told me how she'd seemed fun and kind when they met, but that he wasn't ready for a serious relationship and started to regret getting involved, but then he accepted an invitation to dinner at her home and met Mattie – or Matt as he preferred to be called since turning sixteen.

He was such a troubled kid but had loads of potential. He's a really good artist, Cait. Jack's eyes had lit up when he spoke about the boy. I was proud that he'd made him feel safe and understood how hard it had been to think about leaving him with Lydia.

I thought his issues were linked to his dad dying, which they were, of course, and I understood because of losing Mum, but then I realised it was more than that. Lydia had ruined his young life, and William's life too, had made him miserable. It seemed the poor bloke couldn't do right for doing wrong, and poor Mattie saw and heard it all. It's amazing he's as grounded as he is, but you never know. The damage could be done.

Jack had lost weight because he found it hard to eat, living on his nerves and fear for Matt, and what Lydia might do if he tried to leave for good. *Something inside her is broken.*

I kept seeing Lydia's face as she was escorted away by the police – called by a concerned driver who had seen our cars, one with the doors and boot wide open, then spotted us on the moor – her expression a mix of hatred and contempt it was hard to comprehend. She'd got away with attempted murder as far as I was concerned, but I wasn't surprised when neither Jack nor Matt mentioned the hit-and-run incident to the officers. I knew Jack wouldn't want Matt to be without his mother – however much Lydia deserved to go to jail – and in spite of everything, Matt couldn't bring himself to send his mother to prison.

At least I had something over her now. If she ever came near Jack and me again, I wouldn't hesitate to call the police and tell them everything.

Matt had refused to leave with her, but Jack and I reassured the officers he would be safe with us. He was asleep upstairs in the spare room now, too worn out to do more than eat the makeshift dinner I'd put together when we got back.

In the car, once I'd called Dee and given her a rundown, promising to phone her again tomorrow, Matt had told us his best friend Callum's parents knew how bad things had been at home and wanted him to move in with them until his exams were over.

Jack told him he could stay with us whenever he wanted, and I hadn't argued. It had felt like the right thing to do. Jack was invested in Matt's future, and I wanted to be a part of that. Lydia could hardly object when she'd got off so lightly, and I wanted to believe that, deep down, she had her son's best interests at heart.

I hoped she would get help. Maybe one day, she could have the sort of relationship with Matt he deserved, though, right now, his feelings were too raw. He'd vowed never to speak to her again. Apparently, he had a grandmother he'd never met because Lydia had told him she was dead – had told William the same thing. One night, when Jack had been opening up about how his mum had died, Lydia had told him her mother was dead to her, because she'd not been a good mother or wife and Matt, outside the room, overheard.

Jack wanted to get in touch with her and initiate a meeting – something Matt was keen to do – and I would do my best to support them.

It was hard not to imagine those horrible days that Jack had spent with Lydia, subject to her quicksilver changes of mood, to imagine his confusion and horror that he was being . . . abused. There was no other word for it. He'd felt a deep, unnameable shame when he realised what was happening.

Who lets themself be attacked by a woman? But I couldn't hit back, Cait, I wouldn't. I thought I must be doing something wrong, even though I knew deep down it was her. But I couldn't leave Mattie. Until she came at me with a knife, just because a job I was doing ran late and dinner was ruined. She chased me into the garden, and I honestly thought she was going to kill me. I got the knife off her, but she grabbed it back – that's how she cut her hand – and Mattie saw it all from his bedroom window. He was going to call the police, but Lydia said she would die if she went to prison, and it would be his fault.

I knew I had to get out, but I wanted Matt to know I hadn't forgotten him, that I would find a way to stay in his life, to make it better. And then I woke up in hospital and I'd forgotten them. It wasn't only the trauma of the accident that had wiped his memory that night. Thinking it was Owen he'd seen behind the wheel of the car had been his mind mixing up events – both had represented danger.

Once Matt had gone upstairs for a shower I'd confessed to Jack that my brief relationship with Owen had been more than friendship for a while. 'But not love.'

'I guessed as much,' he said with a little smile. 'But I'd left you, so I can hardly complain.' He shook his head. 'He really cares about you, you know.'

'He thought you were up to no good.'

'He has good instincts. It's just that they were directed at the wrong person.'

'I hate that she made me doubt you,' I said. 'I noticed you'd been looking up symptoms of amnesia online and wondered – I mean, I knew deep down you weren't faking it, but . . .'

'It's OK.' His shook his head. 'She wanted you to doubt me,' he said. 'I was looking for cases where lost memories had come back, wondering whether mine ever would.'

'Do you really want us to stay here?' I'd asked him while we washed up at the sink side by side – an ordinary, everyday task that I wanted to last forever. 'What with Owen around, and his sister not being my biggest fan. Dee keeps complaining that we're too far away.' I slid him a look. 'We could go back to Brighton.'

Jack was adamant. 'This is home now,' he said simply. 'I want to be here, and I think it's a good place for Matt to come to. I can teach him to sail.'

The future was bright for Matt, in spite of Lydia, and for Jack and me too. Now everything was out in the open, we could finally move away from the shadows of the past.

'I think that's enough honesty for one day.' I took hold of Jack's hand and hauled him to his feet, the love flowing between us stronger than ever. 'Let's go to bed.'

Chapter 31

Lydia

Two months later

I checked my reflection one more time, pleased by the healthy glow on my cheeks, and the shine in my hair that matched the gleam in my eyes. I'd gained some weight, thanks to a healthy eating plan, and felt better than I had in a long time.

I checked my phone and saw it was almost time to leave. A smile curved my lips.

I wouldn't have believed I could feel this good a few weeks ago. Rattling around the house on my own, I thought I would go insane.

I got rid of everything that belonged to Jack right away, couldn't stand seeing his things once I was back. I took particular pleasure in getting rid of that old leather jacket he was unnaturally attached to, just as I'd despatched all William's clothes to charity shops after he died. No point keeping them around. The navy jumper of Jack's that I'd worn to meet Caitlin I'd cut into pieces and thrown away.

257

I had attended a couple of counselling sessions, but really, what was the point if Jack wasn't there to reap the benefits? And now I'd accepted he was gone for good, I was beginning to see that he hadn't been right for me after all. He'd brought out the worst in me. I was better off without him. But I would never forgive Caitlin for the way she'd behaved, turning my son against me.

I thought about putting the house up for sale, but this was Mattie's home, where he'd been born and grown up, and I wanted to be here when he returned.

It was frustrating that he still didn't trust me or want to speak to me. I went round to Callum's house and demanded to see him, but despite thinking his parents might sympathise, and be on my side, they threatened to have me arrested if I didn't stop 'hanging about' as they put it. Apparently, I was disrupting Mattie's schooling and it 'wasn't fair'. For his sake, I left him alone after that. Loving someone sometimes means you have to let them go. Easier said than done, but at least I knew it wasn't permanent.

The times I hated most were when Mattie went up north to stay with Jack and Caitlin – as though *they* were his parents, not me. But, despite the burn of jealousy and anger, I made myself remember how good Jack had been with him, and how happy he'd made Mattie for a while, and tried to accept it. At least for now. I might have to try more persuasive tactics to get him to come back if it didn't happen soon, though.

Harriet doesn't live next door anymore, which made it easier to stay. I didn't speak to her when I got back, but she came round the following day to tell me what a terrible human being she thought I was and that she could no longer tolerate being my neighbour. She's moved in with a friend until her house is sold and she finds somewhere new. She told me she'd rather do that than be anywhere near me for longer than was necessary. She said people like me never change, and if she ever saw me with another man she would warn him off, like she wished she had with Jack. It gave me great pleasure to slam the door in her smug, wrinkled face.

But everything changed a couple of weeks ago, when I called Owen Whittaker at his outdoor clothing store. If he was surprised to hear from me, he hid it well. It was almost as if he'd expected me to get in touch at some point.

'I expect you're gutted they're back together for good,' I said.

'Caitlin's happy. That's all that matters to me.' He almost sounded as if he meant it, but I wasn't so sure. On impulse one evening, with nothing better to do, I'd called his ex-girl-friend Victoria Hartwell. She'd been easy enough to track down through good old Twitter, unmarried, same name, now living in Manchester with a job in finance. I told her that Owen had chatted me up in a pub, but when I looked into him I read about the restraining order and was worried about taking things further. It turned out she was only too happy to warn me off.

'Yes, he did ask for his engagement ring back, and he got it, but he also beat up my new boyfriend later on. I bet he never mentioned that.'

I'd worried for Jack afterwards and thought it couldn't do any harm to make contact with Owen to see how things stood.

'I've spoken to them and apologised for being a bit intense,' he said.

'I could have sworn you were hoping for a different outcome.'

After a moment's silence, he asked, 'What do you want, Lydia?'

'You know they've got my son.'

'He stays there sometimes. They didn't kidnap him.'

'You're still keeping an eye on things, then?'

He didn't respond, but I hadn't expected him to admit it. 'Would you look out for Mattie, let me know how he is?'

'Why are you asking me?'

'There's no one else.' The truth of that statement brought me closer to tears than I'd been in a while. 'I miss him.'

'And if I say no?'

'I'll come up there myself,' I said. 'It's not fair they get to see more of my son than I do.'

259

'Maybe it's better this way.'

'What would you know,' I snapped. 'You don't have kids.'

'Like you're parent of the year.'

I'd felt an odd thrill at the way he spoke back to me. Owen was a man who wouldn't take any nonsense. He wouldn't be meek and mild and let me get away with things. 'If you're ever down this way, maybe we could grab dinner,' I said, surprising myself. What did they say about holding your enemies close? Not that he was the enemy. But it wouldn't hurt to get closer – someone keeping an eye on him for a change.

When he didn't reply, I'd felt a blossoming of the ancient urge to push until I got my own way. 'Or maybe I should come up there and take you out.'

'You don't give up easily, do you.'

It was a statement rather than a question. 'I do love a challenge,' I admitted. 'I can be very driven in case you haven't noticed.' The word *driven* made me think of the night I hit Jack with my car, and I wondered for the first time what would have happened if he'd never woken up. *Perhaps my son would still be with me.*

I hadn't expected to hear from Owen again and had almost forgotten about the spark of something our conversation had ignited, so when he phoned a couple of weeks ago to ask whether I was serious about taking him out, I said *yes.*

'Come up and stay,' he said. 'I'll get you some walking boots from the store.' I rolled my eyes at that, glad he couldn't see me. 'I've taken up photography and fancy catching some sunset shots from the coastal trail at Ravenscar. It would be nice if you could join me.'

My enthusiasm dimmed slightly. I wasn't the walking type and thought he knew that – he'd read me more clearly than any other man had – but I decided to give him the benefit of the doubt. Apart from anything else, being in Robin Hood's Bay meant I might get to see Mattie. And it wouldn't hurt for Jack and Caitlin to hear I was dating Owen.

I felt a buzz of pleasure, picturing their reaction. Imagine if Owen and I ended up together, a stone's throw from Sea View Cottage. Though I might not be able to stand living up there for long, would have to persuade him down to London and bring Mattie with us.

Despite my shifting motives, I felt happier than I had in ages. Life was taking a turn for the better, at last. Time to break old habits and make a new start. I always did like a fresh challenge, and Owen was certainly that. I wondered whether Shona would approve. It would be nice to tell her I'd met someone new. She worried about me since I told her my plans to talk to Jack had fallen through as he was back with his wife now. She called me a lot. Sometimes I didn't pick up. Part of me hated her for putting up with my lies. I was certain Mattie had told her what really happened.

I checked the time and picked up my overnight bag. With any luck, I would be staying more than a single night in Robin Hood's Bay. One last look in the mirror to see a smile with twinkly eyes, my flushed and jubilant face staring back. I couldn't wait to get on with the rest of my life.

Epilogue

WHITBY GAZETTE
24th April

BODY ON BEACH

A woman's body found on the beach near Robin Hood's Bay last week has been identified as Lydia Fielding, 36, from Acton, London. It's believed that she arrived in the area for a visit and went walking in wet weather when she slipped, lost her footing, and fell from the cliff top on a popular coastal trail close to Ravenscar.

The body was found by a dog-walker early on Saturday morning. Emergency services were called but Ms Fielding was pronounced dead at the scene.

There were no suspicious circumstances.

Acknowledgements

I would like to thank the amazing team at HQ Stories, with special thanks to my brilliant editor Belinda Toor for all her insight and guidance. Thank you to Helena Newton and Loma Slater for a brilliant copyedit and proofread and Anna Sikorska for another amazing cover, and to Audrey Linton for overseeing the process. Thank you also to the marketing team.

I'm in awe of the readers, bloggers and reviewers who take time to spread the word and give lovely feedback, which makes all the hard work worthwhile – thank you each and every one.

As ever, thanks go to Amanda Brittany for her support, and another big thank you to my family and friends who manage to stay interested and always read my books.

I couldn't do any of it without my husband who has somehow survived this process yet again. Once again, Tim, thank you with all my heart.

**Keep reading for an excerpt
from *My Sister's Child* . . .**

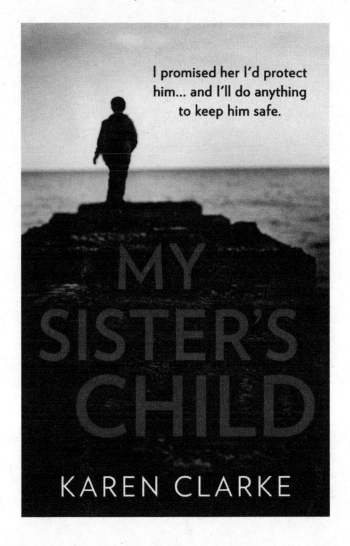

I promised her I'd protect
him... and I'll do anything
to keep him safe.

MY
SISTER'S
CHILD

KAREN CLARKE

Prologue

She was so light these days, bony wrists protruding from her jacket cuffs, her cheekbones too pronounced. There was barely a sound as she hit the water. Only a tiny ripple disturbed the surface.

I stared at the canal as if she might burst upwards any minute, hand outstretched. She'd been drinking before we met. I smelt it on her. So much for giving up. Another of her lies.

I shouldn't have pushed her so hard, but she came at me fast, and the things she said . . . her words like knives in my heart. She wouldn't listen.

I shivered as the wind picked up, my breathing ragged. How had it come to this? I wasn't a bad person. She brought out the worst in me.

My pulse raced as I trained my eyes on the water. How long had it been? Too long. I let out a groan, cold creeping around the back of my neck, settling in my heart.

I recalled the cruel curl of her lips, the way her eyes had gleamed, caught in a streetlight, before she tipped backwards. A flash of surprise across her pale face, as though she couldn't believe it.

Emotion exploded across my chest. Turning, I pushed my hands in my coat pockets to stop them shaking and half-ran from under the bridge, up the steps to the road, crashing shoulders with someone coming the other way.

'Watch where you're going,' I muttered, keeping my head down, resisting the urge to glance over my shoulder as I hurried on.

A fox screamed, tearing the silence. Hard to believe I was in the city. Life, carrying on. The blare of a car horn made my pulse fly. I snapped my chin lower and tried to breathe evenly. Could I continue as though nothing had happened? I had to, or it would all be for nothing, and I couldn't live with that.

It was for the best.

1

'Jess, I'm so sorry about your sister.'

I nodded at the woman who had spoken. Caroline, a neighbour and so-called friend of my mother's from when we lived in London. A memory of her in our kitchen after Mum died jumped into my head, her lips clamped to Dad's.

'Thanks,' I murmured.

Voices ebbed and flowed in the pub around me. Dad was at the bar looking like a wreck, talking quietly to Uncle Denny. Not a real uncle – Dad didn't have siblings – but a childhood friend, and frequent visitor to our home over the years.

I should go to Dad but felt incapable of leaving the leather chair where Adam had settled me, handing me a measure of 'medicinal' brandy before taking Noah into the garden.

'He doesn't like everyone being sad.' Adam's dark eyes had searched mine from behind his black-framed glasses. 'Will you be all right?'

I'd nodded, feeling oddly detached.

Now, I craned my head and looked through the window to where Adam had created goalposts using his jacket and Noah's red jumper. He'd adopted a goalkeeper's crouch, arms spread as he waited for Noah to kick a scruffy football.

Noah would be 6 in a couple of months – a November baby. Watching my robust boy, his brown curly hair a little too long, I felt tears burning my eyes. He was too young for this. *She* was too young. I flashed back to my sister's email two weeks before she died.

Can I come and see you? We need to talk. Rachel.

No context, but that was typical. My heart had leapt, questions flooding my mind. Filled with an unnamed dread, I replied, *Yes. When?* She hadn't responded.

It was the last time I heard from her.

Dragging my gaze back, I scanned the bar of the bland London pub where we'd gathered for refreshments, chosen for its proximity to the crematorium.

'She must have been what . . . 27?' Caroline had settled in the chair opposite, knees jutting from the hem of her black skirt. She knew all about my sister's lifestyle; probably thought she'd got what she deserved. 'Far too young,' she went on when I didn't answer. Her heavy blonde fringe moved as she shook her head. 'I know she put your parents through a lot, but even so—'

'Why are you here?' My voice was even. 'You didn't like Rachel.'

Caroline's head jerked back. 'I'm here for you and your dad.' She flicked a look at him at the bar. 'We've known each other a long time.' Her gaze softened. 'Maybe it's as well your mother's not here.'

I placed the tumbler of brandy on the table in front of us. My hand trembled and I bit back the words I wanted to say. *Don't you remember that day? The day you tried it on with my dad. Some friend you were.* 'It's been a difficult time,' I said instead.

Caroline rested a hand on my trouser-clad thigh. 'I know you all did everything you could for your sister.' I studied the web of veins beneath her skin. 'An accident, the coroner said?'

'I'm sure Dad's told you that was their verdict.'

Caroline's hand pulled away. 'Alcohol does terrible things to a person.'

In that moment, I hated Caroline. She didn't remember the little girl I'd read stories to when she was ill, who would allow only me to wash her hair at bath time – the girl who had so much potential. 'We thought she'd given up drinking.'

Caroline absorbed this for a moment. 'Was it seven, or eight years between you?'

Was it. Past tense. 'Eight.' Mum had thought she couldn't have any more children after me, so Rachel had been a surprise. A *nice* surprise, she stressed, with no idea of the heartache that lay ahead.

I'd assumed that when we were older, my sister and I would establish a relationship that worked, just as my parents had prayed they would reconcile with their youngest child, but Mum's illness had taken hold, and after the final seizure she'd died without seeing Rachel again.

'Your dad did well at the service.' Caroline seemed determined to prolong our exchange.

I nodded, though in truth, I'd barely heard his well-scripted tribute to Rachel that glossed over all the ways she'd let our parents down. Not that there had been many people to listen apart from Caroline and her husband, and someone from the art gallery where Rachel had been working. Rachel had never been good at making friends. In a fog of disbelief I had kept looking at the shiny wooden coffin thinking, *How can she be in there?* while keeping half an eye on Noah, restlessly kicking his heels.

'I still can't believe you upped sticks and moved so far away.' Caroline gave a light laugh.

'It was always on the cards once Dad retired.' My smile felt thin. 'You probably remember we used to holiday in the Lake District.'

Caroline nodded, eyes glossy with tears. 'You scattered your mum's ashes at Windermere,' she said softly. 'Will you do the same with your sister's?'

I swallowed a hard lump of grief. 'I don't know.'

Caroline seemed to gather herself. 'You didn't mind giving up your job in the city?'

273

'Not really.' Finance was the career path I'd followed to live up to my role as 'the good daughter'. When Noah arrived it was an easy decision to follow Dad to the Lakes and be closer to Adam's mum. 'I didn't enjoy it.'

'Your dad still teaching?'

He'd been a professor at the London College of Music until he retired.

'He gives private piano lessons and goes fishing a lot.' I sipped my drink and tried not to shudder as it burnt my throat.

'He always was sociable.'

I glanced over and caught Uncle Denny's eye. He gave a solemn nod and rested a hand on Dad's shoulder as if to say, *I've got this. Don't worry.* Denny had long since retired from the police force, but still had an air of quiet authority.

Caroline seemed about to say more, then rose and moved to the window. 'He's such a handsome boy.' I looked out to see Noah doing a victory lap around the play area. 'He looks so like you.'

It was a throwaway comment, but I felt a tremor of nerves. 'Thanks.' I removed myself from the sweaty clasp of the leather chair, willing Caroline to go back to her husband.

'Well, I'll leave you to it.' As if reading my mind, Caroline summoned a smile. 'Take care of yourself.'

'Thank you for coming.'

As she hurried to the bar, a man materialised as though he'd been waiting for her to leave. I recognized him from the service as the owner of the gallery: Will something-or-other.

'Jess?' I had a vague impression of a teenager wearing his dad's suit. 'Sorry to bother you,' he said, blocking my view of Noah. 'It's about your sister.'

I stiffened. 'What about her?'

'It's just . . .' He rubbed a hand round his jaw. 'There's something I think you should know.'

My heart missed a beat. 'Go on.'

Behind him, Dad peeled away from the bar, eyes seeking mine. His movements were unsteady as he made his way over, closely followed by Denny.

'I have to go,' I said as I watched Dad stumble. 'Tell me.'

Will turned, tracking my gaze. 'It's nothing.' He held up his hands. 'Forget it,' he said quietly. 'I'm sorry for your loss.' He moved away quickly, nodding to Dad as he passed.

'Who was that?' Dad said, as the door swung closed. He was steadier now, Denny's hand on his arm.

'A friend of Rachel's paying his respects.' I pulled out a chair for Dad to sit down. 'We should make a move.'

He nodded, eyes on the table.

'I'll fetch Adam,' Denny said, a smile on his weathered face. I let him go, knowing he wanted an excuse to kick a ball with Noah as Caroline's words came floating back. She was right: Noah *did* look like me, but it was Rachel I saw in his profile. He had the same long-lashed dark eyes as those in the photograph of her at the service, one of only a handful we could find, but the thing Caroline didn't know – that virtually no one knew – was that Noah wasn't biologically mine. He was Rachel's child.

Dear Reader,

We hope you enjoyed reading this book. If you did, we'd be so appreciative if you left a review. It really helps us and the author to bring more books like this to you.

Here at HQ Digital we are dedicated to publishing fiction that will keep you turning the pages into the early hours. Don't want to miss a thing? To find out more about our books, promotions, discover exclusive content and enter competitions you can keep in touch in the following ways:

JOIN OUR COMMUNITY:

Sign up to our new email newsletter:
http://smarturl.it/SignUpHQ

Read our new blog www.hqstories.co.uk
🐦 : https://twitter.com/HQStories
f : www.facebook.com/HQStories

BUDDING WRITER?

We're also looking for authors to join the HQ Digital family!
Find out more here:

https://www.hqstories.co.uk/want-to-write-for-us/

Thanks for reading, from the HQ Digital team

If you enjoyed *My Husband's Secret*, then why not try another gripping thriller from HQ Digital?

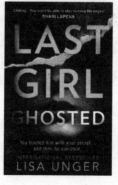
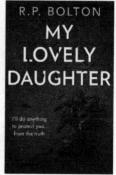